A MYSTERY OF
LOVE AND IVORY

THE SHANGHAI
MURDERS

DAVID ROTENBERG

McArthur & Company
Toronto

First Canadian paperback edition published
by McArthur & Company in 2002.

McArthur & Company
322 King Street West, Suite 402
Toronto, ON M5V 1J2

First hardcover edition published in 1998 by
St. Martin's Press, New York

National Library of Canada Cataloguing in Publication Data

    Rotenberg, David (David Charles)
       The Shanghai murders

    ISBN 1-55278-266-2

    I.Title.

    PS8585.O84344S53 2002   C813'.54   C2002-900453-5
    PR9199.3.R618S48 2002

Design & Composition: *Mad Dog Design Inc.*
Cover Design: *Eugene Kuo*
Cover Illustration: *Alan Dingman*
Printed in Canada by *Transcontinental Printing Inc.*

The publisher would like to acknowledge the financial support of
the Government of Canada through the Book Publishing Industry
Development Program (BPIDP) and the Canada Council for our
publishing activities. The publisher further wishes to acknowledge
the financial support of the Ontario Arts Council for our
publishing program.

10 9 8 7 6 5 4 3 2 1

For Susan, Joey, and Beth

Acknowledgements

I owe a debt to many people for their help with this endeavour. On the practical side, Charlie Northcote, whose support of the original manuscript brought it to Susan Schulman's attention; Ms. Schulman's unstinting faith in the manuscript, which got it to St. Martin's Press; Ruth Cavin, without whose skill this book would have never reached its present form. On the less practical side, the support of my parents and brothers was always there for me when I needed it. Robert's efforts on the part of the book went well beyond sibling obligation. My friends Bruce, Ron, Deb, Amanda, Geoffrey, and Brenda all played far greater parts than they realize. I'd also like to thank the acting faculty at York University who picked up the slack for me when I left on this voyage—especially David and Ron. Finally, I'd like to thank the faculty of the Shanghai Theatre Academy for their patience with this impatient Long Nose, the talent of a brilliant young Chinese actress who played the lead in *Rita Joe* for me, and my fabulous translator and much valued friend (and the original Zhong Fong) Zhang Fang.

A note on Chinese names: They have been simplified as much as possible to resemble the spelling that we would use in the West. There are a few exceptions. For real people and places, the standard spelling is used. With such names, if you remember that x in Chinese is roughly the equivalent of our *sh* you will end up with a pronunciation close to the original. Hence Fuxing Park sounds nothing like an English obscenity. Mandarin is also spoken in four tones so even if you get the sounds right, it is unlikely that a Chinese speaker would be able to understand what you are trying to say. Fortunately, in a novel this is not a problem.

Dearest Sister,

I went on a dead man's walk today, breasting the air that the murdered man had pushed before him, not two days earlier. His name was Ngalto Chomi and he was a six-foot seven-inch black man from Zaire. He was hacked to bits in an alley off Fu Yu in the old city. The temple gods in their shrine around the corner did him no good. This city simply opened a crack and accepted his soul without a pause in its race toward oblivion.

None of this came clear to me until I saw the merchant skin the snake in the marketplace. Skin the snake while it still lived. Skin the snake as he had skinned another snake two days earlier while the black man had watched. Watched because he had bought the snake and taken it with him to a restaurant to be cooked.

But it wasn't the snake that brought home the meaning. It was the skin. Still alive with electrical pulses, it lashed back and forth on the ground, seemingly unaware that its life, its core, was now in the hands of a man with a knife. I thought of Richard. Like the skin of the snake, on the ground, a knife already having removed his life from him with one deft stroke. Dead, but he didn't even know it. Like the chimera of life in the skin of the snake.

Amanda

TO BE SHREDDED

1

DAY ONE

The body on the Hua Shan Hospital's morgue table looked as though it had all the right pieces—but they seemed to be in the wrong places. A divinely challenging jigsaw puzzle awaiting the Maker's few spare moments. At least that's what struck Inspector Zhong Fong, head of Special Investigations, Shanghai District, as he took his pack of Kents from his shirt pocket.

As he lit up, he noticed that the paper of the cigarette was soaked through with his perspiration.

At forty-four, Zhong Fong was the youngest man to head Special Investigations in Shanghai, PRC. He knew he was good at what he did, but he also knew that he was the beneficiary of history. The Cultural Revolution had removed many older police officers who in the past would have stood in his way for dozens of years.

So Mao wasn't all bad, he thought, as he mentally reconstructed the human form in front of him. White male, probably over thirty, definitely under fifty, at one time over six feet tall and probably in excess of two hundred pounds but just now eviscerated, carved up, lopped off and very, very dead. Fong blew out a long trail of bluish smoke while the others waited for him to speak.

Finally he said, "I don't suppose we have any idea who this thing used to be, do we?" The aged coroner only grunted and turned toward the bloodstained industrial sink. The ashen-faced young cop, who had found the body parts only a few hours earlier, felt he had better say something, so he said, "No, sir."

"I would never have guessed," said Fong. This evidently left the young cop confused, but Fong had bigger things on his mind than the confusion of a rookie. "Call the consulates." The rookie took out his notebook and began to write. "Start with the Americans, they like to be first. Tell them what we have here: foreign national, Caucasian, no identification, male, thirty to fifty, cut up and ready for dim sum."

The young cop looked up.

"Don't write that. Say badly mutilated," said Fong.

"Pieces are too big for dim sum," chimed in the old coroner as he spat in the sink and turned on the tap.

As Zhong Fong finished his instructions to the rookie cop and prepared to leave the morgue, he noticed the brownish tap water dripping from the coroner's ancient hands. In a passing thought it occurred to Fong that those hands would shortly take apart what was left of this human being in an effort to find out how, if not why, anyone would go to the trouble of hacking another human being to bits—be they dim sum-size or not.

• • •

Although it was after midnight, the traffic outside the hospital was the normal congested reek of smoke and splutter that was Shanghai. For a moment Fong wondered where he had left his car. Then he remembered that he hadn't taken it since the call had come to his apartment on the grounds of the Shanghai Theatre Academy, just around the corner.

His wife had been an actress who periodically taught at the school, and when they married he moved into her two second-story rooms on the academy campus. The rooms looked out over a small patch of grass on which stood, or rather reclined, a Henry Moorish humanesque bronze with one breast pushed in and one pushed out. It had a doughnut ring for a head.

After a long shower Fong stood at his window, a towel around his waist. In the courtyard two half-drunk student actors were throwing stones at the statue from across the way, each trying to be the first to get one through the statue's head. Since his wife's death, Fong had seen many things go through that metal orifice. Perhaps the most interesting was the erect member of one of the acting teachers, which had been met by the hand of one of the student actresses in a caress that brought out a surge of envy in Fong's heart, like a weed in spring bloom.

The phone rang behind him. He let it ring as one of the boys, tiring of the game's difficulty, ran up to the statue and shoved his stone through the hole. Despite the fact that what he had done took no skill, he celebrated as if he had defeated the elements themselves.

Fong breathed on the windowpane. A slight mist etched and then retreated into oblivion. Like Fu Tsong — the idea arrived full blown in his consciousness. It was followed quickly by the thought that seemed to be his constant companion of late: He had shared neither his wife's art nor her concern. Perhaps all he had ever really shared with Fu Tsong were her rooms. Just her rooms. He picked up the phone on its fifth ring and lived to regret that he hadn't let the thing ring until it tired of ringing altogether.

Some six blocks down Nanjing Road from the Hua Shan Hospital at the Shanghai Centre, built in 1990 by American and Japanese money, Christie's of London was celebrating its Shanghai opening with a gala display of its wares. On view were a third-rate Picasso, a tenth-rate Dali, and several quite notable Chagalls, including *La Sainte-Chapelle*. There were also some turn-of-the-century Chinese scroll paintings and exquisite Qianlong seal-marked vases.

In a smaller case to one side were two customs excise stamps, dated and appraised. Most of the patrons ignored them. But one young westerner with a backpack pointed at the case and said, "Old letters." And indeed they were old letters. Old letters with old secrets. Not the least of which was that one of the two was a forgery.

Passing behind the case with the forgery and making his way toward the back of the exhibit was a small Han Chinese male in a beautifully cut, conservative business suit. His Italian shoes were freshly buffed. His delicate hands (nails polished, right pinky almost an inch long) emerged from his coat pockets. His name was Loa Wei Fen. He marveled at what he saw. So many westerners here now. So pale and with such overripe figures, so awkward in a crowd. And Shanghai was nothing if not a crowd.

He passed by the assembled mass of people around a Pissarro and stopped in front of *La Sainte-Chapelle*. The painting's cityscape blue orb, with a lady in a high window and a rooster looking in both directions as the moon rose over its shoulder, arrested his eye.

It reminded him eerily of earlier in the evening. A man in an alley so full of fear that his head appeared to be looking both left and right at the same time. Both ways. So Loa Wei Fen—Mr. Lo to his business associates—had given him his wish. . . he had first cut him so that he could indeed look both ways at once. And the moon shone overhead, and there was a lady in a window, and the city that grows even as it sleeps moved slightly in its slumbers to permit the passing of another being from its midst. That was just over two hours ago.

The Christie's exhibit was closing. It was one o'clock, late for some businesses in this town to stay open, but not for those that were serious about being part of Shanghai's economic miracle.

Loa Wei Fen glanced one more time at the Chagall, then made his way out of the Shanghai Centre, which sits like a tortoise in its shell over the wall of water that fronts the Portman Hotel. A uniformed northerner nodded toward the revolving door as he approached.

Mr. Lo passed through the lobby, heading toward the

elevator. He got off at the second floor and watched the bank of elevators to see if any other stopped at that floor. None did. He then walked to the end of the hall and, pushing open the stairway door, headed up.

His room was on the twenty-seventh floor. He took the stairs two at a time and arrived without a trace of sweat on his person. The hotel room always surprised him. So much space, so unnecessary. But being a guest at the Portman disguised his mission well.

He removed his clothing and went into the bathroom. He examined his torso in the floor-to-ceiling mirror. Sinew, not muscle, dominated as it should. The lithe movement of tendons beneath the skin as he raised his arms pleased him — like snakes inside. With a breath he released the snakes and felt the life surge within him and flare on his back. The life that for now feeds on others.

He had booked a week at the Portman. He had no idea how much more there was to do in Shanghai. He had been paid a substantial sum of money and hence assumed that there would be more work than just the dismembering of the American policeman. But that was not his concern. He had been paid for the week and for the week's work.

He looked out the small vertical bathroom window. Shanghai sat at his feet, its neon lights blinking a welcome. While across the Huangpo River the new Pudong industrial area was lit by ghostly, high-intensity mercury vapour lights. The better for the night shifts to build by.

After a moment Mr. Lo crossed over to the toilet. He lifted the cover, stood on the rim, and squatted. Like everything else in his life Mr. Lo controlled the working of his bowels with complete certainty. As he climbed down he wondered how a westerner could sit to take a shit.

It would never have occurred to Mr. Lo to think about the incongruity of the two cultures he embodied; evacuating in the way of his Asian ancestors, about to don an extravagant English suit. It would never have occurred to Mr. Lo that he was in the employ of some extremely unsavory people. Mr. Lo was a pure being, an immaculate conception, an idea set into motion when he was taken as a child from his loving mother's arms so many years ago in far off Yan'an province. As the rest of the country went through the throes of the Cultural Revolution, Mr. Lo had been put through the rigours of a different kind of change: The boy who loved was replaced by the man who killed. He never knew the people who paid for this transformation. He only knew the teachers. He had known that he was in Taipei but did not know exactly where. He knew that he was valued but didn't know for exactly what. He knew that he had passed his physical tests and that had pleased his teachers. He knew that he had passed their cultural training and that had pleased them as well. He well remembered the first man that they brought for him to kill. He remembered the resistance of the man's windpipe as he crushed it beneath his heel. He remembered that he hadn't felt anything when the light went out in the man's eyes. He remembered the clean incision that parted the man's breastbone. He remembered the crack as the ribs separated under his fingers. He remembered cleaving the still-twitching heart in two. Then he remembered the taste of the piece of the man's heart that had been placed in his mouth by his favourite teacher.

Mr. Lo knew that he was an investment, a dearly nurtured commodity. What he didn't know was that he was an expendable weapon in the war to bring capitalism to this country of socialists.

The body pieces had been found in an alley off Julu Lu near the former residence of Dr. Sun Yat-sen. As with so many of the tourist sites in Shanghai, Fong had never bothered with it or its historical significance. His wife had dragged him to the YuYuan Garden in the Old City shortly after they were married, but to this day he'd never been to the Temple of the City God, which so fascinated tourists.

Fong didn't expect the crime site to reveal anything of interest except a large red stain and perhaps some small body bits that the rookie cop had missed. The idea of finding something like a fingerprint in a Shanghai alley was a joke.

So Fong was surprised when he entered the alley to find that the crime scene unit had sectored the area with lines of string and was investigating each square meter with great care.

Showing his badge, Fong passed by the cop at the mouth of the alley. The unit had set up three strong over-head lights, which cast hard-edged shadows on the rough pavement. Although late April, it was a cool night and Fong pulled his coat tightly around himself as he moved toward the CSU head, Wang Jun.

He noted that Wang Jun wasn't smoking, which was odd. He also noted that the older man's usually stoic face seemed slightly amused by something.

"What?" said Fong as he came into Wang's light.

"What, what?" snarled back Wang Jun.

Wang Jun was Fong's senior by twenty years, maybe more, and didn't take kindly to the flippancy that he perceived in Fong. However, a grudging respect for Fong had grown, over time, into real friendship. They had worked together on several troublesome cases in the past, and Fong's instincts had proven invaluable in solving some that Wang Jun had thought were beyond solution.

"You look like you swallowed a snake," said Fong.

"I like snake, cooked properly, of course," replied Wang Jun.

He signalled Fong over to one side. When they were out of the light and away from the prying eyes of the others, Wang Jun reached into his pocket and pulled out a wallet in a crime scene plastic bag.

"This is the victim's wallet?" blurted out Fong, openly surprised.

"So it seems," replied Wang Jun with a cold smile.

"Hence the sector search?"

Wang Jun nodded.

Fong held up the wallet inside the plastic bag. "It wouldn't tell us, by any chance, who the victim was, would it?"

"It would if you believed it."

"And you don't?" asked Fong.

Wang Jun popped a cigarette in his teeth and lit it. After a beat, he spoke. "I hate this."

"What? Murder?"

"No. Murder I've grown to appreciate. It's this," he said, pointing to the wallet. "This I can't stand."

"Would you care to elaborate?"

Ignoring the comment Wang Jun charged on. "Did you see the body?"

"Yeah, I saw the pieces," replied Fong.

"Do you know that the guys are calling him the Dim Sum Killer?"

"No I—"

"It's better not to make jokes with rookie cops, Fong," rasped out the older man.

"Point taken."

"Good, now get this," he said, grabbing the wallet.

"The person or persons who sliced and diced this guy were pros. They carved him up like a side of beef, and my bet is they knew exactly what they were doing. It wasn't even that late when it happened and there are people out here at all hours. So this was done fast. This was thought through. This was done by a pro, agreed?"

Fong nodded, noting that Wang Jun had already dropped the "or persons" part of his earlier statement.

Wang Jun held up the evidence bag with the wallet and asked, "Then what the fuck was this doing near the body parts, happy as a leech in a rice field?"

Fong took the bag and used a pen from his notebook to fish out the wallet. Then, laying it flat on the plastic bag, he flipped it open. With a set of tweezers he removed a New Orleans Police Department ID. Holding it up to the light he said, "My guess is that our killer's sending a message. He wants it known that—" Fong tilted the plastic card toward the light and read the name in his singsongy English—"that Richard Fallon of the New Orleans Police Department met his end in a Julu Lu alley and that he was filleted like a fish."

"Wants it known by whom?"

Fong didn't answer but he did step farther out of the light. He didn't want the older man to see his face. "I want statements from every house warden in the alley and from everyone living on the street out front."

"That won't do—"

"Just do it, Wang Jun." Almost as an afterthought he barked, "Interview the street cleaners, they may be helpful."

Fong turned and headed away, returning the wallet to the evidence bag.

"Since you've got my night planned, bring that to Forensics for me, will ya? It'll save me a trip."

Over his shoulder Fong shouted back, "Sure, but I want your completed report on my desk in the morning."

Normally Wang Jun's cursing response would have brought a smile to Fong's face, but not tonight. Tonight Fong's thoughts were very far away as he headed back through the throng to his car.

As Wang Jun watched the younger man's retreating figure, he wondered, and not for the first time, just how Fong managed. Managed to keep sane, that is, after what had happened to his wife in the Pudong.

Before the building boom, which started in 1990, the Pudong across the Huangpo River from the Bund, had been an area of low, ancient homes and twining streets filled with sidewalk vendors and tiny shops. The area lacked sanitation and electricity. Although the police were aware of the comings and goings in the Pudong, they basically left things to the locals to work out. There was opium and even brown heroin but nothing that greatly concerned the authorities.

That was until Shanghai began to enforce the country's single-child-per-family law in 1978.

Within weeks the quacks and mountebanks appeared in the Pudong.

In 1949, on the eve of the revolution, China had a population of under four hundred million. Large, but not large enough for Mao Tse-tung. Soon after stabilizing his victory, he set out to increase the population of his country. By guaranteeing that there would be food enough for all, and granting residency and job bonuses to families with more than five children, Mao opened the proverbial floodgates. In the fifties, sixties, and even into the seventies it wasn't uncommon to see Chinese families with ten or even thirteen children. The great love for children inherent in the Chinese character was unleashed when the fear of having to feed more mouths was removed. The result was that by the late 1970s the Chinese population had more than tripled. Mainland China had more than 1.2 billion inhabitants and a problem that could not be ignored. Promises to feed everyone could be met in the seven years of plenty, but in the seven years of fallow starvation stalked the land. And Mao knew only too well that in the hunger of the stomach is the foment of revolt. So in the late 1970s the Chinese government reversed itself. The single-child-per-family policy was enacted and strictly enforced — and places like the Pudong had a new and thriving industry. It was not hard to find those in the area's squalid back streets who would "diagnose" a female fetus and abort the unwanted fetus for a price.

The day that Fu Tsong, Fong's wife, told him that she was pregnant he grabbed her by the waist and swung her high into the air, feeling that he was holding aloft not only her but also his son. And to his eternal damnation that is exactly what he said to her.

Fu Tsong was tiny even for a highborn Han Chinese, and the doctor warned her early on that she'd have to be careful. That she'd have to cut back both on her work at the school and her performing at the People's Repertory Company.

She sighed and agreed, on one condition.

"And what may that be?" asked her doctor skeptically.

"Assure me that I am carrying a boy."

The doctor put aside his chart and looked at her sternly. Before him was one of the most delicately beautiful women he had ever seen. A woman with a deep fire in her eyes and a strength of will that frightened him.

"Fu Tsong, you know that there is no way I can in all conscience assure you of that. It is beyond my power to know such things. All that is important is that the baby is healthy, and *that* is in *your* power." He reached out to pat her head, and the silk of her hair astounded him.

At that time, Fong was on the rise in the police force. The heir apparent. He was putting in sixteen-hour days trying to prepare himself for the examination that would allow him to head Special Investigations. The hardest part was the English-language proficiency requirement. It was the greatest challenge of his life. He found the English sounds initially incomprehensible and he struggled nightly with basic verb tenses and noun lists. Fu Tsong was a great help throughout, and in the weeks leading up to the exams she drilled him nightly, late into the dawning hours.

One night after throwing aside his English book, she tore open his pants and, hiking up her skirt, straddled his legs while inserting him into her centre. As she rocked he grew within her and she smiled. That smile grew devilish as she threw herself forward and, pinning his arms above his head, hissed, "What if it's a girl?"

She had said it in jest but the look of shock that crossed Fong's face was clear for her to see—a gesture that, once expressed, could not be taken back. She released his arms and leaned back with her hands on his legs.

He saw her close her eyes and sensed her moving far away from him. Then he heard her say, "I know it's a boy, I know it is." She arched her back and threw back her head. Her hair fell to his feet.

In that moment Fong knew in his heart that he had lost her. She let out a low moan, a release. But this was her alone, without him.

As a policeman Fong knew that a moan is the sound

a body makes when it has lost all hope of recovery. As a lover he knew that same moan comes from a woman in the throes of pleasure. What Fong could not understand was what kind of god would make a world where hopelessness and pleasure both made the same sound.

At dawn's first light Fong walked along Julu Lu toward the alley. The city was already alive, the air beginning to get heavy with the fumes of buses and the promise of the year's first real heat. At the mouth of the alley, the police tape had been trampled underfoot. There were still a few policemen finishing off their interviews.

The alley itself was not surprising. There were thousands of these densely populated, teeming side shoots in Shanghai. The five-spice egg seller was preparing her cooking pot as he entered off Julu Lu. He nodded to her. She ignored him and blew her nose onto the sidewalk. At least not into the eggs, thought Fong.

The alley travelled for about eighty crooked yards and was over sixteen feet wide. The buildings were all four and five stories high with basements — most with sub-basement as well. Fong estimated that upwards of three thousand people lived in the buildings that fronted the alley. Bedding was hung from most of the lower windows while in the upper windows shirts, satayed on bamboo poles, projected from the sills like strange nautical signal flags.

It was an alley, so it smelled. But what it smelled of was life, abundant, roiling life.

An angry voice to his left drew his attention. The

warden of the first large building was yelling at him. "Who the fuck you, who?" She'd probably lived in Shanghai since the revolution but she'd never learned Shanghanese, typical. He flashed her his badge and continued on. She muttered loudly, "Too late, all the fun finished, flathead." As he moved down the alley there were similar scenes with other wardens. Some workers were just rising, others were already getting on their bicycles and heading to work. Some were well dressed, others obviously worked as manual laborers. Many wore white gloves to ride their bikes. White woollen gloves had become popular bicycle attire during the winter months and although it was clearly going to be a warm day many bicyclists were still wearing them. Ah, ever fashion-conscious Shanghai. The odd lucky soul had a motorcycle or a bike fixed with a pedal motor. Two of the large hand-driven tricycles for the infirm were chained to a rusting water pipe. The air was thick with the smell of porridge and coal fumes from the outdoor braziers. Electrical wires formed a cross-hatch pattern in the sky over Fong's head — random and as potentially deadly as the poison snakes that fall from trees in distant Yan'an province.

Fong noticed other things as well. Things that angered him deeply. Hundreds of windows faced the alley. Some of the windows contained plank extensions used for sleeping half in and half out of the crammed rooms. So many people! And children. This was a most unlikely place to choose for a murder. Shanghai seldom sleeps, but this place — this vibrant artery of the city — was vitally alive no matter what the hour. This murderer didn't just take a life and then mutilate the body that encased that life—he did it consciously in a place of abundant life itself. As if affronted by the fact of the life here, he had chosen this very spot. Fong looked down to his feet. He knew what he would find. There on the cracked square paving tiles he saw the taped outline of the body, marking its likely position at time of death. Fong was standing squarely on the heart.

The morning after a murder the police station was always a riot of paper. Special Investigations handled most of the murders in Shanghai, a city of fourteen million. Most but not all. Domestic violence was handled by another unit. Shanghai had fewer than two hundred fifty murders a year. Per capita that was less than one one-hundredth of the murders in Detroit. But Special Investigations also tracked major fraud cases, multiple injury cases, and anything that influenced the growing foreign community in the city.

Murder, because of its relative rarity, was newsworthy. Murder of an American was especially newsworthy. And somehow the news about the Dim Sum Killer had already hit the stands.

Fong arrived at his office on Zhong Shan Road, in the old English Concession, in a fury. He hurled the newspaper on the table and exploded with anger at his assistant. "Who the hell let this out? What moron allowed the press access to this material?"

His assistant, a young man who claimed he had been assigned by his commune first to the police academy and then to work as Fong's assistant, was not one to take responsibility for anything, so he did what he always did, he shrugged.

"That's it, a shrug?"

"You want two shrugs?" For the umpteenth time it occurred to Fong that his assistant's story of communal assignation had a hollow ring to it. Fong thought it more likely that this innocuous little rodent probably had good party connections and was there to keep an eye on him. Putting the thought aside, Fong snapped, "I want the editor of the paper on the phone, I want a meeting with the commissioner, and I want the coroner to call me. You capable of arranging that?"

The assistant shrugged again.

"That is an affirmative shrug, right?" Before the assistant could shrug again, Fong spat out, "From now on you hit the desk once for yes and twice for no."

After the briefest pause in which Fong saw the unmistakable traces of hate in the young man's face, the assistant hit the desk once.

"You're progressing." He pointed to a new file on the desk. "Is that from Wang Jun?"

The assistant was about to shrug but decided against it. He hit his desk once.

Fong picked up the file and headed toward his office.

All the lights on his desk phone were blinking as he entered. He punched through to the desk operator to ask who the calls were from. Two were from newspapers and one was from the American consulate. He told the operator to tell all three that he was in the field "avidly pursuing promising leads" and could not be reached at this time. He then turned to Wang Jun's report.

The older man had a terse style that pleased Fong.

PLACE:	Hianpi Alley off Julu Lu
TIME:	Arrival 10:47 P.M. April 18, departure 4:58 A.M. April 19 [then he gave the date in Chinese]
PROCEDURE:	Sectoring, blood typing, interviewing of area wardens and prefects on alley and across Julu Lu.
RESULTS:	Blood samples sent to laboratory. Photos of scene before and after removal of body enclosed.

Fong put aside the document for a moment and looked at the photos. They were taken with standard Wang Jun accuracy. Each was one of a pair—before with the body and after without. Each set was taken from precisely the same angle. There was a series of overhead shots, most likely taken while balanced on someone's shoulders. A series of wide-angle shots of the alley came next. Nothing surprising here. The arrangement of the body parts on the pavement caught Fong's eye. He went back to the wide-angle overhead photo. What was it here? No, it wasn't the arrangement of the body parts as such, but rather some of the parts themselves. He rifled through the rest of the pictures looking at closeups of torso, of legs, of feet, and finally of hands.

Something about the hands. Both had been severed at the wrists then placed back where they should be. Something nagged Fong about the hands, though. He stood up and walked around the room trying to clear his head. What? What was wrong with the hands? He placed his own hands on the window and pressed them flat. Then he released the pressure and was about to walk away from the window when his eyes were drawn to his own curled fingers. Without pressure, fingers naturally curl. Of course they did. He raced back to the pictures on his desk. The fingers on both hands were not curled. They pointed. The killer had arranged the fingers to point. At what? He looked at the shots of the alley and couldn't come up with an answer to his question.

Then he picked up the overhead full body shot. Wang Jun had drawn a grease pencil circle on the photo with a question mark at the side. Fong grabbed an old-style magnifying glass from a side desk drawer and examined the circled area. Between the legs a piece of viscera and a sealing strip came into focus. Neither were in the overhead "sans body" shot. Not a surprise really as they'd probably been discarded or put into the coroner's package. He moved the magnifying glass to allow a further enlargement of the area. He could just make out the writing on the sealing strip. It said "Rip here for air sickness bag." The writing was in both English and Japanese characters so he knew it had to be from a JAL flight. But that wasn't his concern just now. Now he wanted to know what a killer would put into an air sickness bag. A waterproof bag that could be flicked open with one hand. Without putting down the picture he picked up his phone and punched the coroner's extension.

The coroner answered with a cough and the particularly acute clearing of the throat that is the god-given right of every Han Chinese male.

"And good morning to you too."

"Dim sum will never be the same," croaked the coroner.

"Yeah," Fong said, putting an end to this line of conversation.

"I hope to shit you're not calling me for that fucking report at this ungodly hour of the morning. It took me a long time to work this one out."

Still holding the picture in his hand, Fong allowed the older man to vent his spleen. He knew the coroner had probably worked all night at his ghastly trade.

"No, I can wait for the report."

"Good."

"I was just wondering if you checked for all the body parts."

There was a lengthy pause at the other end of the line. Finally, the coroner responded, "I thought we were concerned with time of death, weapon used, that kind of shit."

"I am, naturally, but I'd also like it noted if there are missing body parts," pressed Fong.

In exasperation, part of which Fong knew was aimed at himself, the coroner lashed out. "You guys bring a carcass cut up into dozens of pieces and plop it onto my table and I'm supposed to miraculously put it back together and . . ." He ran out of steam more than stopped. After a moment, Fong could hear him light a cigarette and cough. "I'll haul it out of the freezer and count." The phone went dead.

Fong breathed a sigh of relief. It was hard for him to contradict his elders, especially when it would force the older person to acknowledge making an error.

Before he could even return to Wang Jun's report, the light on his phone came on. Picking it up Fong barked, "Who?"

"The editor of the *Shanghai Daily News*, the paper that ran the story."

"Put him through."

At that moment Commissioner Hu entered the office. His smug look and tailored suit bespoke party affiliation. An affiliation that sat well with his contained manner, square features, thick tinted glasses, and white hair. Before he could speak, Fong punched the speaker phone on his desk.

A silky intelligentsia voice, speaking an almost lisped high Shanghanese, came on the line. "This is Executive Editor Goa Ke Fee of the *Shanghai Daily News*. I have been informed that you would like a word with me."

Fong gave a get-this-guy's-act look to the commissioner. The commissioner chose not to comment.

Fong punched in his response button on the phone. "Yes, Mr. Goa, this is Zhong Fong, head of Special Investigations, Shanghai District—"

"I know who you are," the editor cut in curtly.

Anger surged in Fong. If the commissioner hadn't

been standing there he really would have let this little pisser have it. But controlling himself, he said, "It's about your lead story this—"

"No doubt it is. So what can I help you with, Mr. Zhong, head of Special Investigations, Shanghai District?"

He looked up. Commissioner Hu was watching him closely. Fong turned back to the speaker. "Okay, enough of this shit. Who gave you permission to run this story!"

Without the least hesitancy the reply came back. "We obtained our normal clearances."

There was a stunned silence from Fong. The paper had received clearance for the story? How could that be?

"Is there something else with which you need my assistance, Mr. Zhong?"

"No, well yes, could you send me your authorizations?"

"For the story?"

"Yes, of course for the story," said Fong.

"That's quite impossible. And you know that it's quite impossible. Now if there are no more requests I do have a busy schedule—"

Fong snapped off the phone and looked up. To his surprise, the commissioner was gone.

He quickly read through the rest of Wang Jun's report. The street warden system in Shanghai was still as tight in that section of the city as it had been during the Cultural Revolution. Very little escaped the sharp eyes of these people. The majority were not native

Shanghanese and took great pleasure in exercising their power over the locals. The party always awarded such positions, along with the appropriate housing, to peasants from good revolutionary stock. But, according to the wardens' statements to Wang Jun's men, they had seen nothing out of the ordinary.

Fong then opened the time chart that Wang Jun had provided. There had been a domestic dispute at one end of the alley at 8:40 P.M. The quarrel had ended with the husband yelling and screaming in the alley. Another warden reported that a doctor had been summoned to a dying man's side at 9:30, which would have made him travel the entire length of the alley from Julu Lu. The body was found by the rookie cop at 10:33. There was no possibility that New Orleans police officer Richard Fallon had been murdered and mutilated somewhere else, then carted to the alley. It is one thing to cart body pieces but quite another to haul the blood with them. Richard Fallon's blood was clear evidence that he had been murdered in the alley off Julu Lu.

A shiver slithered down Fong's spine. He got up from his desk and parted the window's ancient curtains. He looked across the river. The Pudong grew even as he watched. The huge cranes of the planet's largest construction project, four times the size of even the dreams of Canary Wharf in London, pivoted and swung like gray metallic herons on an endless quest for food.

Fong pulled himself away from the window. His office, the room in which he now spent a great portion of his life, was large by Shanghai standards and its view of the river was a rare privilege for a non-party member. The building itself sat right on Zhong Shan Road three blocks south of the famous Peace Hotel, on the road the Europeans, who had owned this part of the world for so long, called the Bund. From the turn of the century up until the revolution in 1949, there were four famous streets in the world: Broadway, Piccadilly, the Champs Élysées, and the Bund.

In this very office had sat some of the most powerful men in history. Men who had controlled the trade into and out of the Middle Kingdom. Even the infamous Silas Hordoon had at one time passed through this room.

The phone on his desk rang. It was his private line, so he knew it was Wang Jun. "Yeah, I read it," he said when he picked up. "I think we should meet."

"Good. Look out your window."

Punching up the speaker phone, Fong moved to his window.

There, standing on the river promenade, looking up at him with a cellular phone in his hand, was Wang Jun.

"My new toy, you like?" Not waiting for an answer, Wang Jun continued. "I've got work to do but I think we need to meet. This whole thing stinks."

"Have you found the street sweeper?"

"No, but her shift hasn't come on yet." There was the slightest pause on the phone. "Come down here and take a walk with me. I think what we have to say is better said away from your office." With that Wang Jun clicked off.

For a moment Wang Jun's manner annoyed Fong, but he let it pass. He left his office and, taking the back stairway out of the building, managed to leave without his shrugging, knocking assistant noticing.

• • •

The news of her husband's demise in far-off Shanghai left Amanda Fallon wondering what she should feel. For a moment she didn't understand that she was faint, that the room was weaving and bobbing around her. It was only when the man from the State Department, who had come to her home in the New Orleans Garden District to tell her the news of Richard's death, took her arm, and sat her down that she realized she was going to faint. As her living room narrowed to a single tunnel of light that then moved in on her, all she could think of was, I shouldn't be in shock, I should be thrilled, I should be on my knees thanking fucking God that I'm free of that bastard.

For a moment the government man didn't know what to do. They'd never told him how to handle situations like this. He recognized from the sweat on her face and her ghostly pallor that Amanda Fallon had gone into shock. But even as he picked up the telephone to call for an ambulance, only one thought filled his mind. "This is one of the saddest-looking beautiful women I have ever seen."

Fong spotted Wang Jun near the photography kiosk on the promenade at the base of Nanjing Road. For the thousandth time Fong marvelled at the view of the

European buildings that the raised promenade offered. Because the walkway was almost two stories high and a full six lanes of traffic away from the buildings, the viewer was offered a breathtaking look at the architect's artistry. Gables and domes, spires and bell towers, and mass — lots and lots of elegant cock-proud mass. Although the buildings were completely unlike Chinese architecture, which he adored, Fong had to admit that the robber baron Europeans had created something of lasting beauty in the twenty-one buildings that dominated the Shanghai skyline. Of course it was from those very buildings that these same white men had raped and plundered the wealth of his country for almost fifty years.

There were the usual tourists on the promenade being led around like so many children on a string. Click-click for Japanese, scuffle and whine for Americans, and open haughtiness for Germans. Ah yes, the world's lords had come to gawk at what had been theirs but was no more.

There were also the rural dispossessed. Recently arrived at the train station in the north end of the city and without work or a place to stay, they would wander down to the waterfront to sleep. A peasant can sleep sitting up, head in full profile on the back of his hand which in turn is balanced on a knee. They seem to sleep soundly. But try touching the filthy bag that contains his few worldly belongings and you will see that this delicately posed sleeper can awaken with a roar.

A sleeping peasant looks like a delicate mantis that has fallen into strong Chinese wine and for a moment is stunned into stillness—stunned long enough for the diner to nab him with a set of chopsticks, dunk him in the sauce, and eat him whole. A fate that, at least metaphorically, awaited many of these sleeping men.

There were the con men too. The ones who had enough English to approach white people did so. They all had some supposed family heirloom to sell or their services as guides to Shanghai's many pleasures of the eye, the palate, or the groin. And there were the beggars, not many, not like Kwongjo, the Canton of old, but more than there used to be. The obscenity of his countrymen begging before foreigners always sent a special rush of anger through Fong.

Stretched out on a bench, between himself and Wang Jun at the kiosk, was a clubfooted man. His filthy clothes were pulled up to reveal the stumps that were his feet. A tin soup bowl was near his deformed extremities. Spittle ran from his mouth and there was the unmistakable reek of human waste about him. For a moment Fong's anger subsided as he looked at this poor specimen of humankind.

"Are you in pain?"

The clubfooted man's eyes fluttered open and tried to focus.

"Have you eaten today?"

Slowly the man shook his head.

"There'll be help here in a minute, but you have to promise me that you won't fight them. Is that a promise, do I have your promise?"

The man nodded.

"Good, I'll be right back." With that he made his way quickly through the thickening morning crowd and grabbed the phone from Wang Jun's hand.

"Hey—"

But Fong had already punched in the phone number of special services.

"Is it ringing?"

"I don't think so."

Wang Jun took the phone, listened, and pressed SEND.

"You should think of joining the twentieth century sometime before it's over," he said, handing the instrument back.

Quickly Fong left orders for the clubfooted man to be picked up and brought to a shelter.

"You're a sentimentalist, Zhong Fong, a dangerous sentimentalist. And at your age, really."

"He's sick, he's hungry, our revolution meant something."

"Did it really," snapped Wang Jun. He began to walk.

Fong moved with him. "So?"

"Tell me about the newspapers and how they got the story, Fong."

"They got clearance."

"Bullshit. From whom? That kind of story has to have party approval before it sees the light of day. Surely that takes time. Or didn't that cross your mind?"

Fong resisted the taunt. "They got authorization to run the story and that's that."

Wang Jun shook out a Marlboro and lit it. "I think the murderer was a pro."

"I agree."

"Anything on the wallet?"

"A little blood that will no doubt match the dead man's. If there are prints on the wallet or credit cards I'll bet they'll match Mr. Fallon's as well."

"Why did he leave the wallet? A pro doesn't make that kind of mistake."

"I don't think it was a mistake. I think it was a message."

"If it was, then the sender's pretty lucky that the papers got—" The older man stopped himself. Then he continued, "Pros don't have luck, do they?"

"No, they don't, Wang Jun. There is nothing about luck involved here as far as I can see. Somebody wanted to send a pretty gory message and they used you and me to send it."

"You and me and Richard Fallon, member of the New Orleans police force. Let's not forget that he did his part."

Unable to resist, Fong said, "Parts."

"Dim sum for giants."

Suddenly it stopped being funny. "Yeah, man-eating giants. Cannibals."

Wang Jun stared at his young friend. Fong met his gaze. "I'm not a boy, I'm not someone's messenger boy. I want this lunatic found."

"Who was the message being sent to is the question, isn't it?"

"It's a good question but let's start with the killer. Find the street sweeper. I want her in my office as soon as you get her. Don't let one of your men do it. I don't want her scared. I want her charmed and treated like a lady, so I want you to get her and bring her to me."

"You have great faith in street sweepers, Zhong Fong."

Fong had no interest in discussing his family's long history as night soil collectors. "Just find her and bring her to me." With that he turned his back on Wang Jun and headed toward his office. As he hopped the pedestrian barrier and crossed Zhong Shan Road, he reran his mental tape of the conversation just finished. For the life of him he couldn't understand why that conversation couldn't have taken place in his office.

Geoffrey Hyland handed his Canadian passport over the immigration counter at Shanghai's Hong Qiao Airport. He always arrived in Shanghai with a sense of sadness but also a feeling of coming home. Eleven years ago, he had been invited to the Shanghai Theatre Academy to direct an obscure Canadian play called *The Ecstasy of Rita Joe*. The school's acting faculty despised his non-Russian-based approaches, but to their shock and the delight of both students and audience, the play was a runaway hit. Six months later he was invited back by Shanghai's biggest professional theatre, the People's Repertory Company, to remount the play using the student leads from the first production to play the younger roles and the professional company's members in the older parts. This too proved successful. It was not, however, successful for Geoffrey Hyland. This time in Shanghai he met and fell hopelessly in love with Zhong Fong's wife, Fu Tsong.

That love endured until the day four years ago when,

in his turn-of-the-century house in Toronto's West End, he opened a letter from Shanghai. The words were blunt and seemed to burn, as if etched, on the rice paper. All it said was: *Fu Tsong is dead. Many think her husband killed her. They found her body and the body of a fetus in a construction pit in the Pudong.*

So stunned was he by the words that he never thought to question either the identity or the motive of the writer. Had he in fact been able to decipher the scribbled signature he would not have been able to recall the face of the author. All this was as intended by the writer.

Geoffrey became aware that the immigration officer was standing as he handed back his passport. The young man surprised Geoffrey by extending his hand and saying, "High Lan, yes? Lee Ta Jo, yes?" Geoffrey's eyes brightened. Those productions were a lifetime ago to him, but the repertory company performed them regularly. To him "Lee Ta Joe" had been a time with Fu Tsong. Now was a time without her — a sad homecoming.

He shook the immigration officer's hand and headed toward the airport's lounge where he knew the driver from the Shanghai Theatre Academy would be waiting. The man looked exactly like the late American actor, Jack Soo. Geoffrey had told him that once, over lunch, and thereafter the driver insisted that Geoffrey call him Soo Jack. He also insisted that when Geoffrey needed a car, he be the driver.

As Geoffrey left the immigration counter a note was taken, a phone lifted, and an insurance policy put into motion.

Standing rigidly at attention, the rookie cop waited for Fong to finish reading his report. Fong put down the file and looked at the young man in front of him. He was twenty-two years old, square-shouldered with large usually rounded eyes and short spiky hair. There was some Mongolian in his blood lines somewhere. His name was Ling Che.

"Did you speak to anyone after you left the coroner's office?"

"Yes, as you instructed I contacted the consulates." The papers could have gotten their information from one of the consulates, Fong knew, but he doubted the leak would happen quickly enough to make the morning press. "You phoned them?"

"Yes, sir. Wasn't that how I was supposed to do it?

Those who had no operators working late, I faxed. Isn't that right?"

"Yes, it's right, Ling Che, it's right."

There was a long pause, there was something here that was escaping Fong.

"May I go now, sir?"

Fong sat perfectly still for several seconds. Ling Che didn't know what to do. Then Fong stirred. "Did you use a cellular phone to make your calls to the embassies?"

"Yes, sir."

"Cellular phones aren't secure! Anyone could intercept your call. You're supposed to use the precinct phones!" Fong shouted.

The young man, completely cowed, bowed his head

and mumbled, "I was at my girlfriend's place, her parents were in the country for one night. It was the first time in three years that we—"

Fong held up his hand for him to stop. Privacy, in a city where housing was a major problem even for the well connected and the wealthy, was nonexistent on a young policeman's salary. If you wanted to scratch your ass in Shanghai, you had better be prepared for someone to be watching while you did it. And if the watcher is Shanghanese he will probably offer advice on a better way to go about your task.

He dismissed Ling Che with a nod. He hoped to hell that the young cop wasn't lying to him. He made a note to check.

The light on his phone came up. "Who?"

"The coroner."

After a moment the coroner's smoke-tired voice came on the line. "You'd better come over. I've got some frozen viscera here that you ought to see."

The parcel that arrived at the Jiang Jing Hotel had been left with the concierge. It had not been brought by a courier. In fact the concierge had been away from the desk when it arrived. The parcel had a room number and a guest's name on it. The concierge called up to the room and informed the guest that there was a parcel for him. The guest asked that a bellboy bring it up, knock on the door, and leave it outside.

The bellboy took the small parcel up to room 2430 and knocked politely on the door. Then he placed the parcel, as instructed, on the floor and returned to the lobby.

A full five minutes after the bellboy's knock, the door to the room opened and the parcel was taken inside. Forty-five seconds after that, obscenities in various languages and the clear sound of someone throwing up his lunch on the expensive broadloom came from room 2430 of the Jiang Jing Hotel.

"It's a part of a heart," said Fong.

The coroner nodded at the object in his plastic-gloved hand. "Part of Richard Fallon's heart."

"Where's the rest?"

"There's a good question." The coroner pointed toward a large table on which the pieces of Richard Fallon had been laid out. If there was an order to the pieces, it escaped Fong. The coroner explained: "The body is divided into those things male and those things female, yin and yang if you will. Those that cause heat and those that cause cold. Those that are of fire, those of air, those of water." As he spoke he pointed to different sections of viscera and organs. Then he picked up the heart again. "Only the heart, of all the body's parts, belongs to both yin and yang, both heat and cold, and all of fire, air, and water. That is, when it is whole." He looked at the cleft heart that he held.

"The crime scene unit didn't find the other part?"

"If they did, they didn't bring it to the morgue."

"And nothing else is missing?"

"A cleaver or a knife or whatever was used would have nicked off small bits, which were probably left in the alley, but everything else is here. This one knows how the body is put together, and he attacked it at its weakest places."

"But how did the heart get cut in half?"

After a moment the coroner sighed. "It didn't get cut in half, if you mean by that that somehow in the process of eviscerating Richard Fallon something happened to cut his heart in two. That didn't happen. That couldn't happen. Once Richard Fallon was cut open his heart was cut out of him. Then the heart was cut in two. One half I hold in my hand. The other half is god knows where."

Before he could stop himself Fong found himself thinking, "It's part of the message." But even as he did he reached over and touched the frozen item in the coroner's hand. He ran his finger along the cut edge. The cut was razor smooth for most of its length but near the top there was a jaggedness.

"Did his knife slip here?" asked Fong with his finger on the spot.

"No, I don't think so," replied the coroner with a cold smile. The coroner then put the organ down on the morgue table and removed the plastic glove from his right hand. Before Fong could ask him what he was doing, the old man reached into his mouth and with a tug pulled out a complete set of dentures. With the dentures in his right hand he picked up the heart with his left. Slowly he moved the dentures toward the jagged section of the heart. The jaggedness exactly matched the bite mark that would have been made by the ripping action of the top four front and canine teeth and the bottom six with the eye teeth at either end.

"He chewed it and spat it out. I saw it in the photo," said Fong.

"You saw that in a crime scene snapshot?"

"In one of them but not the others."

The coroner put down the heart and reinserted his dentures.

Fong could hear the fluorescent lights buzzing and just for a moment their greenish cast made him feel a little wobbly on his feet.

"You all right?"

Fong nodded.

"This guy's got a hell of an MO."

"Personal style brought to new heights."

The coroner grunted a laugh.

"Not a word of this to anyone. If by any chance this ends up in the papers, I will have your head, old man."

"More threats of the young? The Cultural Revolution's over or haven't you heard?"

"I've heard. I want your report on my desk by week's end, okay?"

"Sure." The coroner paused and was about to say something, then decided against it and began bundling his gruesome charge back into a large green plastic bag.

When the State Department official handed Amanda Fallon back her passport he flipped it open to show her the forty-day, single-entry visa to China. To him, Red China.

"The State Department picked up the forty-dollar charge for the visa."

Amanda was going to say thank you but she couldn't quite think what for, then said it anyway. He smiled at her and mumbled further condolences for her loss and wished her an easy flight to Shanghai.

When she left the State Department office on Canal Street she turned left and headed toward the Quarter. The intensity of New Orleans's summer had not yet arrived but in the bright sunshine of mid-April it was hanging in the corners of the Quarter's old buildings, waiting to fill five full months with heat and humidity, sweat and loving as only ol'N'orl'ns can. Although she was from the north, she had lived in New Orleans since she was seventeen and a student at All Fun U, known to the world as Tulane University. She had been accepted by the women's college on campus but upon arriving had decided that the men's side offered more opportunities for study in her area of greatest concern. Men. After going through the undergraduate male population in alphabetical order, she decided that forays into the realm of the faculty merited her attention. And despite the published university policy of a total ban on student/faculty "fraternization," Amanda found few who could resist her casual offer of a drink down in the Quarter.

So it was with a series of ghosts at her side that she stepped into the courtyard of her favourite watering hole off Talouse. If the Creole barman recognized her, he never let on. But he wasn't surprised when she ordered a tall rum on ice. A literature professor had introduced her to the glories of this particular drink on hot days. He had consumed several that first day as they sat French style side by side on a banquette with the table in front of them. He talked about Tennessee Williams's work. She had smiled and listened and wondered if there was anything more here than chat and great eyes. Then he had put a hand on her knee beneath the table. She smiled at him and reached down to touch his hand. He started to withdraw it, thinking that she was offended, but as he did she closed her fingers around his wrist. Then sliding closer to him on the banquette she parted her legs and drew his hand up past her thighs. All without taking her eyes from his.

She flushed slightly as she tasted her rum on ice. She had been a wild kid but that was a long time ago. Now she was in her mid-thirties and was about to get on an airplane and head to Shanghai to pick up the corpse of her husband of eight years. A husband whom she had wished dead more often than she could recall. A husband who had "tamed" her. A husband who had in a very real way killed what was most Amanda Pitman in her and replaced it by a creature named Mrs. Richard Fallon.

She had finished her second rum on the rocks when the salesman on the other side of the bar finally decided it was time to make his move. "Can I buy you a drink?" he said in a midwestern twang.

Without missing a beat she called over her shoulder to the barman in her very deepest southern accent, "This Yankee carpetbagger thinks I'm a whore for sale. I could use your assistance."

With a thousand apologies, the scuffling of white shoes and touching of white belt, the salesman made his way to the exit.

Once gone, the barman came over to her table with a tall cold rum on ice. "You got style, lady, this one's on the house."

She smiled wanly at him and took the drink, wondering vaguely if she'd ever enjoy the dalliance of hands under tables and up skirts again, the way she had done so many years ago with the literature professor.

Fong hated being summoned. "Asked to appear," "Could I have a word," "We need to meet"—all were fine, but "In my office now" was not his favourite. So it was with more than a little ire that he approached Police Commissioner Hu's office.

The commissioner's secretary wasn't at her desk when Fong entered. Her computer, a new acquisition, had been left on and its monitor screen was flashing a series of numbers: E-M-29-7976. Fong didn't even know how to turn on a computer, let alone what these numbers meant. With a rush of silk, the commissioner's secretary entered from the main office. She appeared angry that Fong was looking at her screen. Fong momentarily wondered what she would do if he looked at her non-existent tits. With a hrumph, as if she'd been able to read his thoughts, she ushered him toward the commissioner's office. As she did, she refused to meet his eyes. Fong got the distinct feeling that she didn't want to be infected by him.

When Fong entered the office, Commissioner Hu was sitting at one end of a couch, a piece of computer paper in his hands. Upon seeing Fong he quickly folded the paper but in his haste did it inside out, showing the same numbers: E-M-29-7976. A detail that did not escape Fong.

The commissioner signalled Fong to the far side of the couch. As he sat, Fong couldn't get over the notion that they must have looked like the famous pictures of Nixon and Mao — one at either end of a couch — or was it Kissinger and Mao? For the longest time he had had trouble distinguishing among westerners. It wasn't until he headed Special Investigations and had many more opportunities to deal with them that his eye became attuned to the nuances of Western physiognomy.

The commissioner seemed to have just removed a look of dismay and replaced it by his ever smiling, politically connected "good" face. "How are you today, Detective Zhong?"

Swell, he thought. I've been up since five A.M., seen a body in pieces, had a screaming match with a newspaper editor, held half of a heart in my hand and watched a set of dentures munch on it — all before lunch. But he said, "Okay."

"Good," said Commissioner Hu and smiled.

The commissioner had one of those smiles that turned his face inside out. As if the action of smiling was completely unnatural for him and he was practising it. And with intense practice came intense fakery. "Pretending is not acting. Acting is about selecting from what you know," Fu Tsong said in his head. Her voice

43

was so real, so close, so intimate that for a moment Fong lost track of what Commissioner Hu was saying.

Then he caught the drift. His Hu-ness was upset about his not returning the American consulate's phone call. His Hu-ness was also going on about a meeting with the Americans later in the day but that he was to allow the Chinese State people to do the talking. Fine, he thought, the last thing I want to do is chat with U.S. Consulate folks.

"And I thought because your English is so good, you could also translate for us," concluded his Hu-ness.

"Pardon me for saying this but I think that we need a professional translator in a situation like this. I speak conversationally but I cannot claim any real expertise."

"Conversationally is good enough in this case."

"But..." Fong never got to complete his sentence. The smile mask was back on and his Hu-ness was indicating that it was time for him to leave. So Fong got to his feet and headed out.

It was only as he was leaving the secretary's office (the woman still refused to meet his eye) that he realized why he was being asked to act as translator—the powers that be wanted as few people in on this conversation as possible. But why?

On leaving the commissioner's office Fong headed toward the basement of the building and the forensic labs. He knew that there wouldn't be anything to report yet but he wanted to check and see if there were any preliminary responses. Besides, he liked Forensics and the people who worked there. It was the Buddhist end of police work—silent, slow, and patient.

He was waved through forensic security and headed down the long corridor toward the main lab in the back. There was the slightest pop of suction as he pulled open the frosted glass door. He thought to himself that this is probably the only well-fitted door in all of Shanghai. He checked for a manufacturer's label. German, naturally.

Once inside, the hum of the fluorescent lights was about all there was to hear. Several of the scientists looked up and then returned to their work. They knew Zhong Fong but saw no need to distract themselves enough to say hello.

Near the south end of the lab he found Xia Hong Shia, who liked to be called by her English name, Lily. Lily was an attractive, tightly put together woman in her late twenties who seemingly spent every penny on her wardrobe. All to fetching effect. Lily's English wasn't great but she made a real effort and liked to practice, so Fong addressed her in English. "What's up, Lily?"

Momentarily missing the idiom, Lily looked skyward and then smiled at him. "Not a thing fucking." Lily was especially fond of English slang.

Pointing at the microscope in front of her, "May I?"

"Shit, okay."

He put his eye to the lens and squinted. He was always amazed how hard it was to actually see anything through a microscope. After a little fiddling with both his eye and the focus, he managed to get an image of some sort of crystal-based solid.

"What is it, Lily?"

To explain, Lily reverted to Mandarin. "It's standard to ask for a piece of the lung. It usually doesn't show anything, but I found tiny shards of this in the tissue," she said indicating the image on the slide.

"And you don't know what it is yet?"

"Not yet, copper," she said in her smiling English.

There was an unmistakable twinkle in her eye and she stood just a little closer to him than was absolutely necessary. He'd heard rumours that her relationship with her boyfriend had soured but as he looked at her, it occurred to him that his days with younger women were numbered if not in fact over. He didn't know what he felt about that.

"The wallet's in scrapings and should be out soon. Blood typing is almost done. There were a few partial prints on the credit cards," she said in her beautiful Mandarin. Then she added in English, "They're being worked up now."

"Your English is getting very good, Lily."

"I've got CNN. It helps. I think I love Larry King."

"Who?"

"Just an older man with lots of attitude, like someone else I know and also care deeply for." She literally twinkled with her own cleverness.

Enjoying the game, but thrown a little by her forwardness, Fong pointed at the microscope. "Tell me what it is when you find out." Then he turned and headed out.

As he did, he heard Lily whistle at him and mutter, "Yubba Bubla Doo, check out that butt."

Mr. Lo entered the Jade Buddhist Temple up Jiang Ning Road near An Yuan and paid his fifteen kwai. Tourist season hadn't begun yet so it wasn't crowded. The scent of fresh incense was everywhere as the monks passed out bundles of the fragrant sticks to the faithful.

He avoided the main temple in the centre of the courtyard, with its three gaudy gold-painted statues and kneeling chairs, and headed to the east side of the compound where there was a vantage place from which he could see the carvings on the main building's roof—what he thought of as "his statues." The figures formed a unique motif that completed the ends of the upturned pagodalike eaves. On the end of each eave was a long narrow upcurving polelike extension, perhaps five feet long. At the highest point, the farthest from the roof, a tiny robed monk rode a peacock. Behind the monk, following him in a neat line were four lion cubs, each delicately balanced on the narrow pole. All four cubs wore serene smiles. But there was also a fifth lion cub, still on the roof, clearly frightened to make the leap from the safety of the roof to the narrow curving strut. This cub was clearly unhappy. His lack of bravery had kept him from the path—the *tao*. Clinging to the unreal world of apparent safety, the roof, had left him out of the true world—a world of serenity, the *tao*.

As he had so often in the past, Loa Wei Fen willed himself into the eye of the lion cub on the roof. From the cub's eye he looked at the joy of his brothers on the other side. Then, in his mind, he leapt—across the abyss.

Geoffrey's ride in from the airport was as uneventful as a ride with Soo Jack could be. Long ago he had learned that it was better to sit in the front seat and take your chances than to sit in the back and be sure that Jack would spend the entire trip with his head craned around talking to you.

Although he had been in Shanghai only ten months before, the changes were obvious. Huge new hand-painted billboards, behind which were massive building projects, lined Qiao Road and Yan'an as they headed into town from the airport. The air was thick but not as polluted as it would get later in the year. Geoffrey was happy just to watch the city's life.

Shanghai is the largest city in Asia. Its population of fourteen million swells to almost twenty million on any given day because of the people who come into the city to shop and to look for work. The streets, always crowded with bicyclists, taxis, and buses, now had many private cars, some quite fancy, adding to the potentially deadly mix. Jack swerved to avoid a pedestrian who had wandered into the middle of the eight-lane road. He honked.

Everyone honked. Drivers in Shanghai honked to tell you that they were coming. They honked to warn you not to move. They honked to tell you they were passing. They honked to tell you not to swerve. They honked to tell you to go faster. They honked to tell you not to turn. They honked to let the car they were driving know that it wasn't being ignored. Despite all the honking they seldom, if ever, swore or lost their tempers. They honked instead.

Jack was a registered Chinese Driver, not a private car

owner or a cabby. Chinese Drivers were a breed unto themselves. They had real status in Shanghai. They were licensed by the government and knew every road, alleyway, good restaurant, historic site, and pleasure dome within four hundred miles of Shanghai. You want to go to the countryside, you want a Chinese Driver. You want to see the night life in Shanghai, you want a Chinese Driver. You want to shake up your lunch, you want a Chinese Driver.

At the Shanghai Theatre Academy, Geoffrey was met by Deborah Tong, his translator of many years. She showed him to his rooms.

After unpacking his various bags (he'd given up on travelling light years ago) Geoffrey went down the stairs of the guest house and wandered across the compound to the filthy old theatre that he adored.

The invitation from the academy to direct a production of Shakespeare's *Twelfth Night* with a large professional cast and a few talented students came as an unexpected gift. It was unsolicited; usually he had to press the academy for invitations. But as he was to learn later, it was a gift complete with strings.

He'd wanted to work on *Twelfth Night* for years — since Fu Tsong had first begun to talk about the piece. She had said, "Shakespeare has written everyone into this play. We are all there. I know who I am in the play. Who are you, Geoffrey?"

He had managed to duck the question. She was convinced that the play was about love as the ultimate expression of living. Geoffrey's take was more of love as

49

an addiction, a sickness. She had simply smiled at him and continued her analysis. She argued that Malvolio was indeed in love with Olivia, as was Toby, as was Aguecheek, as was Feste. He remembered saying, "That's some woman to have so many men in love with her." To which Fu Tsong had countered, "Oh, not just men. The boy Sebastian as well, not to mention the girl, Viola. All love Olivia deeply." "And what is it that they love so much in this creature?" he had mocked. Totally ignoring his sarcasm she had answered, "Her *chi*. Her life inside."

Ah, yes, her *chi*. Her life inside.

Sometimes, only through absence can a human being tell the value of what was, but is no more. So walking this campus in Shanghai, the People's Republic of China, a country, an academy that no longer contained Fu Tsong's *chi*, Geoffrey Hyland, Toronto theatre director, once more experienced the depth of his loss. How infinitely poorer this place was without its Olivia.

The American consulate's air conditioning was cranked up so high that Fong thought his eyelids were freezing together. He sat between Commissioner Hu and one of the people from the State Department, a trade commissar whom Fong had never seen before. The only American present was the consul general. This surprised Fong.

The business part of the American consulate (known to the people who work there as the real American consulate) was near the seat of true power in Shanghai, the docks. Naturally there was a public consulate, in the pleasant back streets where Huai Hai and Fuxing cross down Wolumquoi, where people of all nations, colours and creeds can apply for immigration visas to the promised land. But nothing of international import got done there. If you wanted to really deal with America, you went down to the docks. Fong found this appropriate. The real American consulate was up the Huangpo River toward the Yangtze. The austere, newish edifice silently hummed its anthem of efficiency.

The size of American rooms didn't seem quite right to Fong. He was used to high ceilings from his own office, but it was the width of the room that unnerved him. Form without function. American.

While translating the "hi, how are ya's" and the "isn't it gettin' hot out there" stuff Fong studied the consul general, a white bear of a man, with bushy eyebrows and a big gut. Fong had known Americans who could play at being American but were in fact quite bright. Such Americans were also quite dangerous, Fong had found.

"So what've you folks found out about the passing of an American citizen, one Richard Fallon?" Fong translated and was told to give the American what he had worked up. Fong handed over an edited version of Wang Jun's report, with copies of only some of the photos and then gave the consul general a list of reports yet to come in and their prospective dates of arrival. There was no mention anywhere of the heart or its missing piece.

"Ghastly business this. You think there's a chance you'll find the guy who did this?"

Again Fong translated and was told to respond.

"It's too early to tell. We have a few leads to follow and a lot of basic investigation to get moving before we can even estimate chances."

The consul general nodded as if in agreement but instead of replying to Fong's statement, he said, "Be careful, sonny boy, you're in way over your head on this one."

Struggling to keep a straight face, Fong smiled. "Would you care to elaborate."

The consul general smiled back and, while nodding, said, "No."

Fong told his colleagues that the consul general understood that things were in their early stages and that he wished to offer the police any services that he could in the investigations. Both Chinese officials nodded sagely. Without asking permission, Fong turned to the consul general.

"Was Richard Fallon an active law enforcement officer at the time of his death?"

"Yes "

"Was he here on any sort of government business?"

"You're cold."

"It's the air conditioning."

"No, no. This has nothing to do with that."

"And what does it have to do with?"

The Chinese officials asked for an explanation and were given an edited precis.

"Will you allow us to use your computers to track his credit cards?"

"I will not."

"Why?" burst out Fong.

The American just smiled, rubbed his belly, and stood.

The Chinese men stood as well and followed him to the door.

At the door, as if it were an afterthought, the consul general put a hand on Fong's shoulder and said, "I've got a teensy favour to ask. Mr. Fallon's widow is coming into town tomorrow or the next day to, well, you know, tidy things up, and I'm sure that she would like to be kept abreast of your investigations. Americans are like that, aren't they?"

Before Gong could translate, the consul general said the exact same thing, in fluent Shanghanese, even getting the complex idiom right. When he was finished, he laughed at the shock on the faces of the Chinese men.

In rapid-fire English, Fong said, "I don't care for this game, if you have something to say to me, say it."

"I thought you Chinese liked games."

"This is not the time—"

"On the contrary. This is absolutely the right time for games. 'At times of change humanity tests the new through the use of games.'"

"Who said that?"

With a smile that had absolutely no warmth, he snapped, "Me. Just now."

At 11:37 P.M., April 19, just over twenty-five hours since the dismembered pieces of Richard Fallon's body were found in an alley off Julu Lu, Zhong Fong called it a day.

As in all investigations at this stage, he had a ton of work ahead of him before he could even guess where to begin. But it would have to wait. Now, he needed time to sit and think so he went out of the office, which everyone else had left long ago, and headed down to Zhong Shan Road. The evening was cool, the oppressive summer heat was still at bay, and the rainy season had not yet come. But it would.

Usually at night, before heading back to his apartment at the theatre academy, he walked the Bund and admired the stateliness of the building where he worked. He'd come a long way, but not in distance. He worked in the former English Concession and lived in the former French Concession but he had grown up in the part of Shanghai that no foreigners wanted, the Old City, the Chinese section of Shanghai. A mere five-minute walk from glittering Nanjing Road or ever-so-chic Huai Hai Road and you found it, just as it had been for so many years, as it would always be, he hoped. The real Shanghai, the Chinese Shanghai.

But it was not there that he headed this evening. Tonight he needed a place to think. Stepping out of his office he turned left and headed toward the confluence of the Huangpo River and the Su Zhou Creek.

Coming to the Beijing Road pedestrian underpass, he stopped and looked behind him. It was an old habit, but on that after today's events he decided to revive. He scanned the faces. Most were Chinese. All were haggard at this hour of the night.

Satisfied that he wasn't being followed, Fong headed

into the cool dampness of the tunnel. Unlike Western cities where these enclosures would have been filled with street people at this hour of the night, in Shanghai the tunnels were both safe and relatively empty. Only one beggar sat there. By his side was a filthy boy child of three or four. In his gnarled hands the old man held an ancient stringed instrument, an arhu. Fong approached him and put two kwai in his bowl. "Play me something, grandpa. Play me something and help me forget."

With that Fong took a piece of newspaper from his coat pocket, spread it carefully on the ground, and sat down. He tilted his head back against the cool tiles of the tunnel and closed his eyes. The unearthly sounds of the arhu filled the tunnel and seemed to echo behind his forehead. They looped and bonged off the hard surfaces of his skull and finally pierced the softness of his brain. And there waiting, as she always waited, was Fu Tsong. Quick and lithe, and fire.

Something plunked down in his lap. Without opening his eyes he felt the tangled hair of the beggar boy. The boy sighed happily as he snuggled into Fong's lap and in the stroke of a bow and the lilt of a melody was fast asleep. For a moment Fong thought that he was losing his mind. Finally the blessing of sleep came to him, borne on a cool breeze, the haunt of the music, and a breath of faith.

Then the nightmare came—again.

DAY TWO

The second day proved no easier than the first. The lab reports came in and to no one's surprise the blood on the wallet matched Richard Fallon's, as did the partial fingerprints from the credit cards. The coroner's report added a few details and confirmed that the most likely time of death was between 9:30 and 10:30 P.M. on April 18. As for the weapon, the coroner concluded that it was a thin instrument with at least a six-inch blade. It was double-sided and, most curiously, it was evidently used with both the left and the right hand. Bones were seldom cut or even nicked in the process; the incisions were made mostly through the joints, severing tendons and levering balls out of sockets. There was a distinct hole in each of the ball joints at the hip which could indicate that as well as having two razor-sharp edges, this particular weapon also had a point capable of puncturing bone.

Wang Jun's men had waited in vain for the arrival of the street sweeper. So now they were trying to find where she lived, a thing harder to do than it sounds since so many people made their homes in alleys and under stairways. Barely places, let alone places with addresses.

The American consulate had finally returned Fong's phone calls and had informed him that the consul general was out of the country on a personal matter and that they were not sure when he would be back. In the meantime, they went on, he could talk to the second assistant for Asian affairs should he need any further assistance from the consulate. Fong declined. Before hanging up he was informed that Mrs. Richard Fallon had boarded a JAL flight in Chicago that morning and should be in Shanghai at noon tomorrow and that the American consulate expected him to make himself available to Mrs. Fallon upon her arrival.

Available for what, Fong wondered. He contemplated calling Commissioner Hu and begging off the Mrs. Fallon chore but decided against it. He'd need to interview her anyway.

The consul general's abrupt departure hadn't really surprised Fong. It occurred to Fong that the Americans were not being represented at the meeting, but rather that a single consul general was attempting to pass on information he knew he could not pass on in any other way. Or perhaps he was just an American piece of shit who enjoyed pulling the coolie's pigtail. Fong knew that it was unlikely that he would ever find an answer to this one, so he shelved it and moved on.

He got up and closed the door to his office, but not before he saw the prying eyes of his assistant, whom he now called "Shrug and Knock." He crossed to his desk and opened the top drawer. Sliding the things in it to one side, he popped open a virtually invisible bottom panel by using the long fingernail on the pinkie of his left hand. From the panel he removed the photographs of the body that were taken before anything had been moved. After a day of investigation he knew what some of the objects in the picture were. The body, although carved up, had been put back somewhat in its godly order. The torso was badly twisted but from above you could clearly see the figure of a man lying on his stomach, his chin in the cement, staring straight forward, his arms and legs spread. The fingers of his left hand were extended unnaturally to point directly toward the alley wall. Directly toward the wallet. The small blob of bloody pulp directly between his legs on the pavement Fong now knew was the piece of the heart the killer had chewed on and then spat out. It was no doubt overlooked as just another piece of viscera and either discarded or thrown in with all the other guts when they were transported to the Hua Shan Hospital morgue. The air sickness bag seal hadn't been found but that didn't worry Fong now that he knew what had been carried in the waterproof bag—half of Richard Fallon's heart. Carried where? That he did not know yet. A left hand that points to a wallet, a piece of heart between the legs—but the fingers of the right hand were pointing as well. To what? Something had been there. Something intrinsic to the message the killer wanted to send. Something that was now gone.

He was about to dial Wang Jun's number when the light on his phone came on. "Who?"

"Gae Fee Hai Lan."

"Who?"

"A long nose who speaks terribly. I think he said Gae Fee Hai Lan."

Fong was still unsure who was calling but decided to take it. "Can I help you?" Fong said in English.

"Your English is a lot better than my Shanghanese, Fong."

With a laugh he did not feel, Fong said, "So you're Gae Fee Hai Lan?"

"I guess so. What does that mean?"

"Water buffalo hill country or something, I don't know, depends how you inflect it."

Small talk dies quickly between men who hate each other. Between two men who loved the same woman.

"What can I do for you, Geoffrey Hyland?" Fong's pronunciation of the Canadian's name was crisp, perfect, and infinitely cold.

Geoffrey did have some shortcomings as a director but the inability to recognize true feelings in someone's voice was not one of them. Fong's chilliness did not escape his attention but he let it pass. "There was a message in my room to call you. So I'm calling. That's all."

"I didn't leave a message for you to call me."

"Well, someone did." Geoffrey's voice rose dangerously.

"And I'm telling you I didn't," returned Fong with the snap of a cracking whip. The silence that followed was slowly filled by the line's electronic hum. The line now connected the two men electronically as surely as Fu Tsong's being had connected them emotionally, in the peculiar erotic bondage of lover and cuckold.

Geoffrey considered hanging up the phone and then thought better of it. "I start rehearsal this afternoon, but maybe we could meet for dinner."

The ludicrousness of that suggestion was clear to both men. Finally Fong broke the silence. "It would be hard for me, I've got a case that's pretty explosive here."

"The Dim Sum murder?"

"You heard."

"The papers are having a field day."

"The restaurants aren't very pleased about the whole thing. Look, Gae Fee Hai Lan, maybe it is time that we sat down and talked, but it'll have to be later. I know where to find you, at least. Once you get going you'll never get your nose out of that damned theatre — or has that changed?"

After a brief pause, Geoffrey sighed, "Things do change, don't they, Fong?"

That hung in the air between the two men like the half a world that separated their home cities. Neither broke the silence for almost a minute. Finally Geoffrey said, "Yeah, I'll be in the theatre a lot, come by sometime."

As Geoffrey hung up, an obscenity ripped up from his gut and tore at his throat. It landed flat and useless in his quiet room.

Fong suddenly felt as if he were somehow falling.

The moment of vertigo passed and he punched Shrug and Knock's line. "Get me all the morning papers and their editors' phone numbers." Without waiting for a response he clicked off and called Wang Jun.

Between Huai Hai and Chong Shu there is a pleasant side street called Dong Lu. About halfway down its curved short stretch is the Long Li Guest House. On the north side of the guest house is a tea house complete with gardens. On the tea house's south side is a small cinema specializing in American action films and soft-core porno flicks. In front of the guest house, extremely expensive, mostly black, late-model automobiles were double and triple parked. All had Taiwanese plates. The Taiwanese, forty-five years after dragging their sorry asses off the mainland thoroughly defeated in war, had returned victors in commerce.

The security here was discreet. The Taiwanese clientele often less so. There was a bar called the Standing Room Only, not twenty yards from the guest house, where the girls were usually kept. They drank and played cards and planned their next shopping spree. Some of them had pock marks on their faces. Many had tracks in their arms. All had the demarcations of transient beauty that had already bloomed and was now on the wane. So the lights in the bar were kept low. The back exit from the Standing Room Only accessed the private grounds of the Long Li Guest House. A businessman could go into the bar, buy a drink, indicate his choice to the bartender and leave his key. The girl then arrived on her own, shortly thereafter, without having to go through the front reception area and potentially embarrass any wives that may have insisted on joining their husbands. The expenses of the tryst were dealt with in confidence through the hotel. They simply appeared on the client's bill as "Cleaning."

But on this day, the men meeting in the back room of the Long Li Guest House were not there to swap stories of favourite whores and bedding techniques. They were there to discuss the death of Richard Fallon and the arrival of half of his heart at one of their hotel rooms.

• • •

At the same time as the meeting was taking place at the Long Li Guest House, there was a more formal gathering across the Huangpo River in the Pudong's newest building, appropriately enough, a power plant. There were no fancy cars here or girls in the bar next door. There were just the simple trappings of power, real power.

Because of the health of the old man who presided, the lights were always kept low. With the lights so dim, the meeting became more about voices than faces.

The ancient cracked Asian voice gulped air to carry its sounds: "Has our message been received, do you think?"

A crisp young European voice responded, "Received, yes, but accepted? That we don't know."

A younger Asian voice chimed in, "These traders have had their way for a long time here, they will not easily be scared off."

There was a murmur of assent around the room.

There had been no murmurs of assent five years ago when the old man had set all of this into motion. There had been just him and his thoughts.

It was a delicate time, a time when nations rose or fell on the decisions of their leaders. He knew that doing nothing would lead to inevitable ruin. The West had invested heavily in China and in Shanghai particularly. But now the big stick of the West, the renewal of most-favoured-nation trade status with the United States, an $8-billion-a-year trading partner, was meeting resistance in the American Senate. The loss of MFN status would effectively end the run of growth in China and possibly plunge it into a savage depression.

The old man with the hoarse voice knew this. He also knew that his beloved Shanghai would be hit hardest. After being ignored by Beijing for almost forty years, the city had finally begun to flourish after Deng's famous cat remark: " A red cat, a black cat, both are cats." This remark was interpreted as meaning money from the East, money from the West, money is money. When four months later Deng casually remarked, "What's so bad about being rich?" the race toward a market economy was on. The five years since had been years of startling growth in Shanghai. Growth and revitalization crowned by the new Pudong Free Trade Region. But now all this was in danger. As quickly as it began it could falter. The old man had seen it happen too many times before. If he had believed in the gods, he would have said that they were fickle and on occasion needed a good laugh. So they played around with our lives — they fully under-stood the idea of irony. But he didn't believe in gods. He believed in planning and thought. He knew what the Americans wanted from China in exchange for MFN status. They wanted what they called progress on what they called human rights.

That they would not get. Ever. China would be governed by Chinese. Never again would a foreign power dictate to China how she was to run her own affairs. This was not 1840 and the shameful Treaty of Nanking where China sold her sovereignty to the English in exchange for opium. And yet, the old man chuckled, he much liked his house in the English Concession and that would not have existed had the English not run Shanghai from the Treaty of Nanking until the Liberation.

He remembered taking up his old writing brush and dabbing it in the ink that had pooled in the well of the stone. He had twisted and feathered the brush on the ancient stone's flattened surface. Then, drawing out a piece of rice paper, he had started his list. On one side he drew the characters for WHAT THEY WANT. On the other: WHAT WE WILL DO.

The list went this way: They want action on, what they call, human rights in China. We will do nothing about this. They want the cessation of export of all goods made by the Red Army. We will stop some but put new labels on most and continue to export them. They want us to stop producing automatic weapons for export. We will protest vigorously and then give in on this point. They want us to stop exporting goods made by political prisoners. We will move the political prisoners to prisons for common criminals and continue their work. They want a cessation of trade in the products of endangered species.

For a moment he had gulped air and sorted his thoughts. Then with a deft flick of his wrist he had slashed characters that read: We will go to any length to stop the trade in ivory in our country.

Rhino horn was not mentioned. Only the old knew the true value of the miracle elixir made from that rare product. He was old. He knew. Knew and would not be denied its benefits.

The cracked-voiced man had been lost in thought. He saw that they were waiting for him. He finally asked wearily, "And this is important, we still agree?"

"If Shanghai is to grow and prosper it is," said a middle-aged Chinese voice. It was affirmed by an American twang.

Once more there were murmurs of assent.

"How can a culture love animals so much?" the old man thought for the thousandth time. He remembered seeing a picture of a German concentration camp commandant tenderly petting a dog while in the background, the dead and the dying were kept behind wire. Like the Japanese at Kwongjo, he thought. Sentimentality is a dangerous thing.

Insurance like that which he had set in motion with the Canadian director was its antidote.

He noted again that the room was waiting for him. It was getting harder and harder to get enough air into his lungs to speak. The operation had greatly drained his powers. Gulping deeply, he forced out, "Then let us authorize a second message." Beneath the massive city, the fibre optic networks glimmered light. And faster than a thought an African man's fate was sealed.

Being a black man in China was like being an extremely expensive pet tiger who refused to wear its leash. The Chinese all stared at you but because you were supposed to be oppressed, like them, they didn't gawk the way they did at white people. Ngalto Chomi, Zairian consul general, had everything a robust young male could ever ask for. An almost inexhaustible supply of money from his private and ever-so-confidential "importing" business, cars, women, and the crucial linchpin of diplomatic immunity. So Shanghai was a playland awaiting his tastes and proclivities. After six months of confinement in the Beijing embassy, constantly under the watch of the conservative ambassador, he had been transferred to the new consulate in Shanghai. He'd been sprung. No more Russians here, just Chinese and a few westerners. Not even many black people. It was a rare day that he encountered another black face on the streets. And he was on the streets of the city all the time. What a city! A candy store of infinite proportions that catered to all tastes, all curiosities. The Chinese were curious about him, too. He felt the eyes of the young women watching him as he moved past them on the crowded streets. He felt the envy as he slid into his sleek Mercedes with its Chinese chauffeur. He felt them — so many of them — all watching him.

The one person watching him that he didn't pick out was a slight-figured Chinese man in a nicely tailored but unremarkable suit. He didn't notice Loa Wei Fen. No one noticed Loa Wei Fen. But Loa Wei Fen was taking note of him, and carefully recording where he went and how long he stayed at each of his stops. Mr. Lo was still the lion cub on the roof, but with every passing day he was getting closer to the edge – to the leap onto that narrow strip.

The large African got back into his car, and Loa Wei Fen slid onto his bicycle. At this hour of the day, a bicycle could make as good time as a car. The large car pulled off Nanjing Road and headed south toward the Old City. Loa Wei Fen guessed he was going to the Old Shanghai Restaurant around the corner from the YuYuan Garden.

He was wrong. But he was close.

Signalling his driver to stop, Ngalto Chomi hopped out on Fang Bang Road just south and west of the popular garden. He was in the heart of the Old City. He liked it here. Here they stared at a black man, and here, he stared back at them. Here his six feet seven inches of height gave him a view of the world of the little people. The people who hacked and spat and called him very "colourful" names. The people who resented his presence. The people who knew so much about opium.

He grabbed a plastic bag of cut-up pineapple off one of the stands, threw down a ten-kwai note and, without waiting for the change, headed north on He Nan smiling and munching as he went. The day was clear but the Old City had its own thickness, not of heat but of intense human experience. Chomi loved it here.

The African's turn off He Nan into Fu Yu surprised Loa Wei Fen. Fu Yu was the famous open-air antiques market. This didn't seem to fit. Besides, it was crowded there and he could lose his prey if he was unlucky. Quickly leaving his bicycle against a post he plunged into the crowd now fifteen yards behind the black man. Only Chomi's height allowed Loa Wei Fen to follow him. But the African moved quickly and, as fortune would have it, a motorized three-wheeled cart pulled out in front of Loa Wei Fen. By the time it was cleared there was no sign of his quarry. Quickly Loa Wei Fen leapt onto a garbage bin at the side of one of the dumpling carts. Ignoring the screams of the vendor, he craned his neck but couldn't see Chomi. Jumping down, he raced through the crowd and ducked into the first available building. He ran through a hallway crowded with beds and up a set of steps. On the first level, he raced down a corridor crowded with more mattresses and threw open the door leading to the front room. An old woman was there with her granddaughter on her lap. She screamed as Loa Wei Fen entered the room. He whirled on her and, in a breath, was an inch from her withered face. The move shocked her into silence. Loa Wei Fen stuck his head out the window and peered in both directions. The black man was nowhere to be seen.

Swiftly descending the steps, he made his way thoughtfully through the crowd. He quickly reviewed the day's events. It had begun before dawn with the e-mail arrival of his new quarry's picture, vital statistics, and addresses. He started his surveillance of the Zairian

Consulate at 7:15. The Zairian consul arrived at 9:50. Just past 11:00, the African emerged from the building and got into his chauffeur-driven Mercedes. Loa Wei Fen smiled.

Now he was racing through the crowd, oblivious to the anger and shouts of those he pushed past. At the foot of the flea market he crossed the street. Once there he looked both ways. There were alleys behind the buildings on both sides. He chose east and sped toward that alley.

About 250 yards down the alley sat Ngalto Chomi's car. His Chinese driver was smoking a cigarette while waiting for his charge to come back from his afternoon diversion. Loa Wei Fen casually strolled down the alley, walking right past the car. Ten yards past the Mercedes and around a sharp bend in the alley he looked to his left, but he needn't have. The smell of the opium cut into the afternoon air, a slight rancidness amid the heady aroma of life in the Old City.

Loa Wei Fen was pleased. As he left the alley, he noticed a squatting father holding his bare-bottomed young daughter under her knees and shaking her gently so that the last of her urine didn't get on her legs. She was oblivious to people watching and sang a little tune as her father completed his task and then pulled up her pants. She hopped over the little puddle of pee and went to help her grandmother clean some vegetables in a small red plastic tub. The father stretched and then hawked a wad of phlegm onto the street. No one gave it a second glance. Evidently everyone found it as natural as . . . as peeing on the sidewalk. Loa Wei Fen liked the Old City too. It was a fine place for a murder.

Amanda Fallon had been told that the JAL flight from Chicago to Tokyo would take thirteen hours. She had no idea what thirteen hours on an airplane meant. Despite the fact that the plane was almost empty, thirteen hours was every one of thirteen hours. The first three hours were tedium incarnate. Flying over the Canadian prairies made even airplane food seem a pleasant diversion. But then just as she was about to drift off, the pilot announced that they were turning north and that their flight path would bring them over some of the wildest regions on earth. The plane in short order passed by Edmonton and entered the Canadian Northwest Territories. The terrain quickly moved from temperate desert cattle farms to a true wilderness. She stayed glued to the window once she caught her first glimpse of the mighty Mackenzie River—still ice bound, etching its glacial path to the Arctic Ocean. She watched in fascination as the frozen striations passed beneath the plane. And then the plane veered west again and range after glacier-capped range of towering mountains leading to Alaska glided beneath the belly of the aircraft. Finally the Bering Strait yawned ahead. Three hours had passed as if in a minute. Amanda's forehead bore a large round red mark where she had pushed up against the Plexiglas window. There was a wildness down there, the likes of which Amanda Fallon had never even dreamed. As the plane crested the Bering Strait and headed south along the Russian coastline, she reached into her bag and took out a pen and a piece of scrap paper. Without preamble or overt thought she began to jot down notes.

She hadn't written for years. She hadn't grown for years. But now she was writing, at first tentatively, but shortly with growing confidence—writing about the glory of what she saw. What she saw after all those years of blindness as Mrs. Richard Fallon.

The second day of a murder investigation was all about what you didn't know. It tended to be depressing, and as Fong entered the musty meeting room with the large round table he looked into the faces of his investigation team and found little to give him solace. Lily was handing out copies of her forensic report, while people were glancing through the file on the coroner's findings. Wang Jun's time chart was on the wall along with several of the photos of the alley—with and without the pieces of Richard Fallon's body. Several of the younger officers held large jars of Tang that they had filled with lutsah, green tea leaves. As the meeting progressed they would refresh the leaves regularly with boiling water from the omnipresent thermoses. The sting of cigarette smoke was in the air. For a moment it occurred to Fong that just such a gathering must have been convened upon the death of his wife. Charts of the construction site would have been hung and pictures of Fu Tsong's . . . He let the thought go and moved to the chair at the head of the table. He had never found out who led the investigation into Fu Tsong's murder but he suspected that it was Wang Jun, who now stood up to go through the crime scene data.

He did it with his normal efficiency. The statement of the doctor confirmed the warden's report. The physician had in fact been at the sick man's side for less than five minutes (evidently proclaiming loudly, "He's dying, what do you want from me?") and then headed back down the length of the alley. He had, as expected, seen nothing out of the ordinary. The man who had been reported for causing a disturbance had ended up in jail that night and hence was easy to locate. He claimed he was so drunk he didn't know where he was, let alone what he was doing. Further coroner and forensic reports added little. The nature of the ambidextrous killer held the table's interest for some time. Fong assigned his best young detective, Li Xiao, to cover this area of the investigation. He was to check into martial arts academies and see what was known about this kind of fighting skill. The coroner suggested that the kind of knife, two-sided and with a significant thrusting point, might be a place to start. Detective Li Xiao took a note and headed out. Lily's analysis of the tiny crystalline shards in Richard Fallon's lungs was still inconclusive. She made the point that with the equipment available to her she might never be able to identify them. Fong authorized a contact with the Hong Kong constabulary and a request to use their facilities. The table was surprised by Fong's willingness to break with tradition and reach out for help to the despised Hong Kong Protectorate.

Wang Jun's people had still not been able to locate the street sweeper so Fong assigned two more people to help in the search and then dismissed the meeting except for Lily, Wang Jun, and the old coroner. Fong's assistant tried to stay behind but Fong sent him out and locked the door behind him.

"That may not be so smart," Wang Jun said.

"I never claimed to be smart, Wang Jun."

"I know that, but try not to be stupid. He's probably on his way to the commissioner's office now."

"That'll give us ten minutes."

After a moment of silence, Lily said, "For what?"

Fong moved toward the time line. As he passed the picture, a copy of the one he had in his desk, he noted that no one had yet mentioned the blob of heart between Richard Fallon's legs or the fingers of Richard Fallon's right hand that were pointing — pointing to what? At the time line he stopped and looked at them. Then he took out a copy of the *Shanghai Daily News* from that first morning with the headline DIM SUM KILLER STRIKES IN JULU LU ALLEY. "We've got a problem." Pointing at the time chart, "The body was found at 10:43 by rookie cop Ling Che. The CSU arrived at 10:52. Right?"

"To the point, Fong, time's a-wastin' here," chimed in Wang Jun.

"Were there any reporters at the scene? Do you remember when the first reporters showed up?"

Lily and Wang Jun were now interested. "Yeah, I remember, because I was surprised how long it took them to smell this one out. I don't think there was one there before the body was already photographed. So not before midnight, at the earliest."

"Right," said Fong. Then turning to the coroner, "And what time did I get to the Hua Shan Hospital morgue?"

The coroner flipped through his pad but Fong interrupted him. "It was 12:49, trust me. And I didn't come up with the Dim Sum crack until at least one o'clock."

The coroner was lost. "So?"

But it was Lily who was on top of it. "Throw me that paper."

Fong did. Lily looked carefully at the masthead. "This is the early edition," said Lily.

Fong nodded. "Right."

The coroner still didn't get it. "So?"

Wang Jun let out a lungful of smoke that seemed to jet across the room. "So? So, the early edition goes to press before midnight. The reporters didn't arrive until after midnight. Even with cellular phones they couldn't possibly have filed the story in time to make this paper."

Then Fong played his trump card. "It's not just a matter of being in time to file their story. They have to clear stories, especially stories about foreigners, with the authorities. I needn't remind you that China does not exactly have a free press."

With a look of shock, Lily said, "Are you trying to say that the paper had this story before Richard Fallon was killed?"

"The story and the clearance for the story," nodded Fong.

After a moment, while this was sinking in, the coroner

added, "I guess they just got lucky with the dim sum stuff."

At that there was a knocking on the door that quickly became a pounding. Fong opened the door to a very angry Commissioner Hu and a smiling Shrug and Knock.

Fong sat in the back of the campus's rickety old theatre that night. His chair squeaked. Every chair in the ancient place squeaked, every floorboard moaned, and the archaic electrical fixtures, which would have closed down most other public establishments, hummed loudly. The large black overhead fans rotated at different speeds (two did not rotate at all) and the sound of the air exhaust system alternated between deafening and concussive. The place smelled of people. Fong liked it. It had been Fu Tsong's favourite theatre and she had played in theatres all over China as well as in Southeast Asia and Japan. In fact she had fought the new thousand-seat theatre on campus, first against the building and then against the design. But it was always hard to convince Chinese people to trust their own theatrical instincts when there were Russian consultants around. Russians used the name Stanislavski like a weapon.

"The proscenium's too wide." "Stanislavski loved a wide proscenium."

"Chinese audiences need the floor of the stage lowered because the average height of Chinese people is less than that of Russians." "Stanislavski always had his stages this height."

"The dimension of this place is inhuman. Brutal."

"Stanislavski said the humanity should be on the stage, not in the house." And so on.

So she had lost. Actually, the city of Shanghai had lost. A lot of money had been spent on a virtually useless theatrical space because a Russian acting teacher who had probably not said a third of the things Russians claim he said was too godlike to be challenged.

Fu Tsong assumed that Stanislavski was a nice enough guy with the odd good idea. She also assumed that he never intended to be quoted and deified. . . although being Russian it's possible he was interested in deification. Be that as it may, Fu Tsong had found it a breath of fresh air when Geoffrey Hyland entered her theatrical life with the line: "Stanislavski who? If I had a dog, I might call him Stanislavski – if he were long dead and gone and irrelevant to the twentieth century art of acting, that is." It had been artistic love at first sight.

Fong remembered Fu Tsong coming home after that first rehearsal with Geoffrey Hyland. He remembered her excitement, her joy. He also remembered his feeling of being outside her world. Outside while Geoffrey was inside.

Now, on the stage, Geoffrey spoke to the *Twelfth Night* cast who sat around old wooden tables. There was a rapt concentration so unlike most Chinese rehearsals, which were often exercises in wasted energy and diffused focus. Fong noted that the academics had been ushered out of the room. This session was not about text. Not even about *Twelfth Night*. This session, the first rehearsal in Geoffrey Hyland's theatre land, was about his passion: acting. Fong had heard Fu Tsong talk about Geoffrey Hyland's first rehearsals. She had said that she learned more about acting in two hours with Geoffrey Hyland than she had in four years at theatre school. So Fong leaned forward and tried to catch every word, to hear what she had heard.

Geoffrey was on his feet—"in full flight" was the phrase that came to Fong's mind—his translator at his side. "For an actor the art form of the theatre is not theatre, but acting. Acting is the art. Because most actors are taught by directors they are usually taught that what actors do is interpret. That acting is not an art but a craft. It behooves a director to have a pliant, obedient actor. And the best way to achieve this is through convincing an actor that his job is to serve the text, the way a brick mason serves an architect. Bullshit! Bullshit, bullshit, bullshit, and more fucking bullshit."

Geoffrey looked out into the house. For the briefest moment his eyes locked with Fong's.

Geoffrey took a breath and allowed his interpreter to catch up. "Acting is not about pretending. Acting is about knowing your instrument and selecting the notes on that instrument that produce the 'most eloquent music.' Hamlet, when pumped for information by Rosencrantz and Guildenstern, takes a recorder from his pocket and offers it to one of them saying, 'Will you play upon this pipe?' To which Guildenstern responds, 'My lord I cannot.' After further beseeching by Hamlet, Guildenstern finally says, 'I know no touch of it, my lord!' To which Hamlet responds, 'Tis as easy as lying.

Govern these ventages with your finger and thumb, give it breath with your mouth, and it will discourse most eloquent music.' Then taking back the recorder he says, 'Why, look you now, how unworthy a thing you make of me. You would play upon me; you would seem to know my stops; you would pluck out the heart of my mystery; you would sound me from the lowest note to the top of my compass; and there is much music, excellent voice in this little organ, yet cannot you make it speak. 'Sblood, do you think I am easier to play on than a pipe?' Like everything else in this play, Hamlet is talking about acting. What an actor does, as Hamlet says, is know his ventages and his stops and plays them in order to create most eloquent music. To do so is an art, not a craft."

Once again Geoffrey let his gaze move to the theatre seats. Fong was still there. Listening. Taking it in. Rapt, as Fu Tsong had been.

Fong felt Geoffrey's eyes on him and knew that with every word Geoffrey was proving to him that he understood Fu Tsong's world in a way that Fong never could. It was a truth against which Fong had no defence. Fong felt the world spinning on its axis. It was several minutes more before he gained enough composure to refocus on Geoffrey's words.

"In *The Empty Space*, Peter Brook begins with a comment that seeing five actors just standing on the stage his eye was drawn to one and not to the other four. He then goes on to make the point that the one able to attract his eye has a gift, is gifted. Fine. Perhaps. But I was sitting in a particularly dull bar back in Toronto one night in 1988. The faces were bland, boring, lifeless. Mr. Brook's other four actors, if you will. And then a strange Flemish lady came on the bar's television and informed Canada that our national hero, Ben Johnson, had been disqualified from the Olympics and that his gold medal was being taken back because he was so cooked up he could hardly find his way back to the dorm after the race or some such. Well, the faces in the bar became electric as everyone of them fell into the pure primary state of being of I AM BETRAYED. In that primary all the faces in the bar would have attracted Mr. Brook's eye. But even as I watched, fascinated by the change in the people, I saw the faces close down as they were unable to stay in the primary of I AM BETRAYED and fell off into the redneck secondary state of being of "We let the fucker into our country and what does he do"—I AM ANGRY—or the liberal secondary state of being of "Well, you know it's hard on a black man in this country and his dad's not here"—I UNDERSTAND. Actors get paid to stay in primary states of being—to stay in I AM BETRAYED and not roll over into secondaries. We pay five bucks or ten bucks or 129 bucks or however many fucking kwai to sit in the dark and watch you stay in primaries. To fully experience for us that which our systems are unable to fully experience for ourselves. Civilians, nonactors, retreat from primaries to the relative safety of secondaries to be able to live their lives, but pay money, sometimes a lot of money, to watch actors stay in primaries and experience live, before their very eyes, that which they themselves are unable to experience. They come to the theatre to watch actors act. To watch them find and stay in primaries. They come to watch artists — actors."

As if coming out of a reverie, Geoffrey looked up and smiled at Fong. Had he said these things out loud or were they only in Fong's head? Fong didn't know. He noticed that the actors, to a man, were hanging on every word. Then, to Fong's amazement, he was sure that he heard Geoffrey's voice deep in his head, as if the late night whisper of a lover dropped into a tilted ear. "Watched her, Fong. We watched her. From down there. You the cop and me the director. We watched her. But at least I appreciated, loved what she did. Loved her. And she loved me." Fong lifted his head from his hands and stared at the stage. Geoffrey was standing to one side. His interpreter was translating Geoffrey's answer to a question about balance between playing actions and maintaining states of being. Evidently a whole section of Geoffrey's talk had passed by as Fong was dealing with the voices in his head. As his translator finished, Geoffrey moved toward her and with the ease of theatre people everywhere put an arm around her shoulders and kissed her. Then to the actors: "I get carried away. We'll pick up tomorrow." There were smiles and thanks and good-byes as Geoffrey shouted, "Ming tien jien, see you tomorrow," as the actors left.

In his seat at the back of the theatre, Fong lit a Kent and tried to release his tension with the smoke that he blew into the musty air.

Geoffrey packed up his bag and stopped as he was

about to turn off the stage lights. He called out, "So do you really know why you're here, Fong?"

Slowly, almost against his will Fong answered, "Because Fu Tsong loved this play."

"She certainly did," said Geoffrey as he struck the lights and headed down the steps into the theatre. "She claimed that everyone in the world was in this play. That all you had to do was allow yourself to know yourself. And once you did you would recognize yourself as one of the characters of *Twelfth Night*."

"And who was she?" Fong found himself asking.

"Olivia, naturally. She who is loved."

"And you?"

"For me to know, and indeed I do know, but seldom admit even to myself, let alone to you, Fong." That hovered in the air for a moment, then Geoffrey added, "You of course are easier to spot in the play. Obvious to all but you, no doubt. You may have to see a few more rehearsals to allow yourself to know, 'what all else do know.'"

The silence between the two men deepened even as the connection grew. Geoffrey felt lumpish in comparison to this thin tight Chinese man. Fong for his part felt outside, outside a world that Geoffrey Hyland clearly knew very well. A world that his wife had loved as she loved her life and the child that had grown within her.

Without prompting Geoffrey said, "Fu Tsong was brilliant when it came to making most eloquent music. I've never seen anyone understand their ventages and stops like her. She was the most artful actor with whom

I have ever worked." He didn't say more but a set of lines from *Twelfth Night* sprang full blown into his head:

> *"Make me a willow cabin at your gate,*
> *And call upon my soul within the house;*
> *Write loyal cantons of contemned love*
> *And sing them loud even in the dead of night;*
> *Hallow your name to the reverberate hills*
> *And make the babbling gossip of the air*
> *Cry out 'Olivia'!"*

For a moment the two men stood in silence in the ancient theatre. An entire world separating them. A woman uniting them forever.

The call came at 3:22 in the morning of the third day. Wang Jun had found the street sweeper. There was a car waiting downstairs.

DAY THREE

I t was 3:46 A.M. as Fong dragged himself into the passenger seat of the car. Wang Jun sat behind the wheel. He had on sunglasses, white gloves, and the hint of a smile.

"It's very early in the morning," sighed Fong.

"It's almost tomorrow in Hawaii," replied Wang Jun.

"I'll take your word for it. That dateline stuff always made me nervous. No matter what time it is in Hawaii, it's too dark to be wearing sunglasses, Wang Jun."

Wang Jun obediently flipped up his sunglasses. His smile broadened.

"Where did you find her?" asked Fong.

Wang Jun set the car in gear and with a laugh said, "Back in the country."

Fong groaned. He hated the country.

"By one of the water towns," Wang Jun added, as the smile creased his face. Fong really hated the filthy water towns.

Pleased with himself, Wang Jun flipped down his sunglasses, sped up Yan'an and headed out of the city.

The drive could take as little as an hour and a half or as

long as six depending on the traffic. At that hour, it took just over two. Along the way they saw some fishermen pulling in their early morning catch from ancient man-made lakes, the odd farmer harnessing his water buffalo for its daily labours, and a great many people trudging their sorry asses toward Shanghai with their lives on their backs. At 4:50 the sun began to rise, and Fong wished that he had brought his sunglasses too. Wang Jun noticed but decided not to comment.

They passed by Grand View Garden in Qingpu County. The massive re-creation was a sort of theme park based on a classic piece of Chinese erotica, *The Dream of the Red Chamber*. Despite protests from the prudish, the place proved to be a magnet to Chinese tourists from hundreds of miles around. They all came, knowing the sordid story of concubine intrigue and couplings. They gawked from one re-created pavilion bedroom to the next, ogling the finery in which these bored slatterns lived or were supposed to have lived. At the time Fong remembered wondering how, as the brochure puts it, the exhibits could be "faithful in even the finest detail." Faithful to what? It was a book. An incomplete book to boot. Fu Tsong howled with laughter when they went the first time. "And here's where she blew the serving boy, and here's where both of the men disrobed for her and did each other to please her. It's beautifully re-created don't you think? I wonder if the chamber pots are full. Those novel characters do use chamber pots, don't they?" A few years after their first visit Fu Tsong, because of her popular portrayal of a young concubine on Beijing radio had been asked to lead a tour of dignitaries to the park. She begged Fong to come on the tour and, after not too much cajoling, he agreed.

He had stood near the back, a pair of dark glasses supposedly hiding his identity, as she led the crowd of politicos. It was a sight Fong thought he would never see. Puritanical, up-tight Communist party officials convulsed with laughter as Fu Tsong insinuated which sexual positions were used in which rooms. From one of the ornate mahogany beds she picked up a beautiful piece of yellow silk with rather hefty knots tied into its length. Swinging it in the air she asked if anyone of the politicians could help her out as to the use of this particular gizmo. They ate it up. She was a dream of desire with just the right taint of smut.

That night she had showed him the many uses of a knotted piece of silk. And each had made him gasp with pleasure. But none more so than when he opened his eyes and saw her joy in giving him that pleasure.

He awoke to a punch on the shoulder from Wang Jun. The sun hurt his eyes and he had a crick in his neck. He looked out the window and saw nothing but fields and a steepish, grassy hill.

"Where?"

Wang Jun pointed at the hill about a half mile off. They got out of the car and began to walk. As they got closer Fong could make out a small chimney on the top of the grassy mound and the slightest of smoke tendrils against the cloudless sky. "She lives in a hill?"

"No, but her brother and his family do," replied Wang Jun as he slid his service revolver into his hand and checked the cylinders.

Surprised to see the gun, Fong remarked, "It's the street sweeper I asked you to pick up, right?"

"Right, Fong, but she ran. People with things to hide run. Or at least that's been my experience, and I'm getting too old to chase them. So this," he said, pointing to the gun, "is my way of being sure that should they try to run, I won't get hurt following them."

"What happened to the gentlemanly touch of a few years ago?"

"It got tired." They were now a mere one hundred yards from the grassy hill. The door would be around the other side facing south, although "door" was probably a misnomer. An opening with a cover would be more likely. However, now with the new market reforms, a peasant could get rich, and quickly too. You never knew what you'd find at a peasant's place. A complete Sony home entertainment system, a Jaguar convertible, a geisha—it was getting out of hand.

The grassy hills were of course man-made. They were the accumulation of the original dirt that had been removed to form the sunken rice paddies. In this part of China several of these mounds were more than eight hundred years old. They had been constantly inhabited since they were first built. Few remained. Of those that did, the truly valued ones were covered in grass like this one. They were said to be remarkably warm in winter and cool in summer and totally waterproof. Yeah, but what about the view, thought Fong.

The path led them to the south side of the hill. The other three sides were covered with freshly flooded rice paddies. Fong shivered at the thought of entering the barrow.

Their reception was chilly, to say the least. The brother, a creature not so differently textured from the thick mud that passed as soil in this part of the world, stood in the doorway and would not let them in. At first he claimed his wife needed time to dress and then he claimed that his humble abode was unworthy of such esteemed guests. Then Wang Jun shoved him hard against the side of the opening and the policemen marched into the barrow.

The first thing to hit Fong's senses was the deep scent of the earth. The domelike shape above him was living earth supporting plants and animals. And he was beneath it. The dampness of the air was complete. Fong felt his entire body coat with sweat. But he wasn't totally sure it was from the air. There was fear here, too. Huddled to one side of the rounded space was a youngish peasant wife and her young son. Across the way was the grandmother. There was also beautiful Danish modern furniture sitting on a silk rug that must have cost several thousand kwai. Behind the furniture were various elaborate fish tanks. Besides the usual tanks that you would see in any restaurant window containing edible fish and eels, there was also a tropical tank replete with godly floating experiments in colour and design. Next to this aquarium was a large glass enclosure sitting on a sturdy wooden cabinet. As Fong took a step toward the enclosure, a mighty serpent, its body as thick as a man's arm, rose a full two feet up and stared at him. For a moment the great animal was completely still and then it flared its hood and lashed at the glass, sending shivers through the panes.

Wang Jun had managed to get some of the basics from the brother. Like his name. After some badgering the man even acknowledged that he knew his sister. But no, he hadn't seen her for years, maybe twenty years. Wang Jun turned to the grandmother for confirmation of that fact and was met with an uncomprehending look.

"She speaks only Cantonese."

"Yeah, and I'm Doctor Bethune," Wang Jun shouted back. That made the child cry. The mother comforted him. Fong noticed that the boy was plump. A fat Chinese peasant boy—the world was changing. Wang Jun took a slow walk around the room and finally said, "You folks live pretty well. It would be a shame to have to confiscate it all as evidence in a murder case." That clearly shook the wife, but the brother stared her down.

Fong watched all this and said nothing. From the moment he entered the barrow he sensed that there was something else present here. There was something wrong with the geography of it all. He looked toward the door opening and then to the cooking fire in the opposite wall. The smell of morning porridge was thick in the room. He walked by the kitchen area and then parted a hanging sheet revealing the family's sleeping mattresses, each a new Japanese-style futon on its own raised wooden platform. Then he crossed back into the centre of the room and stood directly under the apex of the dome. Entrance to the south, sleeping quarters to the west, cooking fire to the north, and silk-rugged living area to the east with its rows of aquariums against the wall.

Something about the aquariums. He walked toward them. The brother shouted at him to take his shoes off before he stepped on the silk rug. He ignored the peasant's protest and crossed toward the aquariums. Three held food fish. Two, food eels. One held tropical fish and one, the great snake. Then he turned back and faced the kitchen.

No Chinese family would keep the aquariums in the living room. They held food. They belonged in the cooking area. He looked at the aquariums and saw that their backs were painted black. The large one with the cobra was almost three feet tall and stood on a solid two-foot cabinet. For a moment, the great snake dared him. It rose up again and flared its hood. The body whipped back and forth as if waiting for its chance to smash the glass and lunge at Fong. Fong took a breath and putting his hand between the back of the glass and the wall, he pushed. The cabinet with the snake slid out smoothly revealing a tunnel, some ten yards long, heading out into the fields.

Over his shoulder he heard Wang Jun swear. Fong raced through the tunnel, the smell of sodden earth all around him. He squeezed out the far end into the knee-deep mud of a paddy. Two paddies over, a figure he took to be the street sweeper was running at top speed along the ridges between the flooded plains. Fong headed right for her, crossing the paddies as fast as he could and shouting at her to stop. She did, for one breathless instant, and then hurled herself across the adjoining paddy. At that moment, Fong's footing gave out under him and he plunged head first into the murky water. He came up soaked and spluttering for air and continued the chase. As he leapt into the second paddy, his hands instinctively reached up to pull what he thought were fat weeds from his lip and neck but the slick stuff refused to come off. When Fong finally got a good hold of the thing on his lip he realized that the weed was alive and not merely stuck to his lip but actively moving toward his open mouth.

In fact his body was alive with fat, succulent leeches.

He bit the one closest to his mouth and spat out half the wriggling thing as he jumped onto the perimeter wall of the second paddy. The street sweeper didn't seem to be making much better progress than he so he tried the wall rather than the paddy this time. As he did, he heard a shriek from the paddy ahead. When he got there he saw that the street sweeper had fallen into the netting that separated the eel section of the paddy from the rice section. The creatures were now actively pouring through the rent in the net, many of them crawling over the street sweeper who was howling in terror. Her howls attracted the locals, one of whom owned the eel section. His howls outdid hers.

Fong finally got to the exhausted street sweeper. He stood on the mud bank and managed to pull the sucker end of the leech off his face. As he tossed it into the teeming eely waters, he couldn't help but thinking that he really hated the country. He really did.

Back in the barrow, the street sweeper faced the two policemen. She was probably in her early twenties but it was hard to tell. Her work on the streets of Shanghai, in the traffic fumes and dirt, year after year, for eleven out of every fourteen days, had taken its toll. It's possible she had hopes and aspirations like the rest of us, but the wheezing in her lungs as she breathed did not bode well for them.

Fong had salted off the remaining leeches and found that he only had one serious sore, near his right hip, which continued to bleed despite the compress from the first aid box in the car. Ignoring the blood, Fong, still in his soaking suit, sat down opposite the street sweeper. Wang Jun had taken the silk carpet and thrown it over the snake aquarium, then cleared the rest of the barrow of its inhabitants. While doing so he took the opportunity to slam the brother across the temple with his revolver "just so that he'd remember next time not to lie to the police."

The street sweeper sat on a low bamboo stool and shivered. Fong was quite calm. He had done many interrogations. His very first had almost cost him his life, when he decided that a young thief needed understanding and a friend, not a swift kick in the teeth. He still carried the scar of the knife wound a blade edge from his left kidney. Fong lit one of the cigarettes from Wang Jun's dry pack and sent a funnel of smoke in the street sweeper's direction. It had its desired effect. The poor creature began to cough violently.

"Where's your face mask?"

She indicated her pocket. "You can put it on if it helps."

She grunted what passed for a thank you, took out the wet mask and put it over her mouth and nose. The street sweepers all wore them — at first just in the latter parts of the day, then all day and finally almost all the time. Some slept with them on. The ever generous state supplied them free of charge.

Wang Jun had already taken the preliminaries from the brother. She was twenty-seven, single, worked the second street cleaning shift on Julu Lu from 5:00 P.M. to 2:00 A.M. Her name was Tsong Shing and it's possible that there was a time in her life when her eyes were not filled with the fear of her own death.

"My name is Zhong Fong and I am head of Special Investigations for the Shanghai District. Two nights ago, between nine-thirty and ten-thirty on the evening of April 18 a man was killed in an alley off Julu Lu. The alley is on your route. It is in fact your responsibility according to your supervisor." There was no response from Tsong Shing. She sat sullenly with her eyes down and wheezed through the mask.

"The dead man was chopped into pieces and left like so much rancid meat to stink in the alley," Fong said, his voice rising ominously. "Open your stupid mouth and tell me if you saw him."

Her mouth, behind the mask, stupid or not, opened and then shut. Like a trapped animal she was looking for a way out. She wasn't sure where the danger lay and hence thought it best to stay where she was, pretty much the way most pedestrians in Shanghai deal with the reality of hundreds of bicycles coming at them on a walkway. Don't move, let *them* avoid *you*.

But Fong was a good interrogator. Some policemen thought interrogations were a joyous opportunity to degrade a suspect. Fong never believed that. He found it base and demeaning to humble another human being. He felt himself a lesser entity each time he walked out of an interrogation room with the suspect broken into mental pieces.

Softly he said, "We know that you didn't kill him." There was the slightest glimmer of hope in her eyes. "We assume that you didn't even see him, the killer, that is." Rushing toward the safe spot she almost screamed. "I didn't. I swear to you that I didn't, I didn't. Honest."

"But you did see the dead man, didn't you, or at least the pieces of the dead man, didn't you?" Slowly her head moved up and down. Then in a sharp nasal tone, with harshly punched consonants, Fong snapped, "You missed his wallet, you little idiot." Tsong Shing literally faltered under the surprise attack. Her body slipped from the small stool as if someone had upended it. Before she could rebalance herself, Fong was on her, so close to her face that he could smell her breath through the mask. "But you found something in the alley, didn't you? Didn't you! His right hand was pointing, wasn't it? What did it point at? What did you pick up in the alley, what!" But this time the trick wouldn't work. He saw it in her eyes halfway through his attack. They had gone dull as she retreated back inside herself. With a hand she pushed him back and then virtually spat into the mask, "I have nothing! I have nothing. Everyone else has something, everyone, but I have nothing. Nothing." Then she crumpled on the ground, moaning softly.

"Finished with the psychological crap, Fong?" Wang Jun was standing across the barrow.

"Yeah, I guess."

"Shall I execute plan B?"

"It seems they leave us no alternative."

Wang Jun then pulled out his revolver and yelled toward the door opening, "Get your fucking ass in here." In a hurry, the brother, his face now quite swollen from Wang Jun's pistol whipping, came to the door.

Wang Jun approached the rich peasant. "Well, comrade, and I use the term guardedly here, I think we have ourselves a situation. It being this." He pointed at the street sweeper but spoke directly to the brother. "Your little thieving whore of a sister over there took something from a Julu Lu alley two nights ago. We as the representatives of law and order in the District of Shanghai want it back." The brother went to speak but Wang Jun indicated that he thought silence the only correct response at this point. The brother stared at Wang Jun's raised gun and said nothing. "Very good, you're a smart guy for a peasant." Reaching for the silk rug, he said, "This will have to be taken in evidence, as will. . ." and he rattled off a list of every valuable article in the place. At the end of his recitation he handed the brother a card and said, "That's my number, if you want your stuff back, you call me and tell me what your slut sister took from the alley." The brother was eyeing his sister with fury. Seeing this, Wang Jun took Fong by the arm and headed him toward the entrance. As they left he said under his breath, "He'll have what we need within a day or I'll eat leech for lunch. By the way I'm hungry and there's a good restaurant in the next water town."

Even as Fong was formulating his arguments against going into the water town, not the least of which was that his clothes smelled like the shit used to fertilize the rice paddies, Loa Wei Fen was watching Ngalto Chomi, Zairian consul general. Once again the agile African completed his office chores and headed down toward Fu Yu. Loa Wei Fen looked to the eastern sky. No rain today, he thought, but dust. The dry hot wind straight off the Mongolian steppes was running strong. The city's grit would mix with the loess from the country, carried by the strong wind—by the cleansing wind of the plains. Loa Wei Fen noted that many people chose to stay indoors to avoid the dust, that the endless strings of bicycle riders on Yan'an were thinner than usual.

As he pedalled his bicycle following the black man's car, he slipped his hand into his inside suit pocket. There the snake-handled Mongolian knife seemed to roll over into his palm as if a thing alive. A day kill in the Old City would provoke the kind of response that his employers wished. A day kill would also move him nearer to the eave of the roof. Nearer to the leap to the curved pole with the other lion cubs.

Amanda found the bus ride from Narita to the JAL hotel vaguely reminiscent of travelling through the clean New Jersey suburbs. At the hotel it took less than a minute to check her in and JAL had booked her bags all the way through to Shanghai.

The deep tub in the bathroom was a joyous sight. She had been travelling since eight in the morning and the trip had taken a total of seventeen hours. So that made it one in the morning her time, although it was 3:30 in the afternoon in Tokyo, but the next day. It didn't matter what time it was. She was tired and a bath would unwind her enough, she hoped, to sleep. On the bed was a cotton bathrobe and a pair of paper sandals. Without bothering to draw the curtains, she removed her travelling clothes and undid her hair. Out the window there were crowds of Japanese men, many of whom would be happy to pay a healthy portion of their monthly paycheques to get a glimpse at what was offered so freely to the late afternoon sun.

The bathwater was softer than she expected. She sank into its warmth and sighed. Then, holding her breath, she slid down farther so that her head was beneath the water.

She didn't know if the tears started while she was beneath the water or whether they began their flow when she came up for air. It hardly mattered. Her body began to heave with sobs. She didn't know if she was crying for the death of a man she had married but had never really known or for all the lost years she had spent with that man. All she knew was that alone in a cubicle of a hotel room in Japan she finally began to mourn.

Loa Wei Fen had made a mistake, but he'd been lucky. The black man had been much stronger than he had anticipated. And the opium had made him physically unpredictable. Once he had managed to cut the African, his knife had done its work with its usual precision. It was not the knife that had faltered. He, Loa Wei Fen, was the one.

There had been no time to dawdle. No time to arrange body pieces. It surprised Loa Wei Fen that Ngalto Chomi carried no wallet. He must simply let the driver settle his accounts. But the wallet was no matter. A black man was not hard to identify in Shanghai.

It was the other thing that he had failed to leave that so angered him. It was not in fact until he was back in his room at the Portman that Loa Wei Fen reached in his pocket and remembered it. His employers would not be pleased. But more important, he was not pleased. He was trained not to make errors. He was trained to be perfect. And here he clearly was not.

He threw the slender white objects at the ceiling.

They shattered. But the sound did not pacify him. To

him the ivory shards were nothing more than snowflakes falling on the roof, making it slippery for the lion cub to jump to the pole.

About the time that Amanda was sinking into her hotel tub, Fong and Wang Jun finally reached the outlying suburbs of Shanghai. Both men would have been amazed to learn that the new housing going up there looked exactly like lower-income homes in Southern California commuter communities.

Shortly thereafter in one of the alleyways off Fu Yu, a five-year-old boy brought a piece of what he thought was "funny dark meat" to his grandmother's outdoor cook stand. The old woman's screams did the unthinkable — they brought Shanghai's traffic momentarily to a halt. This in turn brought the police. Which in short order brought a phone call to Special Investigations.

By the time Fong and Wang Jun got there, the crime scene had been severely compromised. The alleyway off Fu Yu was densely travelled, so despite the best efforts of the local police, it quickly had become almost impossible to tell what was left where and by whom. Fong ordered the evacuation of almost the entire alley and despite the protests of the citizens and a cellular query from Commissioner Hu, he got his way. Then he had construction site searchlights set up all along the alley and quarter-meter sector lines laid down. Seventy-two police officers picked through every inch of one of the filthiest alleys in Shanghai for the better part of twelve hours and came up with almost nothing.

Over and over again, Fong was approached with "What are you looking for?" And over and over again, he said, "I'll know when I see it." So they brought him everything they found. A small handful of one-fen coins, half a well-leafed-through Hong Kong porno magazine, bits of several different kinds of food in various degrees of decay, a sole from the toe of a lady's shoe, and many more things—none of which pleased Fong. He had already found the piece of heart and the strip from the JAL airsickness bag, where he thought they would be. The Chinese driver informed the police that his Zairian charge never carried a wallet, that he, the driver, always went in after his client was finished and paid the bills. So that accounted for the wallet's whereabouts.

As the driver headed downtown with a police officer to make a full statement, Wang Jun approached Fong. "One hand points to the guy's ID."

"The other to the second part of the message," replied Fong.

"Which is?" asked Wang Jun.

"Which is what we are looking for. No! What we'll keep looking for until we find."

Wang Jun slipped a cigarette into his mouth. "Did you notice that the body pieces weren't put together very well this time?"

"I noticed that."

"Could it be that our guy is slipping? Maybe he made a mistake."

"Perhaps."

Wang Jun looked closely at the younger man. Fong's face seemed hard as a river stone. Set. Not looking outward at all, rather turned inward as if probing a memory.

Fong had told her it was nothing more than a mistake. A slip of the tongue. That whatever she was carrying he would love and cherish as he loved and cherished her. But Fu Tsong knew her husband, the cop who loved the actress. She knew the pride he had in coming from the depths of the Old City to his present job, she knew his training in being a man. And she knew that part of that training insisted that he have a son.

Spending her life in the relativity of art, she adored the factual solidity of Zhong Fong. His bluntness pleased her. So did his unrelentingly straight-line maleness. He never apologized for it, yet could easily converse with her many gay and effeminate male friends from the theatre. She enjoyed the pleasure of his touch and thrilled at how after all these years she still roused him by the simple removal of her blouse. She'd catch him in the mirror watching her put on her makeup. Walking into a room with a towel around her, fresh from the shower, provoked a smile from deep inside him. And his smile made her smile. Even the momentary slip of a bra strap outside a loose blouse attracted his attention. As if they were kids—no, not kids, but young lovers who thought their love the only love in the garden of delights.

She also liked his incisive intelligence. He'd read each of her scripts and often had questions that made her see the text in new and different ways. He'd approach things deductively, always starting with "Now what would make someone use that exact phrase?" And then that liquid mind of his would put together backgrounds, often several of them that would lead an individual to say precisely those words. More often than she admitted she used his insights in her work.

But now, as he pleaded his case before her, claiming it was just a slip of the tongue when he said "I'm lifting you and our son," she knew differently. She applied his thinking. What could possibly make a person say that exact line? And there were very few answers. In fact there was only one. A person would only say "I'm lifting you and our son" if what the person wanted was the wife he held aloft to be carrying a son deep in her womb.

Fong was almost ready to call it quits when the brother from the country raced down the alleyway shouting, "I want my fucking carpet back."

"Do you have something for me, comrade?" inquired Wang Jun as he threw an arm around the peasant's shoulders.

"I do, but I want my fucking carpet first."

He wouldn't speak until he was shown his carpet. So Fong, Wang Jun, and the brother hustled into a patrol car and sped off to the police warehouse by the airport. Once inside, the brother was given a glimpse of his carpet and the other pieces of his property. Fong then sent everyone else except the brother and Wang Jun out of the enclosure.

"So you have something for us," said Fong.

The brother hesitated for a moment and then reached into his pocket and pulled out three small intricate white carvings. Taking them, Fong said, "These? These are what your sister took from the alley off Julu Lu?"

"Those."

"There wouldn't happen to be several dozen more of them would there, comrade?" snarled Wang Jun, but Fong waved the question aside and turned to go.

Catching up to Fong, Wang Jun stared at the delicate figures. "Ivory?"

"Yes, ivory."

"Like ivory-from-elephants-type ivory?"

"The same, Wang Jun," said Fong as an idea tickled at the side of his brain but refused to come forward. From far behind them, they heard the brother scream, "How'm I suppose to get my fucking carpet back to my house?" Ignoring this Fong asked Wang Jun, "You don't think he beat the street sweeper to get her to tell him, do you?"

"If it makes you happy to believe that all of a sudden out of the goodness of her heart she fessed up so be it. For me, I hope he didn't kill her. That's all I hope."

The murder of the Zairian consul general was all over the papers. This time, every paper in town had the story and all could have gotten it legitimately. No one jumped the gun. The inevitable call from the Zairian embassy in Beijing was handled at a higher level so Fong never even knew the content of that no doubt unpleasant exchange.

Fong was alone in his office as the dawn crested the river. On the table in front of him was a puzzle. Not a godly jigsaw puzzle this time but rather a number of human events whose points of intersection were still in doubt. One part of the puzzle was the personal data on Richard Fallon, another part was the personal data on Ngalto Chomi—between them were the three small ivory statuettes. Fong took a thick pencil and drew a line to join Richard Fallon to the ivory. Then he circled the ivory and continued the line to Ngalto Chomi. Then he put question marks over each of the connecting lines. He drew a wide arc over the ivory joining Fallon and Chomi. Again he put a question mark over that line. Below the ivory he put the few pieces of data he had on the Dim Sum Killer—weapon specs, a professional, leaving a message, daylight and populous alley kills— and drew a line to the ivory. Then he erased it. He drew lines to Fallon and Chomi and on them wrote the word "contracts." Then he wrote out questions.

1. Who authorized the contracts? He drew a line from the Dim Sum Killer to an empty circle with a large question mark in it.

2. If a message is being sent, to whom? He drew a line from the ivory to another empty circle with a question mark in it as well.

Then he took out a piece of paper and wrote LEADS TO FOLLOW UP. Under it he put:

A. *Shanghai Daily News* publishes story before it happens

B.   American consul tries to warn me of
something, then disappears

C.   ivory

D.   the specs on the weapon

E.   the shards in Fallon's lung tissue

He divided up his personnel. Wang Jun would take the newspaper problem in his usual diplomatic fashion, Lily was following the shards, Detective Li Xiao was already at work on the weapon specs, and he suspected that the American consul was a dead end.

That left the ivory to him.

DAY FOUR

F u Tsong had called it "the Mess." She had labelled it "perfect Hilton Lobby art" and that is exactly where they had first seen it and where Fong was now looking at it again. It was just after 9:00 A.M. and he had not slept. But he knew what he needed. He needed to see the Mess.

The Mess was a white plaster statue about three feet tall and two feet wide that stood inexplicably in a place of honour in the lobby of the Shanghai Hilton, China's only five-star hotel. On the left was a Mongol warrior, complete with shaved head and lengthy braid, who was riding a fighting pony. Fair enough. But this fighting pony was now rearing high on its hind legs because a huge hovering eagle was pulling a long snake from the ground near where the horse's front feet would have been had it not been rearing at the time. Sort of fair enough. But then, just to round out the Mess, the Mongol warrior, braid flying maniacally, had drawn his sword and was leaning over ready to cut the snake in half. Now why exactly was he doing this? The Mongol warrior's dilemma, as Fu Tsong put it, was that he was going to fall on his pigtailed head because his horse was rearing. Now it was logical to assume that the large eagle, not five inches from the horse's nose, could be the thing causing the poor animal to rear and hence should be the object of said Mongol's sword. But no, the sword was raised against the snake. If the horse was frightened of the snake, that danger was taken care of by the eagle. But not if the Mongol warrior had his way. Well. . . as Fu Tsong put it, it's a mess. It had unity but no sense. It's not art, it's kitsch. It's the Mess.

But Fong wasn't so sure that Fu Tsong was right this time, because he saw sense here—not logic, but sense. He saw that the Mongol warrior was at his wits' end. That he was inexplicably at the whim of fate. That he was falling through no fault of his own. That the warrior who was so used to control was going to meet his end completely and utterly as a joke of nature. A cosmic "gotcha." The warrior's reaction to this injustice was to lash out. At the nearest thing. In this case, the snake.

Fong understood that. It was what he felt now. It was why he came to the lobby of the Hilton to see the Mess.

Fong knew that the proverbial shit was going to come down on him today. A second dissection experiment on the streets of Shanghai would not go over well with the powers that be. It was going to be a shitty day, no two ways around that. But like all policemen everywhere, Fong had his sources of information and he was going to tap them before he was handed his head by Commissioner Hu. He was going to tap them until they hurt.

Fu Tsong had called it his "round up the usual suspects"

mood. *Casablanca* was one of the few American movies, which Fu Tsong had insisted he see, that Fong actually liked. Fu Tsong had been surprised. He'd never told her that he liked it because the hero was short, like him. He would never have the chance to tell her that or so many other things, after what happened to her in the Pudong.

He slammed down hard on the brakes of his Volkswagen Santana and flipped off the flasher. With the hint of a smile on his face he crossed the street and entered the favourite whorehouse of one of his "usual suspects." Fate might be throwing him from his horse but he was going to cut the fucking snake in half before he hit the ground.

The gulped air of the hoarse-voiced old man was the only sound breaking the ominous silence in the Pudong power-plant room. Finally he said, "Why didn't we just scare the merchants? They have no honour, no pride, they'd sell their mothers if they thought there was an American dollar to be made in it."

The silence lengthened in the dark room. At last it was broken by an elegant middle-aged Mandarin voice. "We have already discussed this. It is the smugglers who must be stopped. There are too many merchants to frighten into shutting down. But there are a limited number of people with the means to smuggle. So we agreed. Sir, you agreed. That we should send a message to the smugglers, to get them to stop."

"Won't these killings frighten away investment money too?"

"Only for a moment, but that moment will pass. The killer will be caught as we planned," said the elegant voice.

Once again there was a lengthy pause before the old man spoke. "It is a new world. All this because a group likes animals. . ."

"And Shanghai must grow or die."

There was no message on his e-mail and that surprised Loa Wei Fen. His employers were no doubt upset. There had been no mention of the ivory anywhere in the press although the deaths had gotten prominent coverage.

Well, they would contact him, that was a certainty. He looked down at the computer notebook on the bedside table. He affixed the modem jack and turned on the machine. With a few quick commands, he brought up the e-mail concerning the Zairian consul general. Its return address was E-M-29-7976. There was no identified server. That didn't surprise Loa Wei Fen. The People's Republic of China was doing its best to control e-mail correspondence and hence had probably instituted a central server system for the country. With his technological advantage it didn't take Loa Wei Fen long to locate and break into the server's data banks. In short order the street address from which the e-mail had been sent flashed merrily on his computer screen.

He still had three days left on his contract and he thought that perhaps it was time to learn something about his employer. Time to be prudent. No. Now, it was imperative to be prudent.

There was something satisfying about breaking in on a pimp in midcoital pump with one of his girls. Dung Tsu Hong looked every inch a fool as he attempted to cover himself with a pillow while his ladyfriend whined that she was wet and there was no shower here and besides who was this guy?

It was always satisfying to shame them in front of the girls who were so frightened of them. That or rip their fancy clothes. Fong decided that since Dung Tsu Hong was naked, except for the pillow covering his crotch, the clothes option was out. So he grabbed the pillow away from the pimp and smiled.

"I've got a question or two for you."

Dung Tsu Hong sank to the floor, holding his hands over his genitals.

Fong knelt down beside him. "I want information on the two killings. I want it by the end of the week. Under stand me, Dung Tsu Hong! I could come back every day and do this, it gives me so much pleasure. Now if you don't want to see me for a while find the answers to these questions: Who's the knife artist? And where is he?" With that he grabbed a handful of the man's greasy hair and pulled hard. "Those are easy questions for a smart guy like you, Dung Tsu Hong. Who's the knife artist and where is he. Got it? Up and down means yes."

Dung Tsu Hong's head moved slowly up and down. The whore on the bed giggled. Fong shot her a look. This one probably thought her work was fun. This one probably approached Dung Tsu Hong, not vice versa.

In the morning light, returning to his car, Fong felt

none too good. The likelihood that the pimp would be able to find anything was not great. But at least it was something. The punching bag punches back. He turned on the flasher and hit the siren. He had two more calls to make before he went to the office and had to face Commissioner Hu.

Shrug and Knock pocketed his master key and cracked open the door to Fong's office. He surveyed the interior. The Little Turd, as he called Fong, wasn't there. Not usual for him. Then Shrug and Knock's eyes were drawn to Fong's schematic on the table. After a moment's viewing he concentrated on the line drawn from the ivory pieces through the Dim Sum Killer to the circle with the large question mark inside it.

Shrug and Knock knew that this would interest Commissioner Hu.

Fong's next two stops didn't require violence, only the threat of it. The first was to an illegal money changer who frequented the Fu Yu market and also did a franchise operation off Haui Hai in the clothing market near the embassy district. Breaking in on him was not difficult and refusing the casually offered bribe proved that he was in earnest enough for the man to listen to him. The threat to close him down was enough to get the man's full attention. Times were getting tough in the illegal money-changing business. Now that foreigner exchange currency, familiarly FEC, wasn't being issued by the government to foreigners wishing to buy Chinese goods, a healthy chunk of the money-changers' busi-ness, the exchange of FEC for REM (Chinese currency) was gone. Now a foreigner could get REM at any bank, just like a Chinese national. The money changers, for-merly proponents of open markets, now had to compete against the Bank of China. They were learning that com-petition could be tough.

Fong repeated his questions. Who was the knife artist and where was he? The money changer virtually kow-towed as he promised his full cooperation.

Fong's third stop was at the North Train Station across the Su Zhou Creek.

This train station used to be a place of great silences. During the Cultural Revolution, the forced move to the countryside of thousands, perhaps millions of people began here. Their leavetakings took place in the cav-ernous terminus under the watchful eyes of the Red Guards, eyes that did not permit sentiment. Tears were an expression of the bourgeoisie. So silence was the only farewell.

The train station was anything but quiet now, although it was still a place of vast sorrow. Every day thousands upon thousands of peasants from the coun-tryside were disgorged from trains into the huge echo-ing building. They arrived hoping to find work in the economic miracle that was Shanghai. They arrived with sullenness and loathing in their eyes. Had they not fought the revolution to be equal to these execrable Shanghanese? Yet here they were like beggars on the street looking for the right to lift and haul with hands and carrying poles. Water buffalo work.

Only the men came. They came in anger and hate and in the noonday sun; they crowded the station's steps as they sat on their red-white-and-blue-striped satchels and glared at the passersby. At some they spat. At most women they threw stones. At the funny-looking little cop's approach they looked the other way. They might be from the country but they recognized a policeman's walk when they saw it.

Fong passed by the huddled bunches of smoking men and entered the station. Its height always surprised him, but his business was not in the central hall. Flashing his police identification he quickly passed through security and was led to the customs warehouse.

Inside the old warehouse, the sun etched spider webs through grit-plastered windows. Fong took a deep breath and then asked to see Shen Lai. The man who took his request returned in a moment and asked Fong to follow him.

They walked down aisles with three-tiered shelves rising to the ceiling some sixty feet above them. All the shelves were piled high with crated goods. Stacks of electronic equipment from South Korea, Singapore, and Japan. Clothing and food stuffs from America. Heavy machinery parts from India. Coffeemakers from France. Goods from almost every country that Fong could name, all waiting here for customs clearance. At one time this warehouse had been filled with goods from the USSR and Albania. From Romania and North Korea. Now they were the few countries that seemed not to be represented. As the two men passed through the last aisle, Fong did spot an area where the packages were half rotted through and the wrapping so badly put together that it was coming apart. Without looking he knew that this was the Russian section. Some things never changed.

Shen Lai was not happy to see Fong. He was a round-faced fat man in his early fifties with large puffy cheeks and the smallest mouth in the Eastern Hemisphere. Whenever he spoke his mouth looked like that of a goldfish, and that was in fact his *nom de guerre*, the Goldfish. Behind his back they called him Fish Face. Fong couldn't see how the Goldfish was much of an improvement but then again Fong was never up to date on the intricacies of etiquette in the world of Chinese organized crime.

Shen Lai was not one of the tong bosses but he was the appointed access point through which the authorities could reach the tong known as the Small Knife Society. The tongs had controlled customs houses in Shanghai since well before the British came. They took a modest percentage off each and every duty. Those percentages bankrolled almost all their other activities—drugs, women, gambling. They were the cash cow.

Unlike most Chinese men of wealth, Shen Lai smoked a local brand—Snake Charm—and he was filling the air with its pungent aroma as Fong entered the office. Fong took out one of his Kents and lit up. Shen Lai shook his head. "Bad for business, that," he said, indicating the American cigarette. "Not patriotic." He puffed harder on his Snake Charm. The picture of the small cigarette in the tiny mouth almost lost in the enormous cheeks made Fong smile.

"Something funny, Zhong Fong?"

"Not a thing, Shen Lai." Fong crushed out his cigarette against a windowpane. "We're worried about the safety of your workers here."

"Are you really?"

"Yes, we're going to have to close your operations for the better part of a month to make sure that health standards are being maintained. There have been complaints."

A month's closure would cost the tong a lot of revenue and Fong knew it and he knew that Shen Lai knew it.

"You can't—"

But he never got the rest out of his tiny mouth as Fong snapped back, "I can and you know I can. Then I can close down the customs yards at the docks and that would really hurt, wouldn't it?"

"You're crazy, you're out of your jurisdiction."

"Nonsense, I'm the head of Special Investigations. Public safety is part of my portfolio. This place is unsafe. You must have over a hundred workers here, I'm concerned for their health and well-being. I'm closing you down."

There was a beat of silence wherein Shen Lai weighed the threat. He found Fong just enough of a fool to go through with it. Lighting another cigarette he smiled,

"Okay, you've made your point. What can I do for you?"

"I want the knife artist who carved up those two men.

I want him now."

"He's not one of ours, Zhong Fong, surely you know that."

"I do, Shen Lai, he's too artistic for you and yours. But I want him and I want your friends to use all of their considerable power to find him for me. Because if they don't I'll close down this customs house, the one on the Bund, and the new one in the Pudong. Then I'll file so many legal documents that even with the best of lawyers it'll take months to get them reopened. Do I make myself clear?"

Fish Face nodded. His cheeks wagged. His little mouth blew a tiny smoke ring. "Perfectly clear."

It was two o'clock before Fong got back in his car and headed toward his Yellow River. He had been in touch with Wang Jun, who had warned him that some pretty heavy artillery awaited his arrival at the office. Fong thanked the older man and set him to work on the newspaper angle. The coroner and Lily were still waiting for word on the lung shards, but both now thought them likely to be slivers of ivory and there had been no word yet from Detective Li Xiao, who was checking into the martial arts schools. One message that he'd managed to get from Shrug and Knock was that the American consulate had called to inform him that Richard Fallon's wife, Amanda Pitman, was arriving today in Shanghai and that he should make himself available. She was staying in the French Concession at the improbably named Shanghai International

Equatorial Hotel across from Jing An Park, only a few blocks from the theatre academy. Fong called the consulate and left a message indicating his willingness to meet with Mrs. Fallon. He then gave them dozens of police phone numbers that she could call to find him. None of the numbers were his. Fong could live quite well without the intrusion into his life of a grieving widow from America.

Well, his Hu-ness was something to be seen.

Fu Tsong had laughed so hard that tears came to her eyes when she first heard the English term "high dudgeon" — which initially Fong had thought was a basement prison somehow up in the air. Now, looking at his Hu-ness, Fong was sure that he was in fact in high dudgeon. He wondered momentarily what Geoffrey Hyland would call this emotion. Then he wondered why Geoffrey Hyland had entered his mind at a time like this. Then he decided he'd better try to follow what was being screamed at him. Within the general tirade concerning Fong's incompetence, insubordination, lack of administrative skill, and refusal to be part of a team there was a consistent leitmotif: Just find the killer. Don't get diverted. Just find the killer. Don't become a conspiracy monger. Just find the killer. And finally what the fuck was he doing in the customs house this morning? Just find the killer.

Then more high dudgeonness, a demand for a complete report followed by a turn on his heel and exit with Shrug and Knock in tow. If his Hu-ness were a cartoon, and who was to say that he wasn't, such an exit would be accompanied by a puff of dirt at his heels.

After a moment his office door opened and Wang Jun entered.

"You still my boss?"

"I think so. It's hard to be sure with him."

"Lots of words, little substance, huh?"

Fong didn't respond. It occurred to him that there was in fact great substance, but exactly where the substance lay was escaping him. He had Wang Jun call in Lily, and the rest of the team.

Arriving at Shanghai International Airport is not as scary for an American as landing at Sheremetyevo in Moscow, but it's close. It's hard for Americans to overcome their programming and really see what is in front of them. Amanda did her best but she found the bustle and the foreign faces more daunting than she was willing to admit. When offered assistance with her carry-on bag by a young Chinese man, she instinctively refused. At the immigration counter she handed in her form, complete with a "no" answer to the "Do you have AIDS" question. The bluntness of the question galled her. At the counter she waited while the young man—"boy" was the word that popped into her head—put her passport under a light. He looked at the picture, then looked at her, and then down to the picture and at her again. It seemed to her that he was following a set procedure. The catch-a-foreign-devil procedure, no doubt. It also occurred to her that he was probably unable to differentiate Caucasian faces. Be that as it may, she smiled. He didn't, but he handed back her passport and she proceeded to baggage claim.

After a reasonable wait, her bag arrived and she headed into the arrivals lounge. There before her was her first sea of Chinese faces. She took a breath, told herself that she could do this, and stepped forward. Immediately dozens of pencilled cardboard signs were held up and waved in her direction. Although she didn't expect to be picked up she was grateful to see a MRS. RICHARD FALLON in the hands of a young man who took the cigarette out of his mouth to say "Huh-low" and then returned it to his face. He made no movement to take her bag. She followed him out of the terminal into the brightness of Shanghai's late April sun.

The man didn't speak much English and didn't have a car of his own but signalled for a taxi. After what Amanda thought sounded like a pitched battle between him and the driver, he opened the door for her, put her bag in the trunk, and then hopped in the back beside her.

As the taxi started ("took off" was Amanda's impression), he turned to her and said, "Well-come to China."

She thanked him but when she followed her thanks with a question as to whether they were going to her hotel or the consulate, the man just smiled and made a "sorry, no more English" shoulder movement. For a moment Amanda was going to make a scene but she stopped herself. A scene about what? She hadn't expected to be picked up.

The cab swerved and bobbed in and out of traffic as they made their way downtown. The racket was something to hear, the smog something to smell, but it was the look of it all that most impressed Amanda. Huge hand-painted billboards lined the road on both sides. Behind them massive construction projects were under way, cranes turning like weathervanes in the afternoon wind. And bicycles, and people—so many people!

Not greatly to her surprise, the cab came to a stop outside a building with a U.S. federal seal on its outer wall and a line of Chinese people at the entrance waiting to apply for visas that would never be granted. Her escort led her to a back entrance. A marine in full parade dress uniform guarded the door. Amanda eyed the marine coolly. Military types—all spit and polish but not much real style. And forget content.

Inside the consulate, her young escort guided her to a closed door, pointed at it, and with a wave of his hand left her.

The door led to a walnut-panelled waiting room. And Amanda waited. For almost half an hour, during which time she was sure that she dozed off at least once. Finally a youngish Yale type came in with a flutter of papers and apologies. "So sorry that the consul general had to keep you waiting, how was the flight, isn't thirteen hours the worst? Sorry we couldn't send one of our better people out to get you but it's a busy time, lots and lots of business here, blah, blah, blah." She ignored him; if forced to choose she'd take the marine any day.

The consul general stood as she entered despite the fact that he was on the phone. He didn't ask her to sit down and she finally thought "fuck it" and sank down on the leather couch. The consul general was trying to arrange a meeting with a General Electric someone or other and a Shanghai official or something like that. Amanda really couldn't care less. What she cared about at this moment was trying to get some sleep. She felt herself begin to doze off again just as the consul general came around his desk and, extending his hand, began with, "Please accept my sincerest condolences, Mrs. Fallon."

"Thank you. But I think I'd like to go to my hotel first if you don't mind."

"Not at all. I thought they'd brought you there already."

"No, the man brought me here."

"I'm sorry. I'll get you taken to the hotel." He phoned someone and turned to her.

"Perhaps I should see Richard first," she said.

Before that moment Amanda Pitman didn't really know what the phrase "His face fell" really meant. But that's what the consul general's puffy face did. It fell. He recovered in a moment and smiled. "How much did they tell you about your husband's death, Mrs. Fallon?"

"Only that he'd been murdered. And that they haven't found the killer yet."

"Well, that's correct on both points, but I would suggest that you go to your hotel and get some rest and I'll arrange for a driver to pick you up tomorrow morning. There's not really any hurry, is there?"

The words were out of his mouth before he could stop himself. For some reason they made Amanda smile.

They also let her know that there was something here that she hadn't been told.

DAY FIVE

t 8:15 A.M. the next morning the consulate car arrived at her hotel. A young man hopped out and opened the door for her. As he climbed in he said, "Mrs. Fallon, I'd like to offer my deepest condolences."

She was already tired of hearing that. She nodded.

"The consul general also regrets that he'll be unable to meet with you today."

Anger rose up in her throat but she choked it down. "All I want to do is arrange for my husband's remains to be returned to the United States."

"That's already been looked after."

"Excuse me?"

"As soon as the Shanghai coroner's office is finished with its work, Mr. Fallon's remains will be put on the first flight back to New Orleans."

"Is his body at the coroner's office?"

"Yes, as I said—"

"Then let's go there first."

Evidently flustered by this suggestion, but unable to find a reason why they shouldn't go there first, he barked directions to the driver in Chinese. Then he picked up a cellular phone and, with an "Excuse me," dialled a number. He spoke in fluent Chinese. Amanda watched him closely.

Something was wrong with all this.

"Who are you calling?"

"I'm leaving a message with the consul's secretary."

It was only later that it struck her as strange that he was speaking Chinese.

At the coroner's office they were met with resistance. All the talk was in Chinese, but it seemed that the coroner was not in the office and that no one had the authorization to allow anyone into the morgue.

"Tell them I'm the dead man's wife," she said to the man from the consulate.

He translated and immediately the Chinese words took on a solemn tone. Amanda was sure that if she had listened closely she would have heard the Chinese word for condolences several times. Finally the American turned to her and explained that without the coroner present, no one was willing to take the responsibility for letting her in. Then he made some crack about Reds not being able to pick their noses, begging your pardon, ma'am, without a written authorization.

So more quickly than she expected she was back in the car with the man from the consulate. As they pulled away from the morgue Amanda caught a glimpse of a tall building two blocks over that she could have sworn was the Hilton. But that couldn't be, because her hotel was beside the Hilton and the car ride to the morgue had taken almost forty-five minutes.

Out of the side of her eyes she looked at the American.

He didn't seem in any hurry. In fact he looked as if he was trying very hard to kill as much time as he could.

As they drove she asked, "Where to now?"

"I can take you to a funeral parlor. You can pick a casket or arrange for cremation. We've arranged transport for your husband's remains but the actual funeral details we've left to you."

"I'm not concerned about that now. How did my husband die?"

"I'm sorry to say he was murdered."

"I'm aware of that. I've been told that several times. How? How was he murdered?" Like the need to see your mate's new lover and ask for details, she was desperate for specifics.

"I really don't know, Mrs. Fallon," said the consular officer, as if he'd been asked something not discussed in polite society.

"Bring me to my hotel, then."

In a remarkably short time, she found herself disembarking from the consulate car. Once outside she asked, "Can I see the consul general tomorrow?"

"We'll do our best. He's booked tight for a week, but call the consulate first thing in the morning and ask for me and I'll see if he can squeeze you in."

"Can you arrange for me to see the body tomorrow?"

"Of course, if the coroner is there."

Amanda looked at him and thought that he was

joking with her. But upon a closer look it became clear that there was no joke here. Just a bland face that said nothing and implied that you could not get it to say anything that it didn't want to say. As he turned to the driver, about to give him new instructions, Amanda pulled open the door of the car.

"Mrs. Fallon?"

"The Shanghai police are looking after the investigation. Right?"

"Actually Special Investigations, Shanghai District, is."

"And who could I contact there?"

"The head of Special Investigations is a detective named Zhong Fong, but he is a very busy man, Mrs. Fallon."

"I'm sure, all those business meetings he must be attending." With that she less than gently shut the door and turned toward the hotel.

Getting the number for Special Investigations proved more difficult than she thought. Shanghai, unlike Moscow, does have phone books but they are of course in Chinese. They are also notoriously inaccurate. But, with the concierge's help she finally got a number.

She returned to her room intent upon a bit of privacy while she made the call. It took her several tries before she got up the courage to complete the seven-digit number. Like calling a boy when you're a teenager, she thought to herself. Finally she completed the call and was met with a Chinese "Wee" on the other end.

She said, "Zhong Fong please," and waited.

On the other side she heard some talk in Chinese and finally another voice came on the phone with another "Wee." It sounded French this time. Once again Amanda said, "Zhong Fong please." She heard a general discussion on the other side. The discussion stopped abruptly. Amanda called into the phone, "Hello," but there was no answer. Then the phone went dead.

For a moment she felt the unfairness of it all. She wondered what the fuck she was doing there. She wondered what to do next. She wondered if the Chinese breakfast she had eaten that morning was upsetting her stomach.

Later that day she got the concierge to make the call for her. He was told that Inspector Fong was not in at the moment. "Leave a message for him, will you. Tell him that Richard Fallon's widow is in Shanghai and would like to speak to him." The concierge did so and Amanda retreated to her room on the fourteenth floor. The maids had come in and done up her bed. She turned on the TV and got the CNN world service, which proceeded to tell her that if she lived in Hong Kong she could see Larry King Live at 11:00, in Kuala Lumpur ol' Lar came on at 1:00 and in Pusan at 12:00. Amanda wondered briefly where Pusan was and then turned off the television.

She leafed through the hotel directory and found a health club listed on the fourth floor. She called down and learned that she could use the gym, pool, and weight room without an additional fee and also that there were swimsuits there if she wanted to use them.

The health club turned out to have some surprising features. A bowling alley for one. Young middle-class-looking Chinese couples were bowling just as if they were in Toledo, Ohio.

At the pool it looked as if it were "Bring Your Secretary Day." Along with a number of young male executive-looking types who kept hopping out of the pool and using their cellulars were numerous secretaries, all in one piece swimsuits and incongruously floating inside red rubber rings. They were busily frog kicking — perhaps to keep down the cellulite on their thighs? That's the only reason Amanda could come up with for their peculiar behavior. Periodically one or the other of the women would let out a scream as her pretty face slipped too near the water. Immediately her handsome boss would "rescue" her with more body contact than was strictly necessary considering that the pool was never deeper than five feet.

Amanda handed in her room key and was given a large white bathrobe, a purple towel and a locker key on a Velcro wristband. In the locker room, festooned with signs in English and Chinese proclaiming the hotel's innocence should any of the patrons' possessions disappear from the lockers, she removed her clothes and locked them away in her designated locker. Then, with the robe on, she headed for the sauna.

It was clean. It was hot. It took the tension out of her body. With her head leaning back against the sauna's red-wood slatting, she reviewed her progress over the last few days. It occurred to her that having come all the way to Shanghai she might consider leaving her hotel and its westernness even if just for a short while. Then she thought of danger and how unfair it was. If she were a man. . . but then she remembered that Richard had been a man and the one thing that no one was denying was that he was very dead.

She reached into the wooden water bucket and sprinkled a few drops on the coals. They gave off a gratifying hiss and splutter. She rolled her robe into a ball, placed it at one end of the bench and stretched out. The heat of the wood felt good against the back of her legs. The scent of the redwood filled her nostrils. And the heat took her back. Back to a place where heat made the loving so special. "Be cool in the heat, baby," he'd said. "Gotta be cool in the heat or we'll slap and slosh and no one but the laundress will be pleased with the outcome." That was only seven months after she'd married Richard. Seven months of frustration and feeling fat. Seven months of not writing or even really thinking. Just being Mrs. Richard Fallon. Then she'd met this real southerner who hated air conditioning but loved to "do the dance, Cher. Find the rhythm and do the dance." And he was good in the heat. Bodies only touching where they had to. Standing. Leaning over. Mirrors to see. Hands to touch and grace. Joined but not on top or on bottom. A delicate balance in the heat. A blessed relief from the mistake of marrying Richard Fallon.

She'd been told that men changed once they got married but she really only believed that happened to other women. Women who couldn't keep their men's attention. And keeping men's attention had never been a problem for Amanda. The problem was that the Richard she had married became a new Richard after they got married. He became obsessed with money. His interest in the wildlife issues of his work seemed simply to stop. The few friends from work whom she had really liked stopped coming around. When she would call them she clearly got the impression that they were happy enough talking to her but that they no longer cared to socialize with her husband. Richard seemed encased in an invisible shell. As if a deep solitude had descended upon him. Then the calls began to come in the middle of the night and then the business trips. And a secrecy that was not there before came between them, as easy to feel as a Canadian front blowing into New Orleans to relieve the humidity of summer. Their small house in the Garden District filled up with things she'd bought, but none were hers. She no longer really lived in the house in the Garden District with the man named Richard Fallon. For he was not the outgoing warm man that she had married. He was a silent man, a man alone.

The chatter of a Chinese woman entering the sauna, buck naked, with a cellular phone stuck to her ear, broke the spell of the heat and the smell of the redwood. Amanda sat up and headed toward the shower.

After her cold shower she dressed, got her key, and went back to her room. The message light was on. She called down to the desk and was told that an Inspector Fong had returned her call. They gave her a number to call and assured her that it would be answered by someone who spoke English.

She thanked them and dialled the number.

The phone was picked up on the first ring. "Forensicks, Lily talking."

"I was given this number to call to get through to Inspector Fong."

"Dui, right, you called here, good yes. Name please."

"Mrs. Richard Fallon."

For a moment Amanda thought she heard the words Dim Sum something or other said to someone standing near by, then Lily spoke into the phone. "Inspector Zhong not here now."

"When there?" Amanda almost shouted into the phone, annoyed that she'd been reduced to speaking pidgin English.

"Inspector Zhong want to talk to you but not here."

"Where Inspector Zhong?" Pidgin again!

"In theatre. Shanghai Theatre Academy on Hua Shan, 630." Then the phone clicked off.

Fong looked at Lily. He wasn't pleased.

"Lady sound desperate for seeing you, Zhong Fong."

Then, in wonderful saucy Shanghanese, she added, "This lady in front of you is more than desperate, this lady waits in sweet anticipation for seeing you."

Fong's face didn't break a smile.

Finally in English Lily said, "So I shitted up, don't fuck on me."

Fong was unable to top that so he shook his head and headed home. His only solace was the fact that few people, Chinese or otherwise, were clever enough to find the academy, let alone the theatre in the academy compound. And Richard Fallon's widow didn't sound all that bright.

Geoffrey Hyland was winning at a game that he had played since he was first paid to direct a play at the tender age of eighteen. He was guiding human material into art, using a play as a template but not a score. He didn't direct the way a conductor conducts a symphony. He worked more like the lead player in a jazz ensemble. He set the theme, and made sure that everyone else knew the key signature and the tempo and then off they went: improvising freely from each other to create something that lived and breathed, had rough edges — was of life itself. All he demanded was good listening and real talking from his actors. He insisted that they play the "what game." If someone, anyone on stage at any time, spoke a line to them that didn't make sense, that they couldn't believe or in any way seemed "actorly" they were to say "What?" At which point the partner had to redeliver the line, sometimes many times, until some real signal was passed. At first, the actors were reluctant to use this technique; to them it implied condemnation of a fellow actor's work. But once Hao Yong, the brilliant young actress playing Viola, used it against Feste and then used it again and again to get the old charlatan to finally give her something real to playoff of. . . well, they were off to the races. And race was the right metaphor. An emotional race with which everyone onstage and

Geoffrey in the auditorium had to keep up. It was early but already exciting.

Geoffrey's Mandarin had improved greatly from the time eleven years ago when he first worked in Shanghai on *The Ecstasy of Rita Joe*, but he still worked with an interpreter at his side. Even in that first play, by the end of the second week he seldom needed his interpreter's help. Geoffrey, like many stage directors, quickly memorized the script as the actors worked and hence knew where in the text the actors were at each moment. Although he could not exactly pinpoint which Mandarin word was which English word, he could always identify the emotional shifts required in the text and was able to see whether a shift was played by the actor or not. It was for this reason that the language was not a real barrier. If the States of Being were right, and that was something Geoffrey could see, and the actions played were right, then the image (that part of acting contained in the word) would basically look after itself. At least that was true in texts like Rita Joe where the language was not really of the essence. It was obviously less true of Shakespeare texts.

Geoffrey held up his hand for a moment and called out "Hao" (good). He turned to his interpreter and asked Hao Yong to join them. She was now in her late twenties but she still carried herself like the teenager she had been when she played *Rita Joe* for Geoffrey those eleven years ago. Since then, she had been in a show a year for Geoffrey, sometimes more. She was talent that walked and talked. Not pretty, but so alive that when she smiled you smiled with her. In the eleven years she had learned a little English, enough to hold her own at lunch with Geoffrey from time to time. Enough to have been his lover briefly some seven years ago. Before Fu Tsong.

"Help me with the language here." He pointed to the Viola/Olivia scene and the three of them went through it line by line. "When you read this translation, Hao Yong, does it feel like Viola is falling under the power of Olivia?"

For a moment Hao Yong looked at Geoffrey and then with an apologetic shrug of her slim shoulders turned to the translator. There followed a rapid and animated conversation in Shanghanese which left Geoffrey completely at a loss. He loved the way the Chinese actors talked about things like this. For years he thought that every Chinese conversation was a yelling match, but now he didn't think so. Now he knew they were yelling matches.

He watched Hao Yong's face with a growing pleasure. As a student she had been truly brilliant. As a professional actor she was one of the few who was able to overcome her training. She had shucked off the old Stanislavski stranglehold and was in freefall. An artist of true power. But after all these years how little he knew of her. He had never been to her home. He knew that she was married now but he'd never met her husband. He didn't even know if she was an only child; it was likely that she was as she'd been born in the one-child era. But she carried herself and used the knowledge of one who came from a more extended family.

One of the strange ramifications of the single-child policy in China had been the loss of one of the basic communication tools for an actor. Actors use simple family relationships (father/son, older brother/younger sister, husband/wife, lovers, etc.) to convey to an audience the nature of more complex relationships. When an actor goes to work on, say, the relationship between a teacher and a student, the actor playing the teacher chooses father/son while the actor playing the student chooses younger brother to older brother. The ability to find conflicts even on the basic level of relationship greatly enriches performance. From the audience's perspective they 'get' teacher/student because they identify with it as either father/son or older brother/younger brother. But with the single-child policy, the basic knowledge of brothers and sisters has been diluted if not lost. It has removed a potent weapon from the actor's arsenal. Some claim the other loss is that single children never learn how to play properly. Being the only child that the parents will ever have, the child is put under enormous pressure to succeed. Nightly, parents do the child's homework with them. Weekends are often spent preparing for the child's examinations. Getting into university has become an obsession in China. During the final callbacks for entrance to the Shanghai Theatre Academy, the 120 finalists, who had been chosen from over 2,800 applicants from across China, arrived on campus with parents and grandparents in tow. They were dressed and preened and poked like show dogs. It occurred to Geoffrey that the loss of sibling feeling and the loss of the ability to play could have serious effects on a society as a whole. But his mind did not travel comfortably in the world of sociopolitics.

Hao Yong turned to him and touched his hand to bring him back to the present. What an enormous advance in contact that was. They had worked on three shows together before he felt it acceptable to touch her in any way. Her cool hand tapped the base of his palm and in accented, but pretty English, she said, "You think Viola love Olivia?" Her eyes twinkled. After all this time, she certainly knew that was precisely what he thought. "Yes, me too."

"Good," he said, "but does the language support that?"

"No," she said, "but the silences do."

She smiled at him and for a moment he wondered how he ever let her get away. Then he said, "Hao" and was about to let rehearsal start up again when Hao Yong smiled at Geoffrey and said, "Viola is narcoticized to Olivia."

Geoffrey was lost and turned to the translator. A brief moment later, his translator, now embarrassed, said, "She says that Viola is addicted to Olivia."

Seeking clarification that he did not really need, Geoffrey asked, "Addicted but not drugged?"

After a moment of conversation in Mandarin, Hao Yong squatted on the stage, her dress tucked between her knees, so that her face was at the height of Geoffrey's as he stood on the auditorium floor. "No, Geoffrey," she said, her eyes dancing again, "not drugged—addicted." Then a smile erupted across her face. She turned back to Olivia and, spreading her arms, sang out, "Build me a willow cabin at your gates. . ."

From the back of the house Fong watched the interaction between the delicately boned Hao Yong and the awkward white man. He was not surprised. He had been around Fu Tsong long enough to understand the casual nature of contact in the theatre. He had also heard the rumours about these two. Fu Tsong's response to the rumours had been interesting. It had angered her.

Fong held Fu Tsong's massive complete works of Shakespeare in his lap. It had Mandarin translation on the left-hand pages. He was following the text as they rehearsed. He agreed with Hao Yong. Viola was not infatuated, she was addicted. This whole play was about love as a driving need which, once experienced, puts everything else into a false light. Addiction.

Fong took out his note pad and jotted down the word.

Fong's English did not go to the extent of words like serendipity or synchronicity, but as a policeman and as an easterner he found these ideas above questioning. Two murdered men, ivory, and addiction—but how did these pieces fit together?

Loa Wei Fen was surprised when he found out the address of the sender of the e-mail. No, surprised is the wrong word. He was shocked. For the first time in many years, something akin to fear tickled down his spine. He

slowed his pulse and slid his breath into a deeper section of his lungs. The tickle went away. He had learned
this basic trick many years before. As a child in the
monastery he would wake the other children when he
screamed in his sleep. The monks tried everything to
stop him but failed until the Old One took him to his
bed. There in the fastness of sleep, when the dreams
took him, the Old One awoke him and taught him
where fear lives. Taught him the breath that relieves the
fear, taught him how to release his *chi*.

There was never any sexual contact between the two
men. In fact Loa Wei Fen was technically a virgin. His
life energies were directed from the groin, not to it. The
entertainments of the flesh had frequently been offered
to him, but they held no allure, no fascination. His focus
lay elsewhere.

As his martial training continued he slowly learned
how to release the energy of his *chi* into his fighting. On
the day that it first exploded through his arms, he threw
his partner so hard that the other boy's ribs cracked and
a shoulder blade snapped as he hit the floor.

Loa Wei Fen had no idea what had happened, where
this strength had come from. But his teacher knew. The
Old One was brought in and from that day on, Loa Wei
Fen did not see the other boys in the monastery. He
ate alone. He meditated alone. It was only in lessons that
he met others—teachers. Martial arts teachers. Fighters
of every technique. Then one day in his eleventh year,
his fifth at the monastery, his third since he was put into
isolation, a young Mongolian woman appeared in the

fighting room. She appeared alone and spoke none of the common tongue. For days and weeks she spoke at him as he sat in perfect stillness until finally her words began to fall into patterns. Phrases moved into his consciousness and eventually he understood her.

Her broad dark face was a mountain terrain. There was life deep in her eyes. A glimmer of knowledge. At the end of their first month of daily sunrise-to-sunset meetings, she reached into her robe and pulled out a Mongolian swolta—a six-inch double-sided blade with a pin-sharp point made out of tempered steel hard as diamond. A carved serpent coiled around the handle. She was about to order him to close his eyes and turn away from her, but her thought had already conveyed itself to him. *Yes, he was gifted.*

Then, with the swolta, she marked him.

The blade did its work deftly in her hands. An eye on each deltoid and the line of life that joins them arching down toward the centre of his back. The cuts had to be deep enough to mark and the blade was nothing if not capable of such cuts. Then she rolled the knife handle in the blood from Loa Wei Fen's back. Without her needing to ask him, both of his hands reached out, waiting. *Yes, of course, the chosen will work with both hands.*

He put his hands behind his back, palms facing each other and stretched far back virtually closing the cuts. She slid the knife between his palms.

Loa Wei Fen remembered the first touch of the knife. Slick with blood, the serpent had rolled in his hands. Rolled from one hand to the other, finding an ideal perch in each, then rolling back to the centre.

The Mongolian watched with pleasure as the knife, seemingly on its own, moved in the boy's hands, still stretched taut behind his back. After a moment the boy took a slow deep breath and, rolling his arms full circle in their shoulder sockets, brought the knife up over his head. Then he put the bloody hilt of the blade in his mouth and rising, he flared his marked deltoids.

The cuts opened like red rivers on his flesh.

She was pleased. The cobra's hooded mask was clearly carved on his back.

As he stood on the Promenade facing the Bund he allowed the nerves in the skin of his back to trace the line of the cobra. Full circle clockwise on the left eye, then down the line of life and up to the other eye, which he traced counterclockwise. Loa Wei Fen felt the snake's hood open as he looked at the building directly across from him. It housed the District of Shanghai Central Police Administration. It was also the building from which the e-mail had been sent.

Amanda found the streets confusing. The best map that the Shanghai International Equatorial Hotel could come up with was one that showed, in great detail, where all seven of the Esprit shops were located but hardly bothered to name most of the streets. She managed to get reasonably good directions from the concierge and then was forced to ask him, "Is it safe, for me to walk to the Shanghai Theatre Academy?" Being assured that it was not only quite safe but also quite nearby she headed out with a vague idea at least in what direction she ought to head.

Once on the street she came nose to nose with a large street map at one of the bus stops. Labelled OFFICIAL STREET MAP OF SHANGHAI 1989, it was infinitely better than the one that she held. Esprit didn't sponsor the old one. Progress she guessed. Even at ten o'clock in the evening the streets were crowded with cars and bicycles. She stood at the corner of Yan'an and Hua Shan and waited for the light to change. As she waited the world passed her by and everyone from children to old women crossed the street. So she ventured forward. It was a mistake. There is an art to crossing Shanghai streets. An art that she had not yet mastered.

Eventually managing to get to the other side, she walked along Hua Shan knowing that the academy was on Hua Shan. She reasoned that by following the street only three or four blocks as the concierge said she was bound to come across the school. She passed by the Hilton and the Bank of China building and crossed another street, which seemed to lead her to a more residential area.

There were many people sitting on chairs on the narrow sidewalks taking the night air. Fruit stands were still open and small pineapples, which had been skinned and carved to remove the eyes, were on prominent display, their bright yellow orange pulp a tropical temptation. Several times the sidewalks were clogged with bicycles, forcing Amanda out onto the street. And everywhere people looked at her. She was tall in a short world. Blond in a dark one. White in a brown one.

A leather mini-skirted young Chinese woman, with dark brooding eyes, openly evaluated Amanda as she passed.

Continuing, she crossed Julu Lu and sensed that something was wrong. She looked at the street sign on Hua Shan. It was in Chinese characters, thanks a heap. She crossed the street and looking back noticed that the street sign she had looked at was in English from this side. So, she recrossed the street and looked at the sign. It said Chong Shu. What? She hadn't gotten off Hua Shan or had she? She doubled back the way she had come. The leather-skirted girl was still in her doorway and her laughter was not the least bit good-humoured as she saw Amanda coming back.

At each corner Amanda checked the street sign. She discovered that the signs were set up for drivers, not walkers. So at each street sign she grabbed the post and swung out into the road to read which street she was on. She finally came to the corner of Chong Shu and Hua Shan and realized that Hua Shan, on which she had started, simply made a right turn without notifying anyone. By staying straight on you were dumped onto Chong Shu. Okay, fair enough, she thought. Lesson learned.

She crossed the street toward King's Bakery, knowing that the school should be on that side. As she did, movement in a glass window beside the bakery caught her eye.

Her breath stuck in her throat. Several large snakes

were in the window, many rising up to get a good look at her.

She hurried on. She passed the Jing An Hotel, which had a high wall with glass embedded in the top. Then she passed a lengthy area of what looked like stunted scarred elm trees, after which on her right she saw the small polished plaque for the Shanghai Theatre Academy. Thank God it was in English, she thought.

Across the street was the Marco Polo Night Club. Some fancy cars were parked there. And lots of neon suggested untold pleasures within. She turned away from the Marco Polo and back to the school. She was face to face with a problem. A gate. A locked gate. No door and a locked gate. Inside she saw a diminutive old woman pouring hot water from a thermos into a large glass jar with what looked like seaweed in the bottom.

Amanda called out to her. The woman ignored her. Amanda called again. The old lady hollered something back at her, no doubt something nasty, and walked away. When she was gone, an old man hobbled out of the gatehouse and stared at Amanda. His grizzled face wore a smile. Amanda had to stop her immediate revulsion at being stared at and her knee-jerk antipathy to his Mao jacket. Finally he began to point to the other side of the compound. Point and make circular motions of walking with his fingers. After a lot more pointing and much more smiling, she finally got the idea that she was to go around to the other side of the compound. The side that was on Yan'an — a straight, uncomplicated walk up the street from the Shanghai International Equatorial

Hotel! She sighed. Second lesson. Addresses are not addresses are not addresses in Shanghai.

The trip around was uneventful. By the time she had to repass the snake place, its iron shutters had been pulled down. The walk up Yan'an was a little more interesting than the one up Hua Shan. Some stores were still open, as were little kiosks where you could buy anything from beer to tampons. At one point there was a small red car up on a two-story-high iron beam. It sat there at the junction of two streets. Amanda wondered briefly if they were advertising these peculiar little cars or the strength of the beam that held it. Behind the thing was a partially demolished three-story house that at one time must have been quite elegant.

Passing by the raised car she finally found the Yan'an entrance to the Shanghai Theatre Academy. Not fancy like the Hua Shan entrance but open, which was far more important. She walked into the compound and was immediately faced with the fact that she had no idea where exactly she was going. Fortunately for her, the gatekeeper on this side had gotten Fong's message, and as he was to tell his wife later, "It was not hard to pick out the albino." He signalled for her to follow him. She did with only a little trepidation.

They walked past a building whose six stories were completely surrounded by lashed bamboo scaffolding. Amanda had never seen anything like it before. They passed several elegant old Chinese-style buildings with swinging windows on their upper floors and finally she was guided into a low building whose foyer smelled of the washroom which was no doubt nearby. She looked back at the gatekeeper. He signalled for her to go through the next door. She did and was immediately greeted by the scent of thick dust mixed with years of dampness.

The dim overhead lights cast more shadow than illumination but there was a brighter light on stage. And up there was a white male—thank Christ. And he was speaking English to one of the Chinese women. In the theatre several people were sitting around, talking and smoking. Lots of smoking. Onstage the white man was evidently trying to make some point through the Chinese lady whom Amanda took to be an interpreter.

The person on the phone had indicated that Inspector Zhong would be in the theatre, but little else. She assumed that a policeman would be easy to pick out. But there wasn't anyone there who stood out to her in any way except the white man on the stage.

With an exasperated sigh she sat down in an aisle seat. The dust literally rose around her. The broken seat back bit into her. The seat was too low, the arm rest too high. What the fuck was she doing here?

Just as she was about to leave, a smallish Chinese man, square across the shoulders with the casual walk of one used to physical activity, approached her.

If this guy tries to pick me up, I'll deck him, she thought.

But Zhong Fong had no interest in picking up Amanda Pitman. He found her large features anything but appealing and the colour of her skin was like the white sauce that Fong refused to eat when he was a child. The length of her legs, below the hem of her skirt, surprised him. He would prefer to meet this lady sitting down. So he sat in the seat behind her and before she could get up in protest he said in his best English, reminding himself of the *r* sound, "Mrs. Richard Fallon?"

With a sigh of relief, Amanda said, "Inspector Zhang Fang."

They always did that. He thought it proper to start things on the right foot so he corrected her. "Zhong not Zhang, and Fong not Fang."

"Well, while we're at it, Ms. Amanda Pitman, not Mrs. Richard Fallon," snapped back Amanda, none too pleased with the opening gestures of this game.

He saw the flash in her eyes and the rise. It surprised him. What really surprised him was that he liked it. He smiled. "Welcome to Shanghai, Ms. Amanda Pitman."

To which she replied, "Thank you very much, Inspector Zhong Fong."

Turning her eyes to the stage she said, "Is this part of the investigation into my husband's murder?"

"In a way."

"What way?"

Fong was decidedly displeased with the tone of that. She was surprised at her own approach but it was on the table so she let it sit.

"This is China, Ms. Pitman. Perhaps more to the point this is Shanghai. This is not New Orleans. You are not a citizen here. I am seeing you as a personal favour, not in the line of duty, is that clear?"

"Yes, I'm sorry."

"How much did they tell you about your husband's death?"

"Not much. Time and place. They also intimated that an open casket funeral would not be appropriate."

Fong needed clarification on that. His English did not extend to esoteric areas like funeral rites. When he finally got the idea he was shocked. Clearly they had told this woman only the barest details of her husband's demise.

"You are Richard Fallon's wife, yes?"

"I was, yes."

"I could use some more information about your husband. It could prove useful in apprehending his killer."

"Would now be convenient?"

"Not for me, no. I would like to see you in my office."

"Tomorrow?"

"Well, no. Tomorrow I'm going to relive the last six hours of the life of a man who was killed by the same man who killed your husband."

"Can I come with you?"

For a moment Fong missed the idiom and then he got it. His immediate impulse was to say no but he didn't. He paused. His world was changing. Everything was in flux. Why not police procedure too? He nodded then looked toward the stage. Geoffrey was talking about addiction again.

Geoffrey was always aware of everything that went on in his rehearsal, be it on the stage or back in the auditorium. So Amanda Pitman's entrance did not escape his attention. How large she looked in the context of Asian women. How very different from Hao Yong, let alone Fu Tsong. Yet there was something appealing about this big blond American. He was sure that she was an American. As a Canadian who had spent almost fifteen years of his life living in the United States he had no trouble picking an American out of a crowd. Unlike many fellow Canadians, he rather liked Americans. But the total victory of America at the end of the Cold War put America everywhere. Shanghai was loaded down with American images. Everything from the huge Marlboro Man billboard on the Nanjing Road side of People's Park (Mao must be rolling in his grave) to the endless T-shirts with logos for American sports teams that so many Chinese young people wore. Dammit, Sprite was China's national drink!

It was really only the language barrier that kept the Americans at bay. Unlike Europe where English is either sharply on the ascendance or already king, in China there were very few English speakers and English and Mandarin were so different that no amount of goodwill could cross the linguistic barrier.

Geoffrey remembered being approached on the Promenade across from the Bund several years back, before he spoke much Mandarin, by a man who began with "I English. You friend, ho-kay?" Geoffrey had been in Shanghai long enough to know that these seemingly innocent approaches were always the beginning of an attempt to sell services, but he didn't mind.

Geoffrey continued walking but the man kept up with him.

"You tourist?"

"Well, no. In fact, I'm working here at the Shanghai People's Theatre."

That clearly was beyond this man's English, so Geoffrey changed the subject. "What do you do?"

The man smiled and lifted his shoulders. Geoffrey recognized the man's dilemma, being a formidable smiler and shoulder lifter himself in like circumstances. So he rephrased. "Work? What? You?"

A smile crossed the man's face. Why didn't the stupid white man ask that the first time? "Engineer, I."

"Good," responded Geoffrey, more than a little surprised that he had gotten through.

"Engineer, I. You?"

"Theatre director, writer, me." He knew the word for writer although it had taken him several days of practice to get it down, *"Zuojia, wo."* A look of utter confusion blossomed on the Chinese man's face. Geoffrey knew that he had the right word but he could very well have had both the wrong pronunciation and the wrong intonation. Evidently the man believed Geoffrey had said something very peculiar and was going to ignore it. Geoffrey hoped he hadn't implied something rude.

"American?" he asked.

"Mao (no), Canadian."

A smile lit the Asian's face. "Ottawa capital."

The smile seemed to say that all this man's hard work had been worth something. *"Shide* (yes)."

"Married?"

"Shide. You (*ni*) married?"

"Yes, girl."

"You have a girl?"

"*Shide*, just one. Girl one. Government say no more. *Ni?*"

"Two, a boy and a girl."

Conversations with the Chinese always eventually came around to children. He was always saddened when he admitted that he had two children to their one. It was a moment of embarrassment of riches that he couldn't defend. Even saying that he had a son while the man he was talking to didn't, created a moment of real tension. Usually the Chinese person smiled politely, but whatever possibility of communication, of actual contact, however slight, was then at an end. A gulf always yawned at that point. A gulf of culture and reality.

There followed more smiling and shoulder lifting. Eventually the man pulled out a set of stamps and an old coin he had for sale. Geoffrey declined as graciously as he could.

Geoffrey noted that language was clearly not a barrier between Fong and the white woman. Fong's English was good. Fu Tsong had made sure.

Having just arrived in Shanghai, he had no desire to spend his time in the company of white people, so upon breaking rehearsal, Geoffrey hustled out the side door. Besides, he still had his questions about Fong and the death of Fu Tsong. Questions that he was anxious to ask the investigating officer who had, seemingly out of nowhere, contacted him earlier in the day.

The officer's name was Wang Jun.

That night, in the safety of his Portman hotel suite, Loa Wei Fen allowed the memory of the kill to come back to him. The African's heart had wrapped itself around the knife. Its life had surged up the blade and almost thrown Loa Wei Fen back on his haunches. This was a kill that was different from all the others. This was a man with great power. A man whom he was lucky to have surprised so thoroughly. He remembered the tearing sound as the blade cut through gristle and snagged on tendon. He remembered the battle to cut the heart. But most he remembered the pounding of his own heart as for the first time he saw that he was taking a life that was worthy.

He remembered that the black man's heart tasted of bile and Loa Wei Fen knew it moved him farther from the edge of the roof. Away from the leap that would finally put his life on the path—the *tao*.

Ngalto Chomi's half heart received a reception comparable to that of Richard Fallon's. The hotel differed, the men in the room differed, but their reaction, as mentioned, was the same.

Fong had offered to drive or walk Ms. Pitman back to her hotel but she declined. She just asked him to walk her to the Yan'an gate and point her in the right direction. For a moment Fong thought to follow Geoffrey but then decided that his duty was to help Ms. Pitman.

As they emerged from the dim theatre into the clear

night sky a whisper of wind picked Amanda's perfume off her shoulders and tickled it beneath Fong's nose. He was startled by its effect. Up his nose and directly into the rhinencephalon part of the brain and bingo — memory clarion clear.

She was holding out her hand and saying something before he realized that he hadn't been listening.

"Well," she said, withdrawing her hand, "I'll see you at what time?"

Feeling more than a wee bit foolish he covered by saying, "No need to start until eleven. I'll send a car for you."

"I can find my way, just tell me where I'm going."

"Fine. I'll meet you at the entrance to the bird and fish market off Cheng Dou Road."

She tried to say Cheng Dou several times and couldn't get it quite right so he spelled it for her. Like so many Europeans, she learned better from the letter than the sound. So unlike Fu Tsong, he thought, who learned English whole, mostly from movies. Movies she watched on the VCR that Geoffrey Hyland had given them. Movies she watched snuggled in close to him, her perfume whispering memories that he stored in the rhinencephalon part of his brain.

All he could think as he watched them from behind the costume shop was that they made a strange couple. The handsome blond woman and the delicate Chinese man. Almost a reversed yin and yang, thought Geoffrey. Almost.

April 21

Dearest Sis,

Yeah, that's right, it's your big sister writing
you. It must be years since I've written a letter, but if
you recall, sweet thing, I used to write to you all the
time. Shit, I used to write all the time and not just to
you. Well, I feel like writing again and you're the
target so read it and enjoy it or give the stamp to
that nephew of mine or let little Beth chew it into
tiny bite-sized pieces and spit them at her brother.
Do with it what you will.

The Victorians left us a heritage of beautiful
personal letters. What are we leaving? In fifty years
some moronic university type will get a Ph.D. based
on Eccentric Phone Messages of the Late 20th
Century — "Sorry we're not home leave a message."
"This is the house of pain, the house of pain, the
house of pain, leave a fucking message." "If you
don't leave a message at the tone, we'll bomb your
house and dance in the ashes." Stuff like that.

This letter has something to do with flying
over the pole. That's the route JAL takes to Tokyo.
And it's not that "looked at clouds from both sides
now" crap — I always wanted that honey to lighten
up — it's the sense of majesty down there. The endless miles of ribbed ice on the Mackenzie River, the
daunting mountains leading into Alaska, range upon
range upon range, and then the sea — a dream of
chilling no-moreness. But peace too. Solemn and
simple, a rest from the burdens. I thought of Mom.
Her quiet sadness as she padded round and round

the house in those final years. A woman pulled inside with her own quiet. The thing that lived inside her eating her living flesh to keep itself alive. And coffee on the table late at night with her in that tattered bathrobe she claimed belonged to Dad but both you and I know didn't. And the smell of bourbon in her coffee. And the smell of the drugs on her breath. And the retreat in her eyes. She'd never flown over the pole. She'd never gone anywhere.

But I'm here in Shanghai, in an American-style hotel with a bunch of other white folks and some rich Asians. I remember seeing Karasawa's film *Ran*, did I see that with you? It's his version of one of the Shakespeare plays, *Lear* I think. At any rate, I was in New York — having some girlish fun — and it was a cold rainy Wednesday afternoon so I checked into this movie theatre on 61st to see *Ran*. I remember now I wasn't with you. Yes, I surely do remember that I wasn't with you. No, I'm not going to tell you who I was with. At any rate the movie starts and being a Karasawa film it's set in medieval Japan in the period of warring states. Well the thing is almost four hours long but for the first hour and a half each of the actors didn't change kimonos, or if they did they kept to the same colour of kimono, so us westerners naturally were following the characters by the colour of their clothes. But then about an hour and a half in, they leave the country and enter the city, and all of the characters change clothes (and colour). Well, there is a moment of consternation in the audience and then some guy calls out in a loud New York voice: "Ah, come on, give us a break." The place broke up. Everyone began to guess who was who. "No, that's the guy who used to be in the red with the feather on the front." "No it's not, it's the one who was in blue with the flags on his back." It was a hoot.

Well, I thought that then. I don't now.

I met with Inspector Zhong today, a small elegant man with tapered fingers. He's going to fill me in more tomorrow on Richard's death. I know that you thought things were not good between Richard and me. Well, you thought right, they weren't. There was always something missing.

Walking back to the hotel today I passed by a small antique shop on Chong Shu. In the darkened window I could make out the shapes of elegantly curving teapots. All shapes and sizes. In the back there was a velvet case with ten small teapots in declining size from a grapefruit down to a Ping-Pong ball. Each was a perfect thing and complete in and of itself. But together they were a complete "other" thing. Different from the sum of their parts. They were a completed dream, a realized idea, a whole. When I got married I received some very beautiful gifts. Often a lot of thought and care went into picking them. But I kept hoping as I opened the gifts for something. . . something. Richard got angry with me. "What the hell are you looking for? What do you want?" I couldn't explain then. But after looking at that set of ten teapots I now know. I wanted something complete. A whole idea. It's what I think I wanted from Richard but could never have.

I'll buy the teapots tomorrow for Beth.

I'll give them to her on her wedding day.

From Shanghai, with thoughts of you and yours,

Your sister,
Amanda

DAY SIX

The coroner didn't look good. In fact he looked sallow and sickened, thought Fong. As gently as he could Fong said, "You asked to see me?"

"Yes, thank you for coming over at such an early hour."

The old man's politeness shocked Fong more than his pallor.

"Are you okay?"

To this the coroner half sighed, half laughed. "I am in my seventy-third year, how okay could I be?" Then he laughed, spat in the sink, and swore mightily. That made Fong feel better. Crossing to the freezer, the coroner slipped on a pair of plastic gloves and pulled out a dark green plastic bag. Then, bringing the bag over to one of the dissection tables, he let it tumble out.

It was the half of the heart remaining from Ngalto Chomi.

"The African's heart?"

"Yes, and an interesting piece of work it is."

"The heart?"

The coroner looked at him like he was crazy, "A heart's a heart. It's not like a dick or tits. Yes, there's a standard variation in internal organs but this is well within the standard."

"So what's interesting about it?"

"This." The coroner pointed to the cutline the knife had made. It was jagged. More ripped than cut. Fong said as much and the coroner nodded his agreement.

"This is the work of a specialized professional. One whose purpose is to terrorize. Do you agree?"

"Yes, I do."

"Such a person would be highly skilled, yes?"

"Yes."

"Expensive?"

"I'd assume so."

"Professional, highly skilled, expensive and yet he almost botched this one." He took the heart and showed Fong an incision off the cutline of almost an inch and a half.

"The knife slipped?" asked Fong, his interest definitely on the rise.

"If it did, it happened more than once." The coroner pulled back a second flap where the knife had veered sharply off course. "Also, this body, although carved up in the same places as Richard Fallon's, was not done with the same accuracy. There seemed to be a hesitation here. I'm guessing, but I think our man is losing his touch."

"Professional, highly skilled, expensive but at the end of his career. A hunter whose prowess has crested."

"A lion with a limp," added the coroner as his ancient hands slid the half heart back into its bag.

Watching the coroner's slow movements toward the freezer, Fong added, "They get dangerous near the end."

"Like me," said the old coroner. "Like me."

Lily had something for him. The shard in Richard Fallon was in fact a tiny piece of ivory, probably from a carving factory. Fong took a note of that and asked Lily to get in touch with Interpol to check with corresponding MOs. "I've been on my knees to those fuckers in Hong Kong for three days getting the shard crap, do I have to do it again?"

"You're so good at it, Lily."

She playfully punched him on the shoulder. It hurt more than he thought it would. Then assuming she had not paid him back enough she added, "How's the report for his Hu-ness coming along?"

He made a face at her. She made one right back then said, "Maybe it's easier being on my knees in front of the Hong Kong guys than you being on your knees in front of the Hu-man. At least with me it's not a sin against nature."

In English Fong added, "You're something, Lily."

To which she replied, "You bet your picker I am."

Fong was going to correct her but thought it unwise to teach Lily any more English names for male genitalia. So he merely said, "I try not to bet my picker, unless I'm sure of the horse."

Lily was still trying to work out the idiom as he left.

• • •

Passing by Shrug and Knock Fong couldn't resist yelling at him. So he did. Shrug and Knock shrugged it off and smiled. "How's that report coming along?"

In his office Fong found a message to call Li Xiao, the detective working on the martial arts angle. Fong called the number, which was in Kwongjo, Canton. When his call was forwarded to a beeper, he left a message that he had returned the call. Then he checked to make sure that his door was locked and sat down to his typewriter.

The report to his Hu-ness took a solid hour to write and was clear but vacant. It did not muddy waters but it made absolutely no effort to clean them. There was no speculation of any sort in it and certainly no flow chart leading from the Dim Sum Killer to anyone else. When the report was almost finished, his private line rang. He thought it would be Wang Jun so he picked up. "Talk."

But it wasn't the older detective, it was Li Xiao returning his call.

"Sir?"

"Who is. . . Li Xiao, I'm sorry. How's Kwongjo?"

"Like the Wild West in American movies. This place is too close to Hong Kong."

"They really eat lamb's balls down there?"

"Lamb's balls, bull's balls, fuck, they'd eat rat's balls if they were big enough to pick up with chopsticks."

The two men laughed together. Li Xiao was one of the few men on the force, outside of Wang Jun, whom Fong admired. He felt that Li Xiao really had talent and was an incorruptible cop in a force that fought a daily battle against internal corruption. He was the best detective, bar none, who worked under Fong. He also liked the young man. He liked his tough, wide body and his pimpled face. He liked the honest ugliness of him. If there hadn't been such an age difference he would have tried to pursue a friendship with this young man. But age is real.

"You've found something?"

"Maybe, sir. Kwongjo is the centre of so much of this martial arts stuff. We've spread the net pretty wide and have been concentrating on the weapon."

"And?"

"I've got a rumour, is all." He then told Fong what he'd found. He ended with, "If you want me to pursue this I'd have to get to Taiwan. That's where the trail leads."

Few things sickened a Chinese man in authority more than having to ask a favour of the Taiwanese. Fong literally felt dizzy with the prospect of having to go through those channels. "You think that's necessary."

"I'm sorry, sir, I know what a pain this must be, but the trail goes there. There's nothing more on the mainland that I can find. If you want to let it go, then fine, but I can't do more here. I'm sorry."

"Come on back to Shanghai, I'll authorize the airfare, but not a word about this to anyone, okay?"

"Sure. Am I going to Taiwan?"

"I don't know. Just get back here now." Fong spent ten more minutes polishing up the report, trying to make it thick with useless details. Finally satisfied, he pulled it from his typewriter and headed toward the door. He dropped it on Shrug and Knock's desk. "Give this to your uncle, huh?"

Fong was around the corner before there was a smart-ass reply, a shrug, or a knock.

Wang Jun was waiting for him downstairs. He glanced at the sun and said, "Let's walk."

Fong replied, "You have a copy of the driver's statement?"

• • •

Wang Jun patted his side pocket.

"Good. We have a guest this morning."

"Really? Who?" Wang Jun said with a slow smile.

It was not possible that Wang Jun knew about Amanda Pitman coming with them this morning. Yet the older man's smile was troublingly knowledgeable.

"A lady perhaps. A blond American perhaps?" suggested Wang Jun. He licked his thick lips.

"How the hell. . ."

Doing his best hard-boiled American TV detective Wang Jun snapped, "I'm a copper, ma'am, remember that." Clearly unwilling to reveal his sources to Fong, he went on, "We could do a show for the Americans. Shanghai PD. They'd love it. I could play the lead and you could play my short lovable but stupid assistant whom I constantly pull out of problems as I hop in and out of lovely ladies' beds. What do you think?"

"I think two things."

"And those would be?"

"I think you have an active fantasy life and I think you should stay out of my business. All right, Wang Jun?" The latter was said with enough conviction to stop the older man's smile.

Wang Jun had touched a sore point with Fong and he knew it. He also knew other things about his young friend from his interrogation of Geoffrey Hyland the night before — some of them quite troubling.

"So where to first, the bird and fish market?" asked Wang Jun.

"Yes, that's where the driver first brought the Zairian consul," replied Fong.

"We're just going to walk the route?"

"No, I'm going to walk the route, you're going to track me. The killer must have watched Mr. Chomi the whole time. I want you to play the killer. As I go, figure out where he must have watched from. Then we'll see if anyone remembers seeing someone standing and watching."

"It's a long shot."

"Have you got any other suggestion?"

"Hell no, it's a great day for the Bird and Fish."

Amanda knew it was stupid but she didn't know what to wear. It was hot and bone dry out there but she was pretty sure that shorts were inappropriate. She had good walking shoes and as she put them on she was surprised at herself for being pleased that they were low-heeled. So she wouldn't appear too much taller than him? No it couldn't be that, just a practical shoe is all.

She finally chose a simple skirt and blouse and a linen jacket and headed down to the lobby. Over the city map, the concierge insisted that the route was easy. He traced it for her several times with his thumb and finally drew a line on her map with a pencil. Unfortunately the map didn't have the exact street that Inspector Zhong had mentioned but the concierge assured her, "It is right here." Of course he was pointing to a place on the map with no streets whatsoever.

"It's not far, maybe a twenty-minute walk."

"It looks longer than that," Amanda said.

With a ha-you-westerners look he suggested, "Maybe a taxicab?"

That did it. She folded her map and strode out into the hot April morning.

Dust was blowing as she made her way toward the centre of the city along Yan'an. Everywhere there were things that caught her eye. Phrases popped into her head unannounced but pleasing in both their incisiveness and sound.

Because of her height she had a better view of the city around her than she did in the West. She did not tower over people but she was definitely tall. And blond. And the object of many stares and the odd comment. Surprisingly she didn't mind, although she was pleased that she had brought her sunglasses and her linen jacket, which she buttoned across her blouse. They could look but they'd have to imagine for themselves.

After passing by the Russian-built exhibition centre with its Red Star atop a fine spire, she came across a man in green pants who was descending into an open manhole. Three other men, all of whom also wore green pants, watched. As the first man's head disappeared beneath the pavement, Amanda wondered if he would ever return. But before she could contemplate this more thoroughly she glanced down at her watch. Twenty minutes had already gone by and she was nowhere near where she believed the bird and fish market to be.

She picked up her pace. After another fifteen minutes of walking it was pretty close to her appointed hour to meet Inspector Fong, and Cheng Dou Road was still nowhere in sight.

So, taking her courage in hand, she stepped to the side of the road and held up her hand. Several taxis sped past her. The light on the top of the cabs was on so she assumed that they were available. As they whizzed by, though, she saw people inside and realized that the light on the top didn't mean shit in Shanghai. Finally a cab stopped and she was faced with the question of where to sit. She chose the back and climbed in. Inside she found the driver almost entirely encased in a thick fibreglass-like material that separated him from the front passenger seat as well as the back.

He barked something which she took to mean "Where to, ma'am?" She said the name that Inspector Zhong had given her. He turned around and gave her a funny look. She said the name again, slower this time. He sucked on his teeth and looked at her out of the side of his eyes. She tried a third time with a totally different intonation, in fact, what she thought of as Jerry Lewis Chinese and, to her surprise, the cabby's face lit up. He put his hands into his armpits and flapped his arms. He looked like a pimply bird. She smiled and nodded, hoping that they weren't heading toward the zoo.

The car sped into traffic, made the first left and then screeched to a stop. He pointed across a small construction site, in which a woman was washing clothes in a mud pool. Once again he did his bird imitation. Then he pointed at the meter. It had said 14.40 when she got in and it said 14.40 now. She gave him fifteen yuan and was about to get out of the cab when he hollered at her. She stopped in her tracks. She hadn't given him enough tip and he was mad! But no, he was holding out some of the filthiest money she'd ever seen—her change. The little ratty pieces of paper, two two-Jiao notes and two one-Jiao notes gave her a real understanding of the phrase "dirty money." She took the bills and smiled. He pointed, bird flapped again, and drove off. Her cab ride had taken less than twenty seconds.

She looked across the construction site. Like most of Shanghai, this area of town was awash in buildings coming down and new structures rising. To her right an apartment building had been half demolished, exposing once lived-in rooms to the elements. Former life got little respect in Shanghai. On one of the green-painted walls she could make out the silhouette where a picture had hung. On another the mildewed wallpaper peeled forward like a flap of decayed skin.

She heard a tinkling bell close behind her and turned. A man sat on an ancient bicycle with two large round iron buckets attached to the back. Inside was a putrid compost of food waste. His bell may have rung gaily but he was not pleased with the big white lady standing in his way. She stepped aside, barely avoiding an old man whose walking stick landed on her foot as he moved past her. The mass of humanity heading toward the bird and fish market was all being funnelled into one small path in an effort to avoid the water from the construction site.

As she waited her turn to cross the thin dry isthmus of bricks, she looked more closely at the construction site and marvelled at what she saw. Again huge scaffolds of bamboo lashed together with vines and then diagonally supported with further bamboo. And everywhere there were human beings carrying large loads on their shoulders, on their backs, and at their sides. Bricks, mortar, beams, wooden supports, buckets of nails, garbage, all the stuff of building pulled and toted by human beings. The worst was the mud. The ground in Shanghai seemed to be permanently saturated with water so that digging a simple hole was a monumental task. The men's thin arms were stretched to breaking as they lifted their bamboo-handled shovels with the heavy muck.

Crossing the little brick bridge at last, she noticed that the woman was not washing her clothes in the muddy water as she had at first thought. Rather, she had taken the sump pump hose, which was causing the pool of water to form, and had put it into a red plastic tub in which she was scrubbing clothes with a large bar of orangish soap.

Halfway across the bricks she spotted Inspector Zhong. He was standing beside a gruff-looking older man. The two were smoking and looking at their respective watches.

Once across, Amanda strode over to the two men and said good morning. Fong introduced Wang Jun. Then, after consulting Ngalto Chomi's itinerary, which his driver had given them, they set off. Wang Jun dropped back. A quizzical look crossed Amanda's face.

"The killer tracked a man named Ngalto Chomi two days ago. He stalked him, I believe the American phrase is. Because Ngalto Chomi was an important man he had a driver and the driver knew where he dropped off Mr. Chomi and where he picked him up." Pointing to the other side of the small pool, Fong said, "The driver dropped him off there where you got out of your cab and then he crossed, as you did, and came to where we are standing now."

"How do you know he didn't cross and move down that side street? "

"Because I asked that merchant over there."

Openly surprised she blurted out, "And he actually remembered? "

"Mr. Chomi was a six-foot seven-inch black man. Not something we get to see every day in Shanghai. People would remember. Like they will remember you."

"I'm not that tall."

"No you're not, but you're funny coloured too." Without waiting for a response, Fong started down the crowded street. Catching up to him Amanda demanded, "And where's your friend?"

"He's watching us, the way the killer watched Mr. Chomi."

She looked back but couldn't see Wang Jun. Fong,

seeing this said, "This killer was very good. He would pick vantage points that even if Mr. Chomi knew he was being followed he would not be able to spot."

With a big smile she pointed to one side and up a floor. There was Wang Jun. "There."

"The killer was very good, Wang Jun is merely fair." They moved on. It took a while for the idea of walking a dead man's steps to sink in and even once it did, Amanda's eyes were constantly being drawn to the extraordinary array of things around her. It never occurred to her that the bird and fish market would actually sell birds and fish. In fact on the first stretch it sold nothing but tropical fish and things to put them in, things to enhance their underwater worlds and things to feed them. In the crowd people carried little plastic bags with their newest acquisitions swimming in what seemed to Amanda like small clear water bubbles. After the fish came a section of bonsai trees and tropical plants. Her eye was drawn to a display of ancient roots that had been unearthed and polished to a high sheen. The knarls and whorls rivalled the artistry of any human hand. Behind the roots were large plastic buckets of polished stones. Fong pointed out the rocks with red markings. "We call them blood stones. The more red the more expensive they are." Then came several stands selling polished brown Yangtze River stones whose surfaces fit perfectly in the palm and whose heft was particularly pleasing. As Amanda knelt to sift her hand through one of the larger buckets Fong talked to the woman at the stand. Then, as he grabbed a small tub from under the stand, he turned to Amanda. "Stand on that, will you?" She did, wondering exactly what this was about. But then she remembered that the black man had been six foot seven. She was herself close to six feet tall and the bucket was probably another six inches. Which put her close to the dead man's height. She felt a shiver start in the base of her neck and work its way down.

"Can I step down now, please?"

Fong didn't answer her but stared down one of the alleyways. Then he put his fingers in his mouth and whistled loudly. The old lady with the stones yelled at him to stop but he ignored her and whistled again. At that point Wang Jun stepped out from behind one of the fish stands and waved. Fong quickly made his way over to Wang Jun. The woman screamed at Amanda who needed no further prompting to get off the bucket and follow Fong.

Pointing to the alley crossroad, Fong said, "He'd have to assume a position for a little while as Mr. Chomi shopped. He'd have to be able to see down both the road and the alley? Right?"

"Right, so I guess he was either where we're standing now, or cater-corner," replied Wang Jun pointing across the way.

"And if Chomi dawdled, as the driver said he often did, then it's possible that our killer had to wait here or there for quite some time. The woman selling stones remembered Chomi because he, as she put it, 'was a sweet talker who felt every fucking stone, spent a ton of my time, the cutie, and only bought one stone. My best one too.'"

"So he stayed for a while at the stand," Wang Jun said.

"I never got the stone seller to confirm that. She lost interest when she figured out we weren't buying."

"You've got a funny look on your face, Fong."

"It's just the way she talked about him. Stone sellers don't like customers, especially foreign customers. Do they?"

"Not in my experience. What are you getting at?"

"I don't know." Fong mulled the idea around for a moment but still came to no conclusion so he went back to being a plain street cop. "You ask on this side. I'll ask across the way." After only a few minutes, it became clear that no one had seen anything. Some remembered the African, but that was hardly the point.

They worked their way through the extensive market, walking Ngalto Chomi's route and finding places from which the killer must have watched him. When they found these places they talked to the nearby merchants. No one remembered anything. The third alley was where the birds were, along with their racket and smell. Tiny finches and swallows were for sale as were more exotic birds. Once again animals were carried home in clear plastic bags, this time not filled with water but rather with air supplied by punching a hole in the bag, usually with a cigarette. Near the end of the hundred or so bird sellers were the bird food sellers. Large wooden barrels filled to overflowing with live grubs created an ever shifting pattern of transient life. Sellers of gray moth pupas, each with its very own live larva inside, were doing an active business as were the seed merchants. "Do you like birds?" asked Fong. "Not much," replied Amanda. "Mr. Chomi evidently was extremely fond of birds. The Zairian consulate let us look at his rooms. He had a fine collection of finches. Unusual. Here, birds are women's pets. Are you hungry? It's near noon."

"I could eat," replied Amanda.

"Good, because that's what Mr. Chomi did next." Fong set off down the lane.

Catching up to Fong again she said, "And you, do you like birds, Inspector Zhong?"

"I'm actually quite fond of pigeon."

"Really," she asked surprised.

"Yes, the restaurant we're going to is famous for its pigeon."

She swallowed slightly and then stopped as a man thrust a cheap leatherette bag up close to her face and opened the zipper. Out popped the head of a puppy which yapped and tried to lick Amanda's hand. The man with the dog was speaking to Amanda in an animated fashion.

Fong came up beside her. "He says this dog was made for you in heaven. A beautiful lady needs a beautiful dog to augment her beauty."

Amanda looked hard at him. "That's what he said." The man then snapped a volley of words at Fong. "He also told me that no dog no matter how beautiful could make up for the ugliness that I carry with me."

"He said that?"

"Actually no. He asked if the stupid blond lady wanted to buy the dog or not. And if not could she get her big butt out of the way of other potential customers." And looking behind her, there were indeed many other potential customers.

This whole end of the alley was lined with dog sellers. Puppies only. All purebreds. As they left the alley, Amanda asked, "Where are the Heinz 57's, the mutts? And where are the grown-up dogs?" Fong stopped and looked at her with an are-you-kidding-me? look. Deciding that he was not being kidded, he also decided that he wouldn't answer her question so close to lunch.

As they headed toward the old city, the two policemen compared notes. They passed by the place where the driver had waited to pick up Chomi. For a moment they considered whether the killer had a car and then quickly discarded that idea. However, clearly he would need a bicycle. "Great, we've narrowed it down to one of the 7.8 million bicycle riders in the city of Shanghai."

As the men talked, Amanda looked. The entire place was being torn down and put up anew. She'd never seen anything like it. And the faces—everywhere stories etched in human material. An old lady with a filthy child approached her and held out her hand, imploring Amanda to give her some money for the child. Amanda instinctively moved away. The woman followed her. Amanda went to step out into the street to avoid her but the woman reached out and grasped her arm. Amanda was shocked. Despite the enormous crush of people everywhere in Shanghai, touching was a rarity. Even in the cramped quarters of the Bird and Fish Market, people swerved and glided past each other without touching. Unlike New York City where being jostled was part of walking on the streets, here contact was kept to a strict minimum. So when the old lady grabbed her, Amanda screamed before she could stop herself. Both men reacted as if a gun had gone off. Fong recovered first and yelled something at the woman who yelled right back and then Fong stepped between Amanda and the old woman while Wang Jun guided Amanda away.

"I'm sorry, she startled me."

"Country folk don't take kindly to foreigners. They're harmless but a nuisance. You have, they don't, so they grab you to give them something. Simple," said Wang Jun in his slightly lisping Shanghanese.

Amanda got the gist of his explanation. New Orleans had its share of street people too.

Fong came back and apologized to Amanda, who threw it off as nothing. But as they walked, Amanda knew that it wasn't nothing. The old lady had pierced her armour and drawn blood. She picked up her pace to keep up with the men, who had entered another street market and were consulting a map.

"Lost, guys?"

"No, Ms. Pitman, but the driver stopped right here and Mr. Chomi got out pretty much right where you're standing," said Fong.

"I thought you said he went to lunch next."

"That was the next stop but he evidently walked from here to the restaurant."

"Why'd he do that? What's to see here?" asked Amanda.

"I don't think that Mr. Chomi was a tourist in the usual sense of the word. He worked here, lived here. Something attracted him to the Bird and Fish Market — from his home we can assume the birds — and then something attracted him to this street market," said Fong.

"What?"

"That's a good question, Ms. Pitman, one worth trying to answer perhaps." Fong looked to Wang Jun who was pointing across the street to a woman who was taking money for the right to park a bicycle on her ten yards of sidewalk. She wore no red armband so she didn't work for the government. She was just trying to get a little money on the side. What had attracted Wang Jun's attention was the near fight she was having with a young secretary type who wasn't about to pay to leave her bicycle where evidently she'd left it every day for a year.

"You don't think he left his bicycle there, do you?"

"No, our friend kept his bicycle with him. There are too many alleys and ways out of this market for him to chance leaving it and then coming back for it."

"I agree," said Wang Jun.

But there was a shred of an idea here, thought Fong. The killer would need his bicycle to stalk the man. Would he then kill and ride it away? Perhaps. A bike offers speed but removes some mobility. The complex laws in Shanghai about where and when you can ride a bicycle are strictly enforced. Would the murderer chance the attention of one of the thousands of cops assigned to monitor bike traffic? Or would he leave the bike after the murder and simply slip into the mass of people always around in Shanghai?

Both men knew that a bicycle in Shanghai attracted attention if it was left overnight. For the first time, it occurred to Fong that they might be able to find the killer's bike, but not here — nearer the scene of the murder perhaps.

As they walked Wang Jun caught Fong up on his newspaper investigation. It was simple — they were stonewalling him. His many queries had come up short. The whole thing had been handled by the editor-in-chief to whom Fong had spoken on that first morning. The editor claimed to have gotten the story straight off a cell phone report from one of his field guys and then banged out the story almost straight onto the printing press. Naturally, he refused to give up the guy's name.

"But what about clearance? "

"He claims it was one of those things where the Communications Ministry contact was actually in the building at the time and stood over his shoulder as he wrote it."

"The timing's still wrong."

"I told him that. He claims that with the new technology they can alter an edition at the last moment, which allows them two more hours before press deadline."

"Check that for me, will ya?" Fong was not pleased. But at that moment he wasn't sure if he wasn't pleased with the answers to Wang Jun's inquiries or Wang Jun's inquiry itself. They continued in silence for a few minutes. As they entered the heart of the food market Fong stopped and consulted the African's itinerary. "Next thing that we know is that Mr. Chomi bought a skinned snake . . ."

Fong looked up.

Amanda was well ahead of them. She had joined a crowd and was on her tiptoes trying to get a better look at something on the ground.

The skinning of a live king cobra was shocking even if you knew it was about to happen. Amanda didn't know.

Fong raced up, afraid that Amanda would faint.

The children in the crowd screamed in delight as the snake merchant flung the skin, still wriggling, into the air.

Amanda stood very still, very white, and took it all in.

The skinning did not make her faint. It made her understand something — understand it deeply.

Lunch at the Old Shanghai Restaurant upstairs in the Old City, around the corner from the famous YuYuan Gardens, was not all that Fong had expected. It seems that Ngalto Chomi had brought his freshly killed snake to the restaurant to have it cooked. He had done it several times before and the cooks knew him well. For a foreigner, especially a black foreigner, his memory was treated with surprising deference by the staff at the Old Shanghai. Wang Jun suggested that they should have brought a snake too, but Fong didn't respond. Ms. Pitman's silence had been ominous since the snake merchant had displayed his unique talent. Fong wondered how much whiter Amanda Pitman could get. He also wondered if all this was too much for her.

"Would you like me to get an officer to drive you back to your hotel?"

In her distracted state she had to ask him to repeat himself and he did. She declined his offer, but also declined all food at the restaurant. She smoked instead.

Chinese women smoked, but not in public. It would be wrong to say that both Wang Jun and Fong didn't find it just a little bit titillating to be at a table with a tall blond white woman who was smoking cigarettes.

As the men finished eating their lunch Fong turned to Amanda. "You could help us by filling in some of your ex-husband's background."

Through the plume of her cigarette smoke, she said, "Shoot."

"He was a police officer in New Orleans?"

"Not really."

That surprised Fong. "His identity papers said that he worked for the New Orleans Police Department."

"Where's New Orleans?" Wang Jun asked in Shanghanese.

"Ohio, I think," replied Fong in English.

"What's Ohio?" said Amanda.

"Where New Orleans is," said Fong.

"It's in Louisiana, if that makes any difference."

"Fine, Louisiana, but he wasn't a police officer?"

"He technically worked for the New Orleans parish police department, but he was seconded from the federal fish and wildlife department," said Amanda.

"And what did he do there?" queried Fong.

"He specialized in the prevention of the poaching of endangered species." Fong quickly translated into Shanghanese and a bored Wang Jun perked up and took note.

"Ask her if he'd ever been to Africa," said Wang Jun in Shanghanese.

"Later," replied Fong, "after I find out if he was a cop on the take."

"Anyone care to translate for me?" snapped Amanda.

"Wang Jun was just expressing his condolences for your loss."

Amanda looked at Fong for a moment and then viciously spat out, "My husband was a much better liar than you, Inspector Zhong." On Fong's stunned look she rose from the table and, ignoring all the sidelong glances of the Chinese men, made her way to the ladies' room.

Once she was gone, Wang Jun asked for a translation of the last few moments and got them. Then he turned to Fong and said, "We don't need her for the rest of this. The next part is going to get pretty rough. Why do you want her here anyway? Get her a ride back to her hotel. You and I can complete this."

But Fong wasn't listening. He was watching the movement of people in the room. "You figure there's a back way out in the kitchen?"

"There has to be by law."

"Since when do restaurants listen to the law? If he did

leave through the kitchen, the killer must have been waiting by the alley entrance. Someone might have noticed. Check if he left that way."

Wang Jun had just entered the kitchen when Amanda returned. From the glint of moisture on her face, Fong could tell that she had splashed it with cold water.

"Feel better?"

"A little, thanks."

"You don't have to go through with this. The next two stops aren't going to be pleasant, that I can guarantee you."

She didn't say anything. Then carefully Fong moved forward. "How much did the State Department tell you about your husband's death?"

"Just that he'd been murdered and . . . and I wouldn't be able to view the remains . . . and that, uh" — she was getting faint, he could tell from her pallor — "uh, that it wouldn't be possible to have an open-casket funeral." As if having said it relieved the pressure, some colour came back into her face.

Unable to resist her vulnerability, Fong chipped in, "Did you love your husband, Ms. Pitman?"

Her "no" came out so loudly that several other people around the restaurant turned to see who was speaking.

Then a chatter of explanation, *mao, boo she, boo dui.*

"*Mao* what?" said Wang Jun.

"Nothing, just a comment from Ms. Pitman."

"Well it's *mao* from the kitchen too. There's no exit and besides, one of the waiters remembers Mr. Chomi going out the front."

Getting up, Amanda asked, "Who's paying?"

She didn't offer up any cash but moved through the crowd toward the exit as the two men fished out some bills and tossed them to the waiter. Then Fong went ahead to catch up with Amanda while Wang Jun yelled for a receipt. On a monthly salary of under 600 yuan, called kwai by the locals, about $75 U.S., he was damned if he was going to pay 68 kwai for a meal that he didn't enjoy.

• • •

The three headed along Fang Bang Road through the heart of the Old City. Amanda was stunned. Squat hovels fronted the road, seemingly jostling each other for a little light and air. Despite the sunshine it was murky here. And despite the murk and the smell and the dirt Amanda loved it. She breathed in the pungent odour and drank in the dense view. She clearly sensed the life here. Fong looked at the strange American with more than a bit of surprise. The black man had walked this way but even if he hadn't Fong had determined that Amanda Pitman was one white tourist who wasn't going to leave his city believing that Shanghai was nothing more than Nanjing Road and Huai Hai. Nothing more than the Bund and the YuYuan Garden. This was the real Shanghai. Not the English Concession down by the river or the French Concession farther south. This was what was laughingly called the Chinese Concession. A concession that allowed the Chinese to live on the only piece of ground in Shanghai that

Europeans didn't want. They were actually within a few blocks of the house in which Fong had been raised when Amanda turned to him and said, "It's. . . alive, isn't it." For a moment he checked for sarcasm, but he knew there was none. This place. This sinkhole was like a deep stagnant pool. Never good to drink from, often bad to smell, but always teeming with life. There was no need here to figure out where the killer had watched from. There were few alleys here and when there were they didn't go anywhere. So he must simply have followed, pushing his bicycle — pushing his bike until he got to the Fu Yu antique market.

Wang Jun and Fong stopped at the same time. How did he manage to follow Ngalto Chomi into the market? This narrow, extremely crowded place had side shoots and cul-de-sacs everywhere. More important, each side of the building was backed by an alley.

"Where did the driver wait?" demanded Fong. Wang Jun checked his notes and pointed left. With a heightened sense of urgency they moved south on Fang Bang and headed down the first alley. Halfway down Wang Jun stopped and tried to check a dirt-encrusted number sign. It was what he was looking for. "The driver waited here. Back there, around the bend" — he pointed down the alley — "is the rear exit of the place where Chomi was, and farther back is where they found him." To Amanda's surprise, Fong headed back up to the street.

Once there he squatted and using a stick, marked a path in the dust. "Chomi ate at the Old Shanghai Restaurant here, and walked down this way. He must have walked along Fang Bang and come to that inter-section." He pointed back to the entranceway of the Fu Yu market where they had been before they went into the alley.

"The driver said he always went through the Fu Yu market."

"I know, but how does our killer know which way he's going to go? There are alleys behind the houses. How does he cover that?"

"Two guys?"

"Couldn't be. Not with this kind of thing. Wang Jun?"

"I agree. So—" Wang Jun began to walk back toward the entrance to Fu Yu—"so our guy leaves his bicycle here and races into the market to follow Chomi."

"So what does he do with the bicycle? He figures out where Chomi is going but does he know how long he'll stay? No. He may be going into a store or trying to change money or selling something. How would the killer know? So he sees him go into the place and races wildly around trying to find a back exit in the hope that Chomi doesn't just turn around and come back out the way he went in. But lo and behold he comes across Chomi's car and driver and he knows. So he crouches down and waits. Leaving his bicycle where it stood."

"I like it. Let's check out the house first and then fol-low up the bike."

Fong conveyed all this to Amanda as they waded through the dense crowd of Fu Yu.

Wang Jun stopped in front of a vendor and pointed to

the shallow alley behind him. "How do you want to play this?"

"By the book—we're not vice. He wasn't killed there, all I want is to see if there's anyone who remembers Mr. Chomi."

"Show them ID?"

"If they ask, but I don't think they will. No doubt, we're expected."

"Could I be caught up?" asked Amanda.

"Of course. When you were in school did you do any drugs, Ms. Pitman?"

"This from a police officer?"

"Your president did drugs."

"And your president swam the Yangtze."

"He's not our president now and no one, in China at least, believed he swam the Yangtze."

"Yes, I did, as you put it, do some drugs."

"Mr. Chomi did drugs too. Elaborate drugs. And he did them in a rather ancient establishment whose entrance is off this alley. We're going in. Would you like to join us or are you going to stay outside?"

"I'll join you." Then as she followed them she timidly asked, "Heroin?"

"No, Ms. Pitman, this is China. Opium is the drug of choice here."

It was all remarkably simple, Amanda thought. They entered a tiny doorway through which even Fong had to bend down and were greeted as if they had arrived a little late for a casual party. They were asked if they would like to leave their coats. All declined. Then they were asked if they would like some food with their opium. That too was declined. Some alcohol perhaps? No thanks. What about women? Wang Jun beat Fong to the punch with "That sounds like a good idea." Fong flashed him a look. "Maybe next time, I'm trying to cut down," said Wang Jun. They were led by another man back into the recesses of a long corridor with small rooms on either side. The smell of the burning tar was thick in the tight space. Several of the rooms were partially open. Many had no doors, the entrances strung simply with blankets or tattered curtains. As they passed the rooms, Amanda saw men in various states of recline. Some had the pipe held, others were being fed, one with two young half-clad women at his side. The whole place seemed in slow motion. Time alteration was the most immediate effect of the drug and even the tendrils of smoke that Amanda had inhaled were enough to begin the process.

When finally they reached their cubicle, Wang Jun took off his coat and breathed deeply. Then he smiled. "When I get old I'm going to buy a membership to one of these places and spend my days and nights here."

"Better start saving—such a retirement could get expensive."

The curtain opened and an old man with a long braid stepped into their room and lit the brazier in the corner. He was right out of a Hollywood Fu Man Chu film—floor-length black silk robe with large sleeves, small black beanie, long braid and soft green slippers. He carried a beautiful lacquered box in his long-finger-nailed hands. If he was surprised by the constituents of the room, two men and a woman, he didn't let on.

"Do you know who we are?"

"Not by name," said the old man, "but we have been expecting you for some time. Since the large black man was murdered."

"Did you serve the large black man?"

"Once, but Wu Yeh usually did these honours."

"Is she here?"

"Yes, she is always here. Shall I get her for you?"

"Please."

"Would you like. . . ?" He opened the box, revealing several balls of opium rolled and ready, and he produced a beautiful pipe from his sleeve, which he showed, rather than offered, to Fong.

"Is that Mr. Chomi's pipe?"

"Is that the black man's name?"

"Yes."

"Then this is indeed Mr. Chomi's pipe." Fong again noticed the obvious signs of deference to Mr. Chomi's memory. He took the pipe and marvelled at the thing's deep yellowish-white density and the layers of incredibly delicate carvings that saturated its entire two-foot length. Then he saw Amanda's admiring stare and passed her the pipe.

"Is this ivory?" asked Amanda.

"Without a doubt," replied Fong and without missing a beat asked, "Have you seen much ivory in your life, Ms. Pitman?"

"The odd trinket that Richard picked up for me at airports, but nothing like this." She allowed her fingers to trace the pipe's length.

A slender hand parted the curtains and the tiny thing called Wu Yeh slipped into the cubicle. The old man introduced her and then retired. Amanda looked at the delicate girl/woman in front of her—exquisite tapered fingers, skin without a blemish and deep liquid pools for eyes.

Wang Jun looked at her differently. He saw a practised prostitute who knew her craft and the wiles needed to succeed in that craft. Fong saw a masterful liar. He also saw cleverly hidden age and addiction. Unlike Amanda, he was not impressed with Wu Yeh's beauty. Beauty is relative. In Fong's case it was relative to Fu Tsong.

"Do you know that I am a police officer?"

"I have been told."

"I'm not with the vice squad. I'm investigating the murder of Ngalto Chomi, the black man who owned this pipe. You knew him?"

For a moment Fong thought she was going to cry. Then she said weakly, "Yes, I knew him. He came often. Near the end, almost every day."

"Did you always serve him?"

"It was my pleasure to serve him." Fong thought he must be losing his mind. He could have sworn that what the little whore said actually sounded honest. He looked to Wang Jun who signalled that he was at a loss too. Amanda asked to be caught up and Fong did. Then

Amanda looked at the girl/woman more closely. "She loved him, Inspector Zhong. We may be in China, a long way from my stomping grounds, but I have seen that look before on others. She loved him."

And so it proved to be.

Wu Yeh tearfully recounted her last time with her African lover.

Slowly the picture of Ngalto Chomi as a much loved man was coming into focus. Here was a man, who not only because of his colour and his height left a lasting impression on others—stone sellers, cooks, and a whore in an opium den who had been with more men in a week than most women have been with in their lives.

Mr. Chomi is proving to be an exceptional human being, Fong thought, as his eyes strayed to the ivory pipe. A human being whose heart could resist the knife.

They walked out the back door, as Ngalto Chomi had, and instantly knew where the killer must have hidden. The bend in the alley allowed a place from which the killer could have watched without being seen by the waiting driver. Wu Yeh said that she had walked him to the door and that as he lingered with her kiss, he had slid a hand inside her robe and caressed her breast. She had looked up at him and told him that the room was still his if he desired her more. But he had declined—and probably was murdered directly after he closed the door on the whore who loved him.

Wang Jun strung the area with police tape and informed the old man that the door wasn't to be used until further notice. Then the three of them walked to the site itself. It was cleverly chosen but still partially exposed. The attacker had to be fast. Evidently he was. And then no doubt he made his escape away from the place where the driver was parked.

"Which means he left his bicycle back at the foot of Fu Yu," said Fong.

"I agree. It's two days ago, though," replied Wang Jun.

"We might get lucky, swamp the area with cops. I want to find that bike or whoever stole it. I want every bike on that sidewalk claimed and taken away. The one that's left is our man's."

Fong drove Amanda back to her hotel in silence. When he finally stopped the car Amanda turned to him and asked,"Could the bicycle really be valuable in finding this guy?"

"Maybe. A bicycle here is not like in other places. People, you have no doubt noticed, use them all the time. And the roads are rough. No one rides a bicycle without having to get it fixed over and over again."

"That's what all those men with tool kits and pumps are doing on every street corner?"

"Precisely. And I have found that those men with tool kits and pumps, as you put it, have very good memories when it comes to bicycles and faces. There's a man around the corner from the academy that we call the master. He can fix anything. And he never forgets either a bike or a face."

"I see."

He turned to her. Again he noticed the oddness of blue eyes in a white face. Then he said, "I was terribly out of line at the restaurant. I'm sorry for the question about your husband."

"You know, I almost said who, when you said my husband. We were not close, hadn't been for some time, Inspector."

"Do you know what your husband was doing in Shanghai when he was murdered?"

"He was here on business, I thought."

"He was a government employee, wasn't he? What kind of business was he on?"

"He travelled all the time, Inspector. Europe, Asia, Africa—you name it and Richard had been there."

Fong quickly said, "You lied to me about the ivory back in the opium den."

"In a way yes. I never saw anything but trinkets, but I know a lot about ivory. Through Richard—a lot. For some time I'd known that we couldn't be living the way we were on the meagre salary of a government official and the profit from the business I ran."

"Is it possible that he was involved in smuggling ivory out of Africa under the protection of his government credentials?"

"It's possible."

Fong looked at her closely.

"More than possible," she whispered.

"Thank you."

She looked straight into his eyes for an instant. "Now that you know, you don't need me anymore, do you?"

He didn't respond. "Do you?" she pressed.

"No."

"I see. May I ask a favour?" He nodded. "Tell me what you know about my husband's death."

Slowly, with precision but without sentiment, he told her all he knew of the passing of Richard Fallon.

"And that's what the U.S. consulate didn't want me to know?" Fong chose not to answer that question. Amanda took his silence as assent. "So that's everything." It was a statement not a question.

A silence began to fill the space between them. She looked down at her hands in her lap. "So now you can go home," he said.

She thought about that, about "going home." When she raised her eyes his were there to meet hers. "I'm not sure I'm ready to go home yet, Inspector Zhong."

Fong allowed a moment to pass then asked, "Do you like shopping, Ms. Pitman?"

"What are you—?"

"Perhaps you'd accompany me tomorrow. I know very little about ivory and I have a strange feeling that store keepers would be more open to your inquiries than to mine. All right?"

"Fine."

"Tomorrow morning then."

"Fine."

"Dress up."

"You too, Inspector."

•　•　•

That night Fong sat in the back of the old theatre and watched Geoffrey Hyland stage the drunk scene in *Twelfth Night*. It was like watching a master etcher daubing his acid on human material. But this product wasn't set in time and space. It was art in dynamic motion. Art that was molten and tactile. Art that was never the same moment to moment but never random. Never not art.

Hyland began with a simple question: Why is Toby Belch drinking? Answers were posed and tested. No acting was attempted until Hao Yong suggested that Toby needed to escape. Escape what? "A memory," ventured the actor playing Toby, a frighteningly thin tall man in his early forties.

"Good," replied Geoffrey. "Memories do haunt, don't they?" For the slightest moment he tilted his head in Fong's direction and then returned his attention to the actors. "Well?" Finally the actor playing Toby came up with the answer to which Geoffrey had led them. The answer was simple and in line with everything else in this play that parades itself as a comedy but by its conclusion is hardly humorous. The answer of course was that Toby Belch drinks to try to escape his terrifying love of Olivia. To escape even the memory of that unrequited love. Andrew drinks for the same reason. So does Maria, whose love for Toby will never truly be returned. And then there's Feste — the clown who drinks to forget that he ever loved, that he ever had a reason to carry on with his life.

Then Geoffrey repeated Fu Tsong's words, "We're all here. Shakespeare wrote us all in the play. Which one are you?"

Time of day became the next discussion. Geoffrey postulated what he called the witching hour. That time when the Moslem crier, the muezzin, climbs the tower of the mosque and holds up a black thread and a white one. When he can see the difference between the two he calls the faithful to the first prayers of the day. It is the point at which Banquo returns to the castle with his son Fleance to meet his end. It is the moment of night's end, in theory the victory of the light. But in *Twelfth Night*, the long night only leads to a longer day.

The actors began to work. A moment found, a moment lost, a line needing a better translation. Finally Geoffrey stops the group. The faces are flushed, alive. "Let's try working this in vibrating primaries rather than in pure primaries. It's not complicated, just hear me out for a moment. I have two kids, a boy eight and a girl six. They both love playgrounds — you know with swings and slides — they'd go nuts at the Children's Palace on Yan'an. Well, every time we pass a playground my kids go into the pure right-handed primary of I SEE, I LOVE. And if I allow them to go into the playground the six-year-old stays in that pure primary, but the eight-year-old knows in his heart that he is too old to love something like this so much. So when he enters the park he changes from the pure right-handed primary of I SEE, I LOVE to the vibrating primary of I SEE, I LOVE, BUT I KNOW I SHOULDN'T. The six-year-old is a joy to watch in the playground in her pure primary state, but the eight-year-old is downright fascinating sitting squarely in the centre of his vibrating primary. Playing in pure primaries has a tendency to ride an actor's age down creating that kiddy acting nonsense. To be childlike is not to be childish. To keep the work sophisticated the pure primary has to be mated with its opposite which makes the pendulum swing inside. It carves internal landscapes and hence you are compelling to watch without that hideous 'doing things.' By the way, *only* when you're in primaries is less more. When you're in secondary less is only less. Clear?"

A few questions came back at Geoffrey, most having to do with the fear of playing emotions. In each case Geoffrey reiterated that he was not talking about playing emotions but being in emotional states. "You play your actions. You try to make your acting partner feel things that will spur them to do things. But to be compelling— to create density and interest in your work—you must play those actions and release the text's images from a primary state—hopefully a vibrating primary."

Geoffrey's simple, elegant staging of the scene took shape over the next three hours. There were no breaks in Geoffrey Hyland rehearsals. Actors smoked when they were not needed, or drank tea from the omnipresent thermoses, but they never wandered off. This was not a place of idle chatter. It was an artist's studio. They thought and contributed and went into themselves, trying to find their stops and ventages to make most eloquent music.

Only at the very end of the scene do any of the characters drink. Feste takes a sip and it pierces his heart. A cry of pain comes from him that is music itself and the scene ends with the sun rising over a stage of addicted lovers unable to sleep at night or be fully awake during the day.

Fong loved it. Unlike so much spoken theatre, it touched him deeply. Touched him the way that the Shanghanese Opera could. His grandmother had taken him when he was five to the theatre in the heart of the Old City. Shanghanese Opera is a form of classical Peking opera that varies only in interpretation, not genre, from the original. The Shanghanese version has a tendency to be shorter and more melodious. But it is still the singing, tumbling, acting, juggling, transcendent experience of the original.

The very first piece Fong saw took his heart completely. It was *Journey to the West*. The evening began with an oceanside leavetaking of a king and his beautiful daughter whom for political reasons he has to give in marriage to a prince of the western provinces. The scene, although formal, has cracks of tension in it where feeling is implied without being shown. Then a serving man is entrusted with the daughter's safety and off the two go on the three-thousand-mile journey to the West. Their travels begin conventionally enough. The serving man walks as his beautiful mistress rides (indicated by the carrying of a four-tassled stick). She, naturally enough, treats him as a common serf but as the days pass and the adventures of crossing rivers, deserts and mountains, meeting dangerous enemies, dealing with cold, and sleeping in the rain accumulate, a new appreciation for the serving man begins to grow in her.

When finally he is hurt trying to help her safely cross a deep river, she insists that he ride the horse and she walk. After their four-hour stage journey, most of which is done without speech and often with just the two actors on stage, they finally reach the western court and the serving man must hand over his charge. He does and turns to walk back to the East.

The serving man is dressed plainly. He tumbles, dances, sings, fights with both sword and lance, and juggles the complicated war hammer. The princess is played with sleeves and headdress feathers, her lengthened sleeves providing an elongated image and the two long elegant feathers accentuating every head movement by tracing the pulse of the energy from base to tip. Often the feathers are pulled down and put into the mouth creating various configurations. She wears raised shoes, is dressed in red and her face is painted mask white. For many years, she was easily the most erotic thing that entered Fong's life.

When he first met Fu Tsong, he often felt like the serving man in the *Journey to the West* whose job it was to deliver the princess to some great man's bed. It was not until years after they were married that he confessed to her his fascination with traditional Chinese "sung" theatre. He thought she would find it ludicrous coming as she did from the new "spoken word" theatre. But she didn't. In fact she openly acknowledged her great debt to her Peking opera training and said that in the hands of the great actors the opera roles were as real as anything done anywhere. That what the classic form did was find the essence of emotion and then over hundreds of years refine the emanation of that emotion in the body. In the hands of normal classical opera actors this just became a hollow shell, but with a master or mistress of the art the shell held a glowing truth.

So it was with delight that, years later, Fong wangled two tickets for a famous actress's performance of *Journey to the West* at Shanghai's newly renovated Yi Fu Stage. As the evening went on Fong found himself once more lost in the story of the serving man and the princess. Amidst the noise of the audience and the comings and goings, there was real communication. Fong felt as if the actress were reaching out — putting her cool hand directly on his chest. Kneading and pressing toward his heart. Putting his nipple in her mouth and sucking firm and slow. He felt that he saw every quiver of her hand and flash of her eye. He was lost in the embrace of a woman on a stage with white makeup and four-foot feathers on her head.

As the serving man gave her over to her new husband Fu Tsong's hand crept into his. "Special, isn't it?" But he couldn't respond, only nod and hope she couldn't sense the tears welling up in him.

After the show, Fu Tsong excused herself and went backstage to say hello to the stage manager, who was an old friend. Theatre people had "old friends" that way and although Fong understood such things he always felt awkward in a world of people who were intimate but not close. He chose to wait in the lobby and gloried in the photographs of the actress, Su Shing, who played the princess.

That night Fu Tsong took a long time in the bathroom. Fong had already bathed and was in bed, a book open on his lap. But his mind was miles away on a journey to the West. The door to the bedroom opened a hair and he heard Fu Tsong's voice say, "Turn off the overhead light and put my red silk scarf over the bedside lamp." Fong knew better than to argue with her about such things. Turning off the overhead's harsh green-tinged light was a relief. When he placed her red silk scarf over the bedside table lamp the light from the weak bulb diffused enough to cast a pleasing shadowy glimmer.

The door opened. Fong gasped. There in the doorway was Fu Tsong dressed in the full costume of the princess from *Journey to the West*. Her face was made up porcelain white. The feathers bobbed as she moved. It was Fu Tsong but it was also the princess, both the one Fong had seen that night and the one he had seen when he was a boy. The mix both confused and intoxicated.

Fu Tsong moved to the foot of the bed and with an elegant flick of her wrists the sleeves of her gown flowed freely down. Then arching her neck back for a moment she snapped her head to one side and the feathers elongated the shock into a graceful dance of pure energy. She turned, and sliding her hands free of the sleeves, placed a feather in her mouth with a slight cry and a momentary flash of eyes and a pose.

Fong had no idea how long Fu Tsong continued her dance in the softened silk-red light. Nor did he have any idea when exactly she came into his arms. Her kiss at first tasted chemical but as Fu Tsong parted her lips and drew his tongue into her mouth he found himself making love to the princess from the East. She took him on the voyage of his life, to a place far to the west where the erotic dreams of youth meet the adult realities of sex. Where the old and the new meet, and the smell of the earth rises through the shimmer of silken clothes.

The delivery of the second half heart did the trick. All over Shanghai there were hushed conversations in corners of KTV private rooms. The whores were sent away and the men huddled together considering their options. They were traders of every conceivable nationality, race, colour, and creed. They only had one thing in common: the smuggling of ivory. But now, after the deaths of two of their kind, they shared a second thing: fear for their lives.

The phones had been ringing, faxes faxing, and e-mail e-mailing. Decisions were made. And all the decisions were the same. This place was not safe for ivory anymore. Fuck 'em, we'll move it to Singapore or Hong Kong or Hanoi, this place was just too much bother—and too dangerous.

So in private planes, luxury cars, and first-class airplane seats, the smugglers bailed out of Shanghai and headed toward safer ports of call.

That night in the power plant in the Pudong, glasses were lifted and toasts recited. Their spy network had informed them that the rout was on. The smugglers were leaving. After the congratulations went around, the hoarse voice said, "But we are not finished yet."

A chorus of agreement met his comment.

"Now we must proclaim to the West that we have rid the city of these smugglers, that Shanghai will no longer tolerate the killing of endangered species for the edification of a few elite. We must proclaim it loudly so that the conservationists in the West will stop their lobbying against us and allow the money we so badly need to be invested here."

The European voice spoke up. "The stories are already planted in the major presses in the West. By week's end our efforts — well, not our efforts but the results of our efforts — will be trumpeted from the newsstands of New York, London, Paris, and Berlin. The *Sunday Times* is going to do a feature on the eradication of ivory smuggling in Shanghai."

The hoarse voice, gulping air again, burped out, "Good."

There was a strong murmur of concurrence and then the hoarse voice resumed. "We have but two problems remaining. First, the assassin must be eliminated."

"He has already been betrayed. Our people in Taiwan are awaiting the arrival of a Shanghai detective, and they have prepared a dossier on Loa Wei Fen that should lead the police right to him."

There was a pause, and then another voice, unheard before, spoke up. "Is the second problem the detective in charge of the case?"

"It is," replied the hoarse voice, careful to conceal his surprise.

"I have troubled dreams about this Inspector Zhong."

The ancient man made note of the inherent challenge in the voice and then replied, "We have already begun to look after that situation."

"Good." The response was conspicuously neutral.

"To the renewal of most favoured nations trading status. To Shanghai, and growth that will never end. To the New China, strong and powerful," intoned the old man.

Glasses were raised but the owner of the hoarse voice did not drink. He sat and remembered the Shanghai of his birth, the simpler place, the happier time.

That night Geoffrey Hyland sat down for a second time with Wang Jun and went over his evidence again—evidence aimed at convicting Fong of the murder of Fu Tsong. As Geoffrey spoke he felt himself floating, drifting back to that hot summer afternoon four long years ago.

In Shanghai the hot dry days of early summer give way with a vengeance to the rainy season. On average the city is wracked by six to eight full-fledged tropical storms every year between late July and early September.

The fury of the winds that day, four years ago, had rattled the windows in the bedroom as Fong awoke from a terror-filled afternoon sleep to find Fu Tsong, now six months pregnant, gone from his side. He threw back the covers and put on his trousers.

Then the previous night came flooding back in on him.

He shook himself free of the horror and, grabbing an umbrella, headed out into the gathering storm whose darkness had changed day to night.

By the time he got to the theatre he was three leagues wet and none too thrilled that Fu Tsong hadn't left him a message about where she was going.

After last night's fight it was no real surprise.

She'd arrived home late, as she had done so often since her pregnancy began. But it wasn't her lateness that angered him. It was her distance, and if Fong were more honest, her endless bringing up of Geoffrey Hyland's name. Geoffrey had arranged for Fu Tsong to do a play with him in Vancouver. But rehearsals began only six weeks after the baby was due. Fong was amazed that Fu Tsong didn't see this as a problem. She replied that the baby could come with her. That Geoffrey had thought of all that. "It's a great opportunity for me. Geoffrey says my English is good enough and he wants me for the role so I'm going."

"No you're not," came out a lot harder than he intended and sat between them like a solid thing, unmovable, unretractable. After a seeming eternity Fu Tsong snapped, "Does your 'you're' mean me, the baby or both of us?"

"It means you and the baby." In for a jiao, in for a kwai.

"If the baby's a boy, right? If it's a girl, then Fong doesn't give a fuck where it goes, right?"

"Don't, Fu Tsong, we've been over—"

"You've, you've, you've been over and over this but

not me." Then grabbing her belly, "Not us."

"I don't know how to say I'm sorry anymore, Fu Tsong."

"You don't know how to say it because you're not sorry. Zhong Fong wants a son and I'm carrying a girl. One kid. Wrong kind." She screamed the last two sentences so loudly that the windowpanes shook. Then he saw Geoffrey through their open bedroom window. He'd been sitting on the base of the stupid statue, listening.

For a moment betrayal washed over him. This had been planned.

"I'm going to have a girl. I'm going to do the play. I'm going to live with Geoffrey."

Like three perfectly landed body blows, she blasted apart his ordered world and planted chaos in his heart.

Just once he looked at her to confirm that what he had heard was what she had said. Her eyes never wavered. "I'm going to live with Geoffrey," she repeated.

And then, somehow, the big white man was at their open door, now just Fong's open door. Fong heard himself saying in Mandarin, "There is no place here for you."

But Fu Tsong was already moving toward Geoffrey and pulling herself close to his side.

Fong didn't remember reaching for the VCR or hurling it across the room. All he remembered was the dent in the plaster and the red and black connector cables embedded in the wall from which the unit now dangled.

He remembered the give in the white man's chest as

he charged him and the thud as they went through the open door and crashed against the darkened corridor wall. The drip from the hallway air conditioner landed on his face as he screamed at the white man to leave his wife and baby alone.

Then he heard his name called. For a moment he didn't recognize Fu Tsong's voice. She called him sharply a second time and he turned to her. She stood in the door and said simply, "I'll see you tomorrow at rehearsal, Geoffrey. My husband and I have much to talk about tonight."

And so they did. In tears and twisting tongues and rage and tenderness they tried to find each other again across the abyss. They made love, had sex, fucked, and tried to hurt each other. They closed their eyes and fantasized that they were still in love. But tomorrow loomed and the girl child in her womb was a night older as the thunderous dawn approached.

Fong's welcome at rehearsal was chilly to say the least. Geoffrey was sporting a cast on his right wrist and Hao Yong was reading Fu Tsong's role, book in hand.

"She's not here, Fong," snapped Geoffrey.

"Where is she, then?"

"She said she was going to fix everything. That she was going 'to get everything fixed' were her exact words."

Fong responded weakly, "Do you know where she went?"

"She's your wife, Fong. You tell me. She left rehearsal over an hour ago."

As if on a cue from the heavens, a crack opened high in the theatre's south wall and a slender river of water, like a free-flowing tear, made its way to the floor.

Fong controlled his rising anxiety. His years of training as a cop came to the fore. "When exactly did she go?"

The stage manager said, "Forty-five minutes ago."

"Was she carrying a bag?"

"Yes, a small one," the stage manager said. "I called her a cab."

Geoffrey stared straight ahead.

"Which company?"

The stage manager gave him a name and he turned and ran toward the exit. As he left the theatre he heard Geoffrey's voice call out, "If anything happens to her, I'll chase you wherever you go. Wherever you go I'll find you and get my revenge."

"'Wherever you go I'll find you and get my revenge.' You said that?" asked Wang Jun. The white man nodded and continued to talk but Wang Jun wasn't listening. Geoffrey Hyland's story had triggered a memory in the old cop. A memory of another room, one in the Pudong, later on the day that the theatre director was describing.

Wang Jun took a deep breath to clear his head. It was getting light outside and Wang Jun was tired, vulnerable. When he had been ordered to interview the Canadian director he had been skeptical that anything new would come of it. Now, after his second interview, he just wanted to be sure before he proceeded. Before he reported that it was time to reopen the case against his friend Zhong Fong. Yes, Hyland had seen a terrible fight and been attacked by Zhong Fong the night before Fu Tsong's death in the Pudong. Yes, Fu Tsong had asked the director to contact Soo Jack the next afternoon, the afternoon of her death. No, Geoffrey Hyland had not been able to get in touch with Soo Jack so the stage manager had gotten Fu Tsong a cab. Yes, Fong had shown up at the theatre that afternoon, asking after Fu Tsong. Yes, Geoffrey had seen Fong the day after Fu Tsong's death and asked after Fu Tsong but Fong had ignored the question. And finally yes, Geoffrey had had an affair with Fu Tsong.

"Do you think Fong capable of killing his wife?"

"I guess anyone is capable of such a thing."

Then, as if it were an afterthought, Wang Jun tossed in, "You did know that Fu Tsong was pregnant, didn't you?"

Wang Jun watched the white man's face carefully.

"Yes, I knew, but . . ." Geofffrey himself falling – deep in the big white room. His mind did the simple arithmetic, the calculation he had never done before. Fu Tsong died in August four years ago. He had last slept with her in March of that year. The child could have been his.

Loa Wei Fen's breath was coming in slow, ragged bursts. His heart was racing. The sheet he slept on by the side of his bed at the Portman Hotel was dripping with sweat. "I must have been poisoned," he thought. It was the only thing that could explain what was happening to him. The clock on the bedside table said 2:07 A.M. He'd been asleep for almost twenty-two hours. He turned to the window, unwilling to accept the clock's assessment of the time. He fully expected to see daylight as he parted the curtains, but no. The blanket of night was full upon the city.

He had made an error when he killed the black man. He didn't know why he had made the error, but he did know that everything in his world had changed since.

Two days ago, after discovering that the source of his e-mail commands was police headquarters on the Bund, he had headed back toward the Portman. He went via the Old City, intending to pick up his bicycle from where he had left it the day of the killing. But as he approached, he sensed rather than saw the watchers. After a moment's examination, he spotted the police officers everywhere asking people about bicycles. He veered into the Fu Yu antique market and found himself somehow drawn toward the opium den where he had seen his quarry kiss the Chinese woman.

The image of the Chinese woman materialized more lovely than his memory, when she parted the curtains, a pipe in her elegant hands. That image exploded in his heart when, after preparing the opium, she put her tongue in his mouth. That image implanted itself as the liquid dream floated into his lungs and the impossibly small woman inserted him into herself bringing the clouds and the rain.

As if the two of them were part of something else. Part of a whole thing, he thought.

On the floor of the Portman Hotel the memory hurt him. Hurt him more than the scarring on his back. More than the rigours of his training. Something was ripping open inside him. Then Wu Yeh, his opium whore, was there in his hotel room—although he knew she couldn't be. The slender Chinese woman, pipe in hand, her robe open, awaiting him. As she approached, all Loa Wei Fen could think was that this isn't true—what has happened to me? And the great beast carved on his back flared its hood, its eyes blood red, and sank its fangs deep into Loa Wei Fen's heart.

Even as he toiled in the midst of his nightmare of love, Loa Wei Fen's computer was collecting data from the ether. A name appeared and an address. A photo likeness and a long set of names, dates, and places. The message ended simply. "Kill him any way you wish, and then disappear for a very, very long time."

DAY SEVEN

Shanghai, PRC, An April Dawn

Dearest Sister,

In Shanghai, I wear my westernness like an overcoat. As the sun crests the horizon in Fuxing Park the long gray amoeba shadows of the old men doing tai chi glide in slow motion across the cracked pavement. A woman in stirrup stretch pants is conducting a ballroom dance class to the sounds coming from a crackly beat box. Couples are learning the steps to a rumba. To my left two men in old-fasioned undershirts are playing a game of go while six or seven other men crowd in to offer their unsolicited advice. I am left alone with pen and paper and a head full of phrases running this way and that. I saw a girl in love yesterday, mourning the death of her lover. Back in the hotel room at Narita I thought that was what I was doing, but now I know for sure that it was not. I was pushing my past out of me or it was rising out of me by itself. I saw a little boy peeing by the roadside yesterday evening and I wanted to run over to him and hug him and tell him to figure out how to love someone with that thing. But I didn't. I just smiled. I do a lot of smiling here, sometimes when I don't feel like smiling much. After spending the day walking with Inspector Zhong, I spent a large portion of the evening walking alone. I found an area down Wolumquoi Road, near the consulates, where the city is a little less hectic. I sat and watched and dreamed of being alive here in a city where life is all there is for most people.

Tom Waits talks in a song about hiding in a hat, hanging in a curtain. I feel like I've been doing that for a long time. But, here I feel my time of hiding is almost over. That I have finally got to the brim of the hat, the hem of the curtain.

There was a dry wind yesterday all the way from the Mongolian steppes, they say. A fine loess sifted into everything. The city was bone dry, parched. But this morning, at dawn, there is a mist over the mighty Huangpo River and the hint of the promise of summer rains to come.

Love ya a hunk, squeeze those kids for me will you? —

A.

At the office that morning, Fong read the fax a third time, still unable to believe the words on the page. The Taiwanese government had okayed his request for assistance! And in less than a day to boot. On top of which they offered open access to their files and help in any way they could. It didn't make sense. Unless. . . A thought began to tickle its way toward the surface of his consciousness.

He had Shrug and Knock arrange airplane tickets for Li Xiao and confirm visas. But even as he spoke his mind was elsewhere. Tickling, tickling, the thought was coming to the air like a bubble from a still lake bottom. Unless. . . someone very powerful wanted the killer caught and ordered the Taiwanese to cooperate. Then it came to him clear. The messenger had delivered his message and was now expendable.

And from that moment, Fong stopped trying to find the killer. Now he wanted to find the man who hired the killer. Who owned him. Who put the knife in his hand just as surely as the ivory pipe had been put into his own hands in the opium den. He recalled the heft of the pipe and the last vestiges of the tickling stopped. He knew in his heart that ivory was somehow the link that closed the chain between those killed and those who ordered the killings.

He was waiting in the lobby of the International Equatorial Hotel later that morning when Amanda came down.

As he requested, Amanda had dressed up. Zhong Fong had not. Amanda lifted her arms with a so-what-do-you-think? gesture.

"Very nice, just right."

"Thanks. You on the other hand look like a cop."

"That bad, huh?"

"Worse."

They started with the hotel gift shops working their way from the arcade at the Equatorial to the Jing An

Hotel to the Hilton. In each shop they found helpful but totally uninformed sales people. Selling they could do. Telling you the history of the ivory pieces that were on display or even the source and type of the material was beyond their limited knowledge. One of the older sales-women asked if they were concerned about importing a piece back to America.

"Why? Should we be concerned?"

"No, not really, it's small. The embargo is really on large pieces."

"How old is this piece?"

"Old enough you can be sure that it was made before the ban on elephant products came into effect."

Leaving the store, Amanda remarked, "She was lying."

But Fong wasn't so sure. "There's a lot more places to check out."

They walked east to Hua Shan and followed the road past the popular bakery near the hospital. As they stood in the middle of the street trying to cross, the traffic momentarily stopped to allow two young orderlies wheeling a patient on a stretcher. One of the orderlies held an IV bottle aloft. "Traffic accident," said Fong.

"I would never have guessed," snarled Amanda as the cars whizzed pass them on both sides.

"You think the traffic is dangerous here?"

"I do think that, Inspector Zhong, yes I do."

"It's statistically safer than all American cities. You North Americans have this myth about Asian drivers."

"Fine, but you have to admit that drivers here don't

seem to stop for anything. Except children. I've seen them stop for children."

The small man at her side all of a sudden became beautiful as a delicate sadness crossed his features. The sadness and the beauty disappeared in a moment. Then, with a wan smile, Fong replied, "We have a great fondness for children here in Shanghai. A great fondness."

On Hua Shan Road they finally got lucky. In an antiques store that displayed a turn of the century elephant tusk whose two-and-a-half-foot surface was entirely covered with Buddhist religious etchings, they found an elderly man who, with a bit of prodding, gave them their first real lead. "Yes, the ivory is very hard to come by now," he said. More questions and more subtle evasions. For a moment the older man thought these two were dealers themselves. He distracted them with his collection of thin-necked perfume bottles whose designs had been painted on the inside of the glass. The woman was momentarily fascinated by the bottles but then brought the subject back to ivory. The salesman showed them an ivory ball about four inches across, with lace patterns carved into its surface. Inside the ball were thirty-four other balls of ivory, each and every one carved as delicately as the outside sphere. Finally the man, who by now the salesman had determined was a policeman, asked, "Who did the carving?"

"Fen Shen Lo and Tong Tsu." Then he supplied their addresses.

The policeman said thank you and turned to go but the old man reached out and stopped him. "Don't hurt these men. They are both very old now. And they are artists, see?" From beneath the counter he brought out a newish tusk, which unlike the scrimshaw etching style of the one in the window was carved into a three-dimensional rural scene of such intricacy that, totally unassisted by colour, the figures appeared lifelike. "This is the last piece I received from Fen Shen Lo. Is it not exquisite?" It was a question that required no answer.

Tong Tsu's home was closer so they went there first. The old carver's daughter, now herself an old woman, answered the iron door leading to the inner courtyard. She too knew a cop when she saw one. "You're looking for my father." It was a statement, not a question.

Fong acknowledged that they were, that they would like to talk to him.

"You people call it talk now. What happened to hound, harass, and terrify?"

"We would just like to meet with your father and talk about his art," put in Amanda.

"Well, you're too late for that. After they raided his workshop six months ago and took away the piece that he'd been working on for over four years, he packed up and left without even saying goodbye. Someone from his village got a message to me that he had managed to get there but he was sick. They say he's dying and I can't manage to get enough money to go see him. They say his hands shake so badly he can't drink his tea without it scalding his lap. This for a man whose hands could do this." With that she pulled on an ordinary string around her neck. Off the string hung a three-dimensional ivory cameo of a young man in a top hat and tails beside his young wife with a baby in a frilly dress seated on her lap. All in extraordinary detail. All no more than an inch high and three-quarters of an inch across.

She did not have to say that the woman was her mother, the man her father, and the baby herself. The cameo father had the woman's eyes and nose, the mother the mouth, and the baby the shape of face.

The cameo was a frozen moment in time caught by the artist through the living material called ivory.

As they left the courtyard Amanda turned to Fong. "Would she accept money from me?"

"No, but a train ticket to her father's village would probably meet her approval."

They were luckier with Fen Shen Lo. He was a modest man who lived in a new apartment on the outskirts of the city. His advanced age and artistic reputation had allowed him a little more space than others. He answered the door with a smile and a greeting. He had been expecting them; the owner of the Hua Shan store had called him.

Amanda immediately sensed a gentleness in this man.

They had tea with him in his small sitting room. He apologized for not having sweets to offer them. Amanda liked the tea, the way the leaves sank to the bottom of the cups like seaweed by the shore. For the first time she understood the notion of reading tea leaves. There they were, as accurate a reckoning of the future as any other. Finally Mr. Fen turned to Amanda and said, "So you think us very cruel, do you, in the West?" Amanda went to protest but he raised a strong but gnarled hand. "Cruelty is such a complicated subject. Does the beauty you make from cruelty make the cruelty acceptable? Is it cruel to force the body into the contortions of your ballet dancing, or our Peking opera? I don't know. I just know that there are things a carver can do in ivory that cannot be done in any other material. Let me show you."

With that he got to his feet and went through a simple door that opened to, for Shanghai, an extremely large studio space. There, mounted on end vises, were six large tusks. Each was an incomplete work. He directed them toward the largest of the tusks.

"I have been working on this piece for almost eight years. Thirty years ago there were over three hundred registered ivory carvers in Shanghai. Now there are fewer than ten. And most of us. . . elderly." He loosened one side of the end vise so that the tusk could be rotated. It was like looking into a living cave peopled with animals and plants and magic beings—all impossibly detailed. His work had progressed out from the fullness in the centre all the way to one end of the tusk and was now expanding toward the other side. His fingers touched it lovingly. He pointed toward a largish figure of a woman twirling, her dress floating out behind her, her sash out in front of her, her hair flying back. "Only in ivory. The material is so dense, so intrinsically solid and yet soft enough to work with hand tools. Only ivory allows this."

The sadness at his loss was clear.

"I could tell you that all these tusks come from Chinese elephants in our southern Hunan province who died natural deaths but you would not believe me. No one believes. The papers say that ivory is smuggled into Shanghai. The papers want it stopped. Save the elephants. Perhaps they're right."

"Where does this elephant tusk come from, Mr. Fen?"

In a dull voice, almost not there anymore, the old man said, "From our Hunan province, in the south, it was taken from an elephant who died from natural causes."

Fong withdrew a photo of Ngalto Chomi from his pocket and put it on a table. "You know him, don't you, Mr. Fen?"

The old man's eyes slid across the picture, the recognition clear on his face.

"Did he supply you with some of these tusks?"

Slowly the old man looked at the strange couple before him. It was a different age. He took a deep breath, then said, "Some? No. Not some. All. All my beauties."

When he shook their hands at the door, all that Amanda could think of was that his hands felt like rice paper. And his eyes were so sad that tears would never leave them.

Fong saw it too, but read it a little differently. Fong saw them as the eyes of one in love. The eyes of one addicted to the thing he loved, who knew that the source of his addiction had dried up. That when his work on these tusks was finished, he would have no further reason to live.

Just as Li Xiao was about to board the plane for Taipei he was summoned to the front desk by a page. When he took the offered phone from the hand of the airline hostess he noted her nails were painted blood red. He smiled at her and said his name into the phone. He listened briefly. "Yes, I've kept the records. No, I'd prefer to be there when they're examined. I'll be back tomorrow. It can wait, Wang Jun. The woman died almost four years ago, so it can wait another day."

He had slammed down the phone harder than he had intended. Red Nails looked at him, "Bad news?" she asked meekly.

"Yeah, bad news. Thanks," he said, handing back the phone. Fucking bad news, he thought. He liked Zhong Fong, but there were still too many unanswered questions about his wife's death. Too many for Li Xiao, who had been in charge of the investigation since its inception four years ago, to ignore.

Amanda and Fong walked along Chong Shu in the silence left from their meeting with the old carver. Fong was turning an idea over and over and over again in his mind. Ivory was being smuggled into Shanghai. Both of the dead men were connected to ivory smuggling. Someone was killing ivory smugglers. Why? To stop ivory smuggling. Why? It wasn't a big business. To corner the marketplace in ivory? Is this killing off the competition? If so, why kill them that way and leave messages who they are and that this has to do with ivory as witnessed by what the street cleaner found? Two dead ivory smugglers as a message to others to stop smuggling ivory into Shanghai. But why? Who would benefit from the stoppage of the smuggling of ivory? Not the jade sellers or anything like that. This couldn't have to do with business that way. Fong went back and turned the "idea bauble" another way. Who opposes the smuggling of ivory into Shanghai? In other words, who would be made happy by the stoppage of said smuggling? Friends of elephants. Anyone else? He racked his mind but could come up with no one else who would be made happy from stopping the smuggling. Only the friends of elephants. Fong searched for the English word for such people. And found it: conservationists. Who's killing the great smugglers of ivory? Conservationists? No! For a moment vertigo enveloped him like a sickly cloud.

Amanda turned to look at him. "Are you all right?"

"Yes, no, I'm just a little tired."

"You are a terrible liar. Come on, we'll get you some tea."

Sitting in the window of the quiet restaurant, Amanda put up her hand as Fong began to order. Then she said to the waitress, "lu tsah" (words she knew meant green tea). For a moment the waitress's face fell into a pattern of shock, and she was about to say something harsh to Amanda when Fong interceded with a few Chinese words and the waitress with an icy smile turned on her heel and left.

Amanda looked at him. He smiled. "Right words. Wrong sounds, wrong stresses, wrong tones."

"She looked like I insulted her."

"You did"

"Well, I didn't mean to. What'd I say?"

Not wishing to allow Amanda to pursue her line of inquiry, Fong posed a question of his own. "How strong are American conservationist lobbies?"

"Now, quite strong," she replied, surprised by his question.

"Strong enough to sway the United States government?"

"Their opinion carries weight on some issues, yes."

Fong thought for a moment. "Would the conservation lobby be pleased to hear that Shanghai was no longer in the ivory trade?"

"No doubt about that."

Fong put both his hands flat on the table. For just a moment he smelled Amanda's perfume. He stared right into her eyes and said, "What are the American concerns about investing in China, Shanghai in particular?" Then he counted them off on his elegant fingers. "One, the fear that the Communist government of China will at some future time nationalize their businesses. Two, what happened at Tiananmen Square, what you call civil rights. And. . ." here he held up three fingers and circled his thumb and index finger, "three, the accusations of conservationists that ivory and rhino horn are still being used in China. Are there more?"

"I'll let you know if I think of any."

"Do that," he said. But he wasn't awaiting an answer. He was completing his own thoughts out loud.

"Premier Deng in 1987 opened the doors to the West with a remark which was taken to mean that money from the East is no more valuable than money from the West. That began it all." He swept his arms wide to encompass the notion of all the building in Shanghai. "Surely there must have been assurances given at the highest possible levels to Western business that there would be no takeovers. I may not like Western business-men but they have never struck me as foolish when it comes to their money. Do you agree?"

"I guess. So that leaves only Tiananmen and smuggling as obstacles to western investment, right?"

"I agree. Tiananmen and smuggling. American secretary of state Warren Christopher broached this human rights business the last time he was here but got nowhere. He was quoted as saying that he wished the meeting was as good as the lunch."

"Who would have thought it possible: wit from a secretary of state."

"Perhaps, but not funny. China will not be bullied on this issue. Tiananmen will continue to stand as a barrier to some western investors."

"Some, I guess."

"More when you add the conservationists' concerns about ivory to the civil rights concerns. Civil rights concerns, Tiananmen if you wish, won't go away, but ivory will. When the smugglers understand that they chance being carved into—" He stopped himself. "I'm sorry." For the slightest moment Amanda couldn't figure out what he was apologizing for. Then she did and turned away.

He sensed that she was able to hear the rest so he went on. "The ivory trade will continue but not here, not in Shanghai. Shanghai will be free of ivory. And the West will be pleased with us. The smuggling of ivory may be a small issue but it is a strategic one and if you put it together with Tiananmen it could be enough to close the floodgates of western investment in Shanghai. And make no mistake, every building project you see here is leveraged to the tip of its bamboo scaffolding. It all depends on a continuing and growing stream of Western money. Money that the smuggling of ivory endangers."

"Are you saying that Richard and that African man were killed to stop the ivory trade?"

"No, they were killed so the money pipeline from the West to Shanghai will not spring a leak." His eyes trailed across the street. On the other side of the traffic was a massive construction site, its I-beam bones protruding above the wicker fence.

Leaving Amanda at her hotel, Fong called the office. A joyous Lily picked up.

"Are you at my desk?"

"No, I've had all your calls forwarded down to me, hoping that I'd be the one to break the good news. Now you have to ask me, 'What's the good news, Lily?'"

After a moment, really in no mood for this, "What's the good news, Lily?"

"I'm free for dinner, I have new satin sheets, and I've practiced tai chi for a month to get my sexual tension level up to yours."

"Lily!" he yelled into the phone.

But she cut him off. "We found the killer's bicycle."

The whole bike had been dusted for prints but none were found. Wearing white gloves for riding bicycles was very fashionable, so it was not surprising that the killer's hands were covered. But he had left other tailings. Several threads from garments, a partial shoe tread on one of the pedals, specific samples of mud from tires. The length of the frame and lowered seat gave them the killer's height. Photos of the bike were given to hundreds of policemen who headed out to the sidewalk bicycle repairmen throughout the city.

That night Fong watched Geoffrey stage the scene at the end of the third act of *Twelfth Night*. This production had many unique features. It began with Orsino dressed like Mozart banging away at a piano with a quartet trying to keep up with him. At a given moment, when the music is clearly not coming together, Orsino lifts his hands from the keys and slowly the others stop playing. The effect is like a deflating bagpipe. There is a moment of silence and then a furious Orsino yells at the quartet, "If music be the food of love, play on." And they do. But once again the music degenerates quickly into notes and numbers. Orsino stops playing and the notes become noise. Then silence.

Throughout the production Orsino keeps returning to his piano and working on that same melody but to no effect. However, at the end of the third act, Viola (Hao Yong) creeps beneath the piano, curls up and falls asleep. Orsino, not seeing her, sits down to play. The moment he puts his fingers on the keys, the failed melody that we have heard several times before comes pouring out of the piano. The noise has become music again. The presence of Viola has returned music to the world of Orsino. Love knits the notes together and makes the harmonies joyous.

Fong felt his heart leap in his chest as he heard the music swell. And he felt his heart break at the truth that Geoffrey Hyland saw. Only love made the mathematics of sound into the glory of music. But in Hyland's *Twelfth Night* Orsino never sees Viola asleep beneath the piano and hence never knows that Viola is the source of the love that restores music.

Fong almost leapt from his seat as a hand landed on his shoulder. When he whirled around it was Amanda Pitman.

"Sorry, I didn't mean to startle you."

He was going to deny that he had been startled but thought better of it. "I was someplace else for a moment there."

"Me too," she said looking up at the stage.

In the musty theatre Fong could smell her perfume again and he sensed her closeness. Was it possible that after four years he was beginning to feel again? That this strange westerner could see what he saw, feel what he felt, know what he thought only Fu Tsong could know.

Geoffrey was pleased with the scene. It didn't make him cry or leap for joy but it was deeply satisfying to find a theatrical moment so fully realized. He also knew that the moment touched those watching in the house. Even the cackling house manager and costume mistress had shut up for a moment. He knew that the blond woman was in the back, one row behind Fong. He knew that she had put a hand on Fong's shoulder. But he didn't really care. The moment he had staged was something that he and Fu Tsong had planned for their production of *Twelfth Night*. The one they had never gotten to do.

The moment was broken for actors and viewers alike when the house manager decided that she just had to talk to the costumer — in a voice that could cut cheese at thirty paces. When Geoffrey first came to China he let this kind of thing pass. But not anymore. Without a moment's hesitation he turned and pointing at the woman, yelled in fluent Mandarin, "If you have something to say, you cow of a woman, pick up your fat ass and say it outside."

She yelled something back at him, which he assumed had to do with him being a stinking long nose who was lucky to be invited into the Middle Kingdom and if he didn't mind his manners she'd grind up his dick and serve it to his children as dumplings. . . or something like that.

Whatever it was, he ignored it and turned back to the actors. It pleased him that she was upset, but when he looked back out into the house a few moments later it was he who was upset. Upset to see that Fong and the blond woman had left the theatre.

Nights in April in Shanghai can be chilly, especially if the dampness from the sea comes inland. And this was such a night. Amanda was wearing only summer clothing and she shivered slightly in the damp. Fong saw it and for a moment thought of offering her his coat but stopped himself. Somehow the offer of a coat was a first step in a process that he was not sure that he was interested in, or even capable of completing. So they walked side by side without contact, but closer to each other than either would openly admit.

This did not escape the eyes of Loa Wei Fen.

The very fact of their closeness awoke a pang of jealousy deep in the assassin's heart but he controlled it. This would not be like the last time with the black man. There was no time limit on this kill. He would do it properly. He would be patient. Resume control. And when completely sure of his quarry, strike. This way he could once more move to the edge of the roof. Perhaps even leap to the slender path with the other lion cubs.

Dearest Sister,

I spent a large part of today with the head of Special Investigations, Shanghai District. I was his "ivory date." I'll explain another time.

This evening I sought out his company in the back of a darkened theatre, and later still he walked me back to my hotel through the never empty, but gratefully quieter, night streets of this enormous city. The air was cold and I was wearing only a blouse and a cotton skirt. I know that he saw me shiver, and

I know that he thought of offering me his coat, but I know he didn't offer because it would appear forward. We did not touch all the way to the hotel. Nor did we talk, not a word. But as we approached the lobby I picked up my pace so that he had to hurry to keep up with me—through the door and directly to the bank of elevators, one of which, thankfully, was open. I do believe he followed me simply to have a chance to say good night. To be polite. Nothing more. But with the elevator door closing I noticed that it was now he who chose not to speak. He followed me silently to my room. Once inside I sat down on the bed and turned to him, I would guess a flush was on my cheek. He looked at me as if I were a series of lines and planes. As if he were at an art gallery and I was a piece on view. It was a unique and wonderful experience to be looked at that way. Then he drew up a chair at the end of the bed and sat on it. I don't know the directions but if I was facing west he was facing east, our heads were side by side. I leaned toward him and could smell the earth. He didn't kiss me. His hands touched, no, *explored* my face, as an artist does a piece of granite he is about to sculpt. Then his right hand slowly moved down my neck between my breasts and he lifted my skirt. I parted for him as his hand, inside my panties, encompassed me. Cool fingers, knowing fingers. With a shock I realized that I had my eyes shut. I opened them. He was looking into my face and inviting me to look back into his. Searching. So I did, first look and then touch. His hand still on me, a finger now gently inside, a thumb performing magic—I reached for him. A shift, a button loosed, a zipper pulled and he was in my hand, cool and hard to the touch.

He found a rhythm for me and I for him. Fingers stroking, coated, our eyes locked together, no speech except the symphony of touch and intent.

Asians call it the clouds and the rain.

It poured that night.

Pray for me, Your Sister, A.

Loa Wei Fen took note of Amanda's hotel room number. Then he headed back down the stairs and, although he knew he shouldn't, raced toward the release he knew he could find only in the arms of the opium whore, Wu Yeh.

The man with the hoarse voice read the e-mail report from Loa Wei Fen. He appreciated that Mr. Lo wanted to go slowly this time. He turned to his assistant and, handing him the printout, said, "Has Taiwan supplied the necessary information about Mr. Lo to the police?"

"They will do as you asked."

"Good. Now let us twist the arm of the local police a little to throw off Inspector Zhong Fong—just in case Mr. Lo is not up to the task."

There was a polite bow, and the plan was put into action—the end now in sight.

DAY EIGHT

hrug and Knock was smiling as Fong came into the office the next morning. The smile was so startling that Fong knew something was seriously amiss. So, without entering his office, he walked right past the door and exited down the exterior stairway. Once outside he crossed over to the promenade and waited in line at the crowded phone kiosk. When his turn finally came he called Lily.

"What's up?" he queried in English.

"Really, but I think that's unlikely, don't you?" replied Lily uncharacteristically in content, tone and her use of Shanghanese.

"Someone's there so you can't talk?"

"Yes, I believe we in this office have answered that request before." She then pretended to rifle through some files and continued, "Yes, we have, and what you say is true."

"What's wrong, Lily? Come on, tell me, what's his Hu-ness up to?"

"Well yes, we are approaching an indictment in the case of that woman's death in the Pudong. Yes, in fact we are waiting to make an arrest even as we speak."

Fong didn't need to hear any more. He understood. He didn't know how long she continued to talk, he simply held the phone in his hand with no words coming to his mouth. The young man behind him claimed with a piercing yell that his beeper was getting heavy he had so many calls to return. Fong looked at the man as in a dream and, handing over the phone, walked to the river side of the promenade. The Pudong was booming across the water. Rising like a live thing taking sustenance from the very ground. . . the very ground where his wife and unborn child lay buried in cold obstruction.

He walked to the north end of the promenade and then crossed the Bund and walked up Beijing Road, the longest hardware store in the world. For over two and a half miles, the stores on both sides of the street sell nothing but hardware—all kinds and sizes, but in Fong's experience never the piece you needed to fix the broken light switch in your room. Beijing Road was less travelled than most of the east-west roadways and Fong felt exposed. He crossed the street and headed north a block to the Su Zhou Creek. In fewer than twenty steps he was back in old China—sampans and river barges, people cleaning their clothes in the filthy stream. It calmed him enough to allow him to think.

He knew they had investigated Fu Tsong's death. He knew they still had questions. He didn't know who was in charge of the investigation.

That being the case, he may have already made a fatal error by calling Lily, but he didn't think so. It occurred to him as he watched an elderly woman washing her dishes in the brown water that it was Lily he chose to call, not Wang Jun. He couldn't justify his choice, nor at this moment did he wish to think about it. He'd try to contact Lily again. There were certain pieces of information that he needed. Today was the day he was to hear from Dung Tsu Hong the pimp, Shen Lai the customs broker/tong connection, and from the money changer. He was also anxious to get Li Xiao's report from Taipei. But as he walked along the river, *Why now?* was the only real thought in his head.

Why were they reopening the investigation into Fu Tsong's death now? Because I was getting close? It had to be. But close to the killer? No. Now they were trying to give me the killer. They had gone so far as to make Taipei cooperate, no mean feat. I must be getting close to the one who bought the killer's services. Who owns him.

"Power," Fong said aloud.

He headed back, away from the creek, toward the book shop on Han Kou, which in the thirties had been the fanciest brothel in Shanghai. He went to the newspaper section in the back and began reading through the papers. The coverage of Ngalto Chomi's death was still front-page news. This truly loved African had touched the hearts of so many that there was a constant stream of testimonials to his goodness and the horror of his death. The papers also had more of the specifics than before. Still nothing about the heart, so the old coroner was clean—for the time being.

The death had even made it into the *International*

Herald Tribune under the headline ZAIRIAN CONSUL MURDERED IN BUSY SHANGHAI ALLEY. The word was getting out. The message was disseminating worldwide. They'd hit the mother of all communication with this one. No one gave a fuck that Richard Fallon was dead but the world seemed to mourn the passing of Ngalto Chomi. An ironic twist on the usual story, thought Fong. White man ignored, ethnic gets all the attention. Well, maybe the world was changing.

As he was about to leave the shop, he saw an edition of the *New York Times*. He picked it up. On the back page of the first section was a full-page advertisement telling the Western world that Shanghai was free of smuggled ivory. That Shanghai cared about the endangered species of the world. That Shanghai was their kind of town. The only thing missing was the phrase Invest Now! Two murders was a small price to pay for the continuation of the lifeblood of Shanghai, Western money.

Fong felt sick. He and Richard Fallon and Ngalto Chomi had been nothing more than pawns in a game. But now he was on the run, and he knew that they were serious about getting him. One more bloody stain meant nothing to these men.

Loa Wei Fen felt the smoke curl down his throat, slither through his belly and clutch at his groin. He felt the beast on his back rear in angry protest. But then she was there to lull the monster and awaken the man.

She'd been awakening this man for several days now Slowly the man had spoken of things in his opium dreams. Dark things. The opium works differently on different people. The keepers of the drug know this and are wary of the signs that the drug is opening deeply placed, often hidden, doors in the smokers.

On his first night with her he had screamed in his sleep, "Old man, you stink of rotted paper," and pushed her away. Later he had curled up and suckled at her breast for almost an hour, which seemed to give him peace and allow him to sleep. Lately his "reachings" had been incoherent jabs of speech and slashes with his body. But yesterday he had cried out in anger at her, "You love the black man, not me." For a moment she was sure that he had awakened, that the opium had trailed with the dawn. But as she looked, his eyes had rolled all the way back in his head and the drug had taken him on another dream-filled loop.

She remembered all of that as she inserted him into herself. She also remembered the card that the policeman had given her. As she rocked to his rhythm she watched the drug take effect. The violent carving on his back calmed. As it did she wondered if she should call the number on that card.

Li Xiao had never been out of the country before and as the police car with the polished young driver took him into Taipei, he tried not to stare. All around him he saw wealth. Housing far superior to his present living situation in Shanghai or to any he could ever hope to have. Cars the likes of which Shanghanese policemen could only dream about. And these were the remains of the defeated Kuomintang who forty-five years ago had fled to Taiwan! The dogs who had retreated with their tails between their legs. The vanquished who for forty-five years had been supported by the United States and the immense treasure that they had plundered from the real China.

Their prosperity disgusted him.

As the car turned into the new central administration building, he saw two little girls holding their pregnant mother's hands as they waited to cross the street. Three children! The ultimate injustice.

Inside, the building whispered and purred. Li Xiao was guided along carpeted hallways to the commissioner's office. There were handshakes and nods and a lot of false smiles but quicker than he expected they got down to business. They handed him a computer-generated file. It started with a detailed report on a secret school that specialized in the kind of knife training that matched the old coroner's data. There followed a few pages on the history and use of the school with a note that although the school was secretive it was not illegal. Names of the teachers came next and their present whereabouts, followed by names and ages of former pupils. Of the pupils, only seventeen were considered to fit the specifications forwarded by the Shanghai police. Of those seventeen, fifteen were accounted for during the period in question, which left just two men.

Two photographs followed.

Li Xiao flipped over the first. It was of a youngish teenager.

"How old's this boy?"

"Fifteen when the picture was taken, seventeen now."

"And he's in China now?"

With a noticeable wince, the Taipei police commissioner said, "On the mainland, yes."

"In China," Li Xiao corrected him, then went on without waiting for a rebuttal. "And this?" He was referring to the second photograph. The one in which Loa Wei Fen stood in the Shanghai airport's arrivals terminal.

"Taken less than two weeks ago. In the Shanghai Airport."

"Yes, it was convenient to get the Shanghai Airport sign in the picture." The commissioner stifled a response. Li Xiao knew a setup when he saw one. He was getting the sick feeling you get when you know that you're being used but you can't avoid it. "What's this fucker's name?"

"Loa Wei Fen. He's a hired assassin, we've tracked him for some time." Then with a broad smile, "He's on the mainland even as we speak."

Li Xiao looked at the man. At his finely tailored clothes and his expensive shoes. His eyes momentarily lingered on a large ring on the man's hand.

"Is there anything further we can do to be of assistance, Detective Li?" asked the commissioner, still smiling.

"No, well yes, I guess there is."

"And what's that?"

"Tell me how you manage to sleep at night, get up in the morning, look in the mirror, and still believe you're a man." Before there was an answer, Li Xiao turned on his heel and left.

As he slammed his way down the marble-walled corridor, he couldn't help feeling the injustice. This asshole was going to live a long and fruitful life while Zhong Fong, a cop whom Li Xiao truly admired, was going to take a big-time fall. He looked at the picture of Loa Wei Fen in his hand and said out loud, "And you, my friend, are going to wish you'd never been born."

Fong had always considered Shanghai home. He'd known its physical intricacies since his boyhood and its metaphysical realities since the age of majority. But now it was a place of strangeness, a wary watching place about which he seemed to know little. Every intersection with its white-jacketed traffic cop, every block with its red armbanded street warden, every second block with its strolling brown-jacketed pair of patrol cops. . . In all these places all would soon be looking for him, if they were not already. So he headed for his home within home: the Old City.

As he entered it his pace slowed and, as if answering a call, he dropped his cop walk and became a part of the dankness of the ancient place, a member of the swamp. He had a long day to wait out, realizing that darkness might be the best friend he had left in his hometown.

His Hu-ness sat at the head of the table in the musty meeting room. At his side Shrug and Knock smiled a smile that upset the rest of those present—Lily, the coroner, and Wang Jun.

"Detective Li Xiao will join us shortly, I've been told

his flight from Taipei landed an hour ago," began Commissioner Hu.

"Then let's wait until he gets here," said Wang Jun.

Shrug and Knock smiled. "That's not necessary, is it, Commissioner?"

"No, it's not. I've ordered an all-points bulletin sent out for the arrest of Zhong Fong and he should be brought in shortly," said the commissioner.

Wang Jun was not pleased. He knew that much of what was being said was a reminder to him that his IOU had come due. He was snapped out of his personal concern by the arrival of Li Xiao, who literally burst into the room. "I am heading this investigation. Who called this meeting in my absence?" he demanded.

Shrug and Knock nodded toward the commissioner. Li Xiao almost spat but decided against it. With barely concealed anger he barked out, "This is my case—the least you could have done is wait for my return."

"I thought it proper to act quickly on this urgent matter," responded his Hu-ness.

"What exactly made this matter urgent all of a sudden?" snapped Li Xiao.

"The new information that Wang Jun received. Perhaps you'd care to fill in our young detective, Wang Jun," said the commissioner with the confidence of a gambler holding four aces.

Wang Jun quickly repeated the highlights of his two conversations with Geoffrey Hyland. Upon his completion, the room was quiet for a moment.

"You found Zhong Fong four years ago with his dead

wife didn't you, Wang Jun?" asked Li Xiao.

"I was there first. He'd called me and I tried to trace the cab that took his wife to the Pudong. I was there first, that's all," said Wang Jun.

"Yet you saw no reason to arrest him then, did you?" asked Li Xiao.

"No, I didn't," said Wang Jun.

"Despite what Zhong Fong did with the body and the baby, you saw no need to arrest him then?" pushed Li Xiao.

"I'm not on trial here, Li Xiao," snapped back Wang Jun.

Li Xiao looked at the older man and wondered what was in it for him. He'd always assumed that Wang Jun and Zhong Fong were close. But a sixty-year-old cop staring a pension in the face in a city whose inflation rate might shortly skyrocket was an easy mark. Easy to turn — even against a friend. Out of the side of his eye he saw Shrug and Knock smile. The crosscurrents in the room were intense. Clearly Shrug and Knock was having a good time. The commissioner was staring down Wang Jun, and it seemed that both the coroner and Lily were unnaturally silent.

"Any new physical evidence?" Li Xiao barked out.

"We only found pieces of the two bodies from the construction site. Small fragments. Cement was never intended as a preservative of human flesh. But nothing new has come to the morgue, so I wonder why I am here," the coroner said.

"Nothing new has landed in Forensics either," said Lily.

Li Xiao looked around the table and finally bellowed, "Then why are we all here?"

After a moment the commissioner rose. Shrug and Knock followed suit. "You are here to arrest and convict Zhong Fong for the murder of his wife. That is why you are here. I want him apprehended and brought in with all haste. I want our case against him made as quickly as possible. In the meantime, when you catch him, he's to be kept in Ti Lan Chou Prison." Then directly to Wang Jun, "Is that clear?"

Wang Jun nodded. The commissioner and Shrug and Knock left the room.

Ti Lan Chou was the political prison perched on the east reach of the Huangpo near its confluence with the Yangtze. It was the largest prison of its kind in China and hence probably the largest of its kind in the world. People were held there for crimes against the state. Sentences were long. Never commuted. No pardons or bail. Lots of time spent in sweatshops making goods that the state sold to the West. It was not a prison with which Special Investigations dealt. This was federal police territory. Even in a hardened policeman like Li Xiao, the threat of Ti Lan Chou Prison struck a rich vein of fear. Li Xiao knew why Zhong Fong was to be held there. It would give the feds time to rig a case that would be presented to the public in photographs, which were referred to as object lessons and could be viewed in various strategic locations throughout the city. These sets of photographs, which detailed crimes and punishments, were immensely popular during the Cultural

Revolution, a regular people's art form. Li Xiao's favourite had been the one that was up for months near Jing An Park on the Nanjing side. It consisted of several gory photographs of the murder victim followed by photographs of an arrested suspect, photographs of the suspect tried, and finally photographs of the suspect executed—a complete morality play on six yards of fence. It was indeed very impressive and bespoke tremendous efficiency on the part of the police and the judiciary. All well and good except that Li Xiao had worked on that case and they'd never caught the perpetrator. What they had found were photos of him which had been cleverly doctored into this cute little political lesson. The photo technicians had advanced their art mightily since the days of Mao swimming the Yangtze.

Li Xiao knew that with the priority APB issued by the commissioner they would catch Zhong Fong. That was for sure.

Li Xiao was troubled, though. Troubled by the timing of it all. Troubled by the arbitrariness of it all. Troubled by what he felt was the betrayal of a friend.

Wang Jun's new portable phone rang in his pocket. Li Xiao looked at the man. Would a man sell a friend for a phone line? In Shanghai, maybe? But no, it would have to be bigger for Wang Jun. He was alone in the world. No wife, no children. And age with its inevitable inevitability was working its terror on him. Where was honour in this city of greed? Things were truly getting out of hand.

He almost didn't hear Lily guide the conversation

round to the Dim Sum Killer case. She had information on the bike and interesting tidbits from three informers. As she went through these Li Xiao pulled out the photo of Loa Wei Fen and put it on the table.

"And this is?" asked the coroner, at last interested in the conversatIon.

"A man trained to work with a swolta, a six-inch double-sided blade with a piercing point. He also is in Shanghai as you'll note by the airport sign in the photo. He's ambidextrous too," said Li Xiao.

"Distinguishing marks?" asked the coroner.

"A cobra carved into his back. That distinguishing enough for you?" Then turning to Wang Jun, "I guess you're the chief on this one now, do you think that's enough for an APB on a real killer?"

Lily took the phone out of her mother's hands before the old woman could say hello. She knew who it'd be. Before the caller could say anything, she rifled off a phone number and an address and then said, "Half an hour on the dot. I won't call twice. Don't call here again." As she hung up she said to her mother, who was looking shocked, "A date, Mom, your little girl's got a date."

Exactly half an hour later Lily dialled the number of the payphone in the kiosk at the corner of Delicious Food Street and Huai Hai. It rang once and Fong picked it up. He was dressed in an old blue padded Mao jacket and wore a cap. His hair had been cut off and dirt was worked deep into his palms. There was a nasty cut across his cheek as if he had shaved that morning in cold water. He looked older. Worn. He wore army issue spectacles. Fong listened to the news about the meeting. He openly gasped when he heard about the idea of arresting him and putting him in Ti Lan Chou Prison but he managed to control his fear.

"Can you get me the picture of this Loa Wei Fen and the reports from our snitches?"

"How?"

"I don't know, Lily, you're the devious one—think of something devious."

"Do you remember the case of the boy with the bike?"

Fong certainly did; it was one of his first cases as a member of the Shanghai Police Department. A plump, six-year-old boy had taken a bicycle from a fourteen-year-old neighbour and ridden it on the sidewalk. The bike, being too big, was too much for him to control and he had run right into an old man. The man staggered onto the street had a heart attack and died on the spot. His family went nuts.

When Fong arrived, the dead man was still on his back in the street, snarling traffic. His wife, completely ignoring him, was screaming at the boy, whom she was holding against the wall with her strong peasant hands. Her aged sister had slipped a clothesline over a tree and then around the boy's neck and was heaving mightily, trying to hoist the boy off his feet and hang him in the middle of the busy block. A crowd had gathered around them and was offering unsolicited advice on the art of hanging fat kids. It took all of Fong's moral authority and the help of three block wardens to break up the would-be lynching.

After calling for a coroner Fong had walked the boy, who still had the rope around his neck, back to his home. As soon as he handed the boy over to his doting parents he turned completely unrepentant. He snarled at Fong and screamed that he should arrest those stupid old ladies and that the old man had had his turn and was better off dead. One less old revolutionary idiot. He was only sorry he didn't get more of them. But he would with the next bike he took. He was going to be a businessman and drive a big car, his fat little mouth said. Not some stupid policeman.

At that comment Fong grabbed the roll of fat around the child's neck, pulled him toward a park down the way and would have beaten the daylights out of him had Lily not happened to have been there flirting with her boyfriend.

She took the boy from Fong and brought him home. "I know which park you're talking about," said Fong.

"I'll leave the things you want in the garbage can by the statue of the Long Nose. Give me an hour. I don't want to see you, understand?"

"I do Lily."

"In the meantime, the whore from the opium den called in. I don't think anyone else got the information. You check her out and by the time you're finished with her you can go to the park to pick up the stuff."

"Thanks, Lily."

"Good luck, short stuff."

The old man in the opium den was hesitant to allow this peasant-looking man into his establishment. But when Fong removed the cap and eyeglasses and showed his police ID the old man bowed and led him down the smoky corridor. Once in the room Fong broke with the formalities of the place and immediately asked for the little whore, Wu Yeh. She arrived quickly. She was clearly frailer than before. She seemed drugged. Her robe hung limply about her, open in the front. Her pallor was now a ghastly white. He introduced himself gently. She smiled a little smile as if she didn't know what else to do.

"You have seen the man named Loa Wei Fen?"

"The one with the snake on his back?"

"Yes, him."

"Yes, he comes here often now." There was no love in her words, just retreat. She seemed to be singing softly to herself. Fong reached out and touched her arm. An unusual gesture for Chinese people. It seemed to centre Wu Yeh. Her internal singing stopped. There was a light in her eyes for a moment.

"You can bring back my man, can't you?" she said.

"The man with the snake?"

"No, not him, not him. He hurts me. Bring back my man, my beautiful black man, you can do that, can't you?"

If he were still a believer he would have said, you blaspheme. But his faith had died with the death of Fu Tsong. So he just shook his head.

"If you see the man with the snake on his back, you call me. You call me when he comes here."

She was lost in her thoughts again. The light in her eyes was almost gone. The song was returning.

"If he comes you call me, okay? Call me at the number on the card. Ask for Lily. She'll get a message to me."

She nodded but said nothing, actively retreating into her world of loss. Fong stood to go and was already out in the corridor when he heard her say as if to herself, "He wants me to come to his hotel now. Doesn't want to come here. Wants me to go there."

Fong looked at her in wonder and asked as simply as he could, "Which hotel?"

"The Portman."

As he slowly walked toward the park where Lily was going to leave him the information, Fong allowed himself to really look at his city. The knowledge that if he were caught he would not see it again for a very long time seemed to sharpen his eye. What he saw thrilled and appalled him at the same time. Life in transition. Complicated. Intricate. But endlessly alive. Everything seemed to catch his attention. Hidden gardens behind high, broken-glass-topped walls. Shopkeepers splashing water from red plastic tubs to keep the summer dust down. Laundry hanging across the sidewalk dripping onto an oblivious teenager's glutinous rice treat. Stained quilt sleeping mats draped over cheap folding chairs on the sidewalks. The Old Feeling Restaurant on Shan Xi — which old feeling was not specified. A young clerk eating ice milk on a stick within which black rice chunks were embedded — as if ants had ventured into the freezer. Restaurant windows stocked with suckable cured chicken feet. Hunchbacks and dwarves. In the open air market: strawberries and eels, pigs' feet and squirming baby crabs, bamboo hearts and a man holding a live chicken by its wings. And a five-spice egg, although supposedly cooked in boiling water, rocks gently as the chick's beak pierces the shell and a new life seeks the sunlight. A scrawny Shanghanese cat, with wide cheekbones and a yellow stare, wary and watching. The brutal Russian architecture of the hotel on Yan'an with the Kaige sign on top. A young man strutting with his double-deck Aiwa boom box incongruously encased in purple velvet. Large flower displays in wicker baskets outside a newly opened business, hoping for good luck. The Shanghai 21st Radio Factory. (Fong had lived his entire forty-four years in Shanghai and had never seen Shanghai Radio Factories One through Twenty.) Black velvet equestrian hats, which were all the rage for motorcyclists. Car owners dusting their pride and joys with three-foot-long feather dusters. Former great houses of the wealthy now laundry bedecked and packed — people in every closet and stairwell. And everywhere construction. Bamboo scaffoldings mounting the walls in impossible leaps and bounds, all seemingly festooned with electrical wires swaying in the late afternoon breeze. Street cobblers with rows of ladies' shoe heels laid out on the sidewalk beside their portable benches. Street barbers. Street food sellers. Street bicycle repair men with bulbous red inner tubes exploding from black tires like fat snakes refusing to be stuffed back into the darkness. People rushing for the accordion-joined buses.

Men wearing two-tone brown-and-white shoes. A waiter charging out of his restaurant with a large squirming freshwater eel in his hands. With a quick motion he slams the lithe creature against the sidewalk. There is a wet slap and the creature moves no more. The waiter smiles toothlessly. Men wearing cheap pants too large but kept up by belts which are wrapped around and around their thin waists. Practical. Chinese practical. No doubt both the pants and the belt were bought on sale. Young people sporting T-shirts with English writing on them. For some reason "Hug Me I'm Lonely" was a popular shirt. It hardly mattered. The shirt could have said Fuck Me I'm Slavic or Eat Me I Taste Good Broiled, they wouldn't have known the difference. Near the park Fong noticed an old man shaking a Russian-made pocket watch. Fong thought this the ultimate definition of old-style faith. Not even the Almighty could have made that piece of junk work again. He saw a pregnant woman walking her belly with the special pride of those who procreate in a single-child town.

He stopped at a street vendor and bought a piece of twisted fried bread. It burned the roof of his mouth as he tried to eat it. The laughter of the woman vendor told him in no uncertain terms that he was no longer being taken for a cop. Now he was just another sucker who had bought a piece of refried dough, perhaps refried for the third or fourth time that day. He turned to look at her and was about to complain but he stopped himself. He needed his disguise. Bigger fish to fry today.

Still a little early, he passed by the mosque on Chang

Le which was now a stock market. The other one, on Xinle Lu at Xiang Yang Lu, was a nightclub. He couldn't decide which was a more unfortunate fate for a religious building.

It was after dusk when he finally neared the two small parks in the triangular patches formed by the diagonal crossing of Fuxing and Huai Hai.

In the eastern park there was a stone statue of two children dancing. There were beds of flowers but nowhere to sit. In an action that could only be described as cruel, the sittable cement sides of the flower beds had been studded with sharp iron prods, lest one needed to rest one's weary bones. The western park was dominated by a cast iron statue of a Long Nose, his arms raised as if either teaching or pleading, it was hard to tell which. On the pedestal were the dates 1912-1935. During the Cultural Revolution all other means of identifying the twenty-three-year-old westerner had been obliterated. Old men huddled around games of Chinese checkers, not the game with marbles children play in the West. This is a complex game that resembles a cross between go and chess. The game near the statue had drawn a crowd of watchers, each sagely advising what he would do were he the player whose move was next.

Fong approached as if to watch the game and spotted the manila folder in the trash can. Lily had slid it down one side so that it was clearly visible but not easy to pluck out. As Fong moved toward the can he saw to his horror one of the city-paid scavengers approaching the basket. These people carried a wicker basket over their shoulders and an iron pincer in their hands with which they plucked specific materials out of garbage cans for recycling. One of the assignments was paper.

But as Fong approached the recycler he could smell that paper was not this worker's assignment. This scavenger was collecting compostable materials. The odour of rot enveloped her like a thick haze. As she walked away Fong moved toward the basket and plucked out the manila envelope. As naturally as a man on his evening stroll, he moved out of the park, passing the old men doing tai chi and the elderly women doing the old-lady version of it, "shake a leg."

Fong sat in the growing darkness of Fuxing Park reviewing the material that Lily had left for him. Most of it was highly suspicious. The picture of Loa Wei Fen at the airport supplied by the Taiwanese screamed "set up." The one piece of information he found untainted was from the opium whore, Wu Yeh. The pimp's information was of little use, as was the money changer's — both coming up with save-their-skin suggestions but no hard facts. But the tong connection, Fish Face, provided surprisingly exact information — troublingly so. It was as if the Taiwanese and the tongs were trying to outdo each other in their efforts to give Loa Wei Fen to the police. The data from the two sources was almost identical but there was an open mockery in the note from Fish Face. His ended with the phrase "Get him before he gets you."

As Fong headed toward the park's exit he could smell burning refuse. It was 7:00 P.M. and Shanghai was adding the pungent scent of burnt garbage to the already potent mix of the city's air. He thought back to Wu Yeh in the opium den. He thought of the brightness leaving her and the blurred opaque dullness replacing it. Opium replacing love. One addiction for another. But the addiction of love added light while the addiction of opium simply clouded. The light was dimming in her soul, that was plain to see — as the lights had dimmed in his with Fu Tsong's death. Dimmed but not extinguished. Now his light was reviving, thanks to a blond American sitting at a desk in the Shanghai International Equatorial and writing a letter to her sister.

Dearest Sister,

I wasn't unhappy to find him in my hotel room when I got back. I was shocked, though, at his appearance. He'd cut off his hair and there was a gash across his face. And he wore an old quilted coat. He looked — well, he looked Chinese. I know that sounds strange but that's what I thought as he stepped out of the shadows. For a moment I didn't recognize him. Before I could do anything he passed by me and stepped out into the corridor. Then he returned to the room and turned out the lights, shut the draperies and pulled me into the bathroom. Before I could say anything he said as explanation, "There are no windows in here." Well it's hard to deny that. He pulled a picture out of a manila envelope and putting it on the sink said, "Have you seen this man?" The Chinese man in the picture was young and silkily handsome. He wore an expensive suit. "Have you?" Fong asked a second time. I told him I hadn't although it was hard for me to be sure and who was this guy anyway? He replied without batting an eyelash, "He's the man who killed your husband, Ms. Pitman."

The mention of Richard's death and Fong's formality chilled the air. "So arrest him."

"I don't want to arrest him. I want to talk to him. I want to find out who put him up to this."

"So talk to him. Or don't you know where he is?"

"He's staying at the Portman Hotel." Before I could stop myself I heard my voice saying,

"He looks Chinese."

"Hotels are not segregated in Shanghai now. A Chinese man with the right money can now stay where he wishes, even eat in the same restaurants as whites, and fuck in the same beds. One would hope that the sheets had been changed, but it is hard to regulate such things. It has been a while since we have seen NO DOGS OR CHINESE ALLOWED signs in Shanghai."

He had caught me. Nailed me for my assumption that any man with enough money to stay in the Portman would have to be European or Japanese. The silence between us began to grow. I'd lived in a marriage of wide and complex silences. I did not want this relationship to be like that, so I forced myself to reach out to him.

"It scarcely matters if I say that I'm not guilty, does it?" His silence was a succinct answer but much to my relief he was not continuing to fade into the background, to move away. "If you know where he is and you want to talk to him, go over and pay him a social call."

"He'd kill me."

"You're a policeman. You know how to defend yourself."

"Not against this kind of man. He'd kill me . . . but he might not kill you."

I laughed at him. I told him to forget it. I told him this was his problem, not mine. I told him to get out of the bathroom, I needed to take a pee. He told me to go ahead but he didn't move. So I hiked my skirt and peed.

Then he did.

Then in the deep tub of the Shanghai International Equatorial Hotel I came alive with a Chinese man I'd barely known for five days. As the shower beat down on my back and head I rode him to an oblivion that had been denied me for many years.

When I awoke it was after midnight. He had just finished dressing and was heading toward the door with a promise to return—a promise I extracted from him when I said I would find the room number of the man who killed Richard.

Pray for me, A.

To Fong the school's old theatre, late at night, echoed of life past, finished. Joy and laughter huddled in the corners of the ancient building, hiding from the emptiness lest their potency be sucked dry by the void.

That evening the top of the proscenium arch was

emblazoned with a red banner proclaiming the vital role of the theatre workers. There must have been a political meeting in here earlier in the day. That's a wee bit redundant, all meetings are political. Especially in China. The theatre, which of course belonged to the people, could be taken over by the "people's representatives" whenever the people's representatives decided that the people needed further encouragement in their labours, studies, or work habits. Meetings were also called whenever these representatives needed to remind the people how very important it was to be represented by representatives.

The meetings occurred frequently enough in the theatre that a special rigging for the banner had been drilled into the plaster on either side of the arch: a strangely archaic set of heavy pulleys and ropes. As if the banner, which could not weigh in excess of two pounds, somehow, no doubt because of its weighty message, assumed untold mass.

As Fong stood in the empty space, he heard the flick of an electric switch and in a moment the sound of a compressor pump. Slowly a dim light bathed the stage set—a scene of a Victorian garden. On stage left going downstage and then across the front was a shallow stone-bordered stream. The compressor pump was forcing water into the stream. Fong was not surprised when Geoffrey Hyland walked out of the wings into his Victorian *Twelfth Night* world. What did surprise Fong was that he was holding a bottle of Jack Daniel's.

Geoffrey gestured to the set and the water. "Do you like?" he called out. Fong chose not to respond. "Ah, your silence speaks volumes. Long time no see, Fong old bud. I'd begun to look forward to your cryptic presence in the back of my rehearsals."

"Why?"

"You give it all a kind of edge. After all, you're the real thing aren't you, Fong?"

"What real thing?"

"The real thing. That which would kill for love. You are Orsino in action. Willing to kill your love before allowing another to touch her. I told you that everyone could find themselves in this play. I told you that."

"You truly believe that?"

"I do, I've said so twice now."

"And you believe I'm Orsino, willing to kill for love?"

"Once again I say, I do," pronounced Geoffrey with a mawkish bow. A wobbly mawkish bow. Fong had never seen Geoffrey drunk before. He wondered why he was drunk now. He was afraid he knew.

"Are you all right, Geoffrey?"

"Couldn't be better," he said, righting himself. He waved at the stage. "Do you like my pathetic little stream?" Then he pointed downstage right. "Malvolio sits down there, dangling his footsies in the cool stream, like this." Geoffrey crossed to the corner of the stage, and kicking off his shoes put his stocking feet into the water. "It's surprisingly cold. Be that as it may, the conspirators put the letter, folded like a boat, in the stream up there. The water carries Malvolio's demise right to him. It hits him on the foot in fact. We've practised. It works every time." Then smiling, he said, "Neat, huh?

The poor ass does nothing, but God's water brings him his doom. Like me. No? I just sat in this fucking theatre and in walked your wife. But then you know all about that, don't you, Fong?"

Very slowly, without any inflection, Fong replied, "No, I don't, Geoffrey."

Pulling a mock look of shock Geoffrey said, "Why don't you come up into the light like the rest of us love-lost buffoons?"

"I'm not an actor, Geoffrey."

"So you say. So you say, Fong."

"You have two children, don't you Geoffrey?"

Geoffrey quickly corrected him. "*Had* two children, a boy and a girl."

"Why had?"

Then in a voice filled with self-loathing Geoffrey yelled back, "Had because after I met your wife, your fucking amazing wife, I could never really go back to them. Not really. Children know. Everyone knows. Even you know, don't you, Fong? Look into your heart, Fong! You know, don't you!" He took a long pull from his bottle.

The stream pumped water. The ancient lights flick-ered. And Fong knew that Geoffrey Hyland was adrift in an ocean of pain and recrimination. Enough of both to have driven him to the police. So at least Fong had learned that much.

Leaving the theatre Fong hugged the sides of the buildings as he made his way toward his apartment. Untalented students rehearsing scenes; an extraordinar-ily loud television set in the open-sided faculty room;

the staircase leading up to the apartment. No guards, no police. It wasn't possible that they would have over-looked his apartment with an all-points-bulletin out for his arrest. He pushed open a basement door and tiptoed past the couple asleep on a mattress on the damp concrete. Then he ran up a back stairway to the second floor.

Even as he opened the door to his apartment, he knew that he had not been the first to open that door this evening. Lived-in rooms, especially rooms of love, have a consistency to them. A firmness that links one object to the next in a continuous flowing idea.

There was no flow here now. At first he thought it was because of him and Amanda but quickly his eye lit on the telltale clues of another kind of brief but serious intrusion. The bathroom door, always hard to close, now left slightly ajar; the puff in the drapery fabric that always results when opened and not given the necessary attention when subsequently closed—but more than these telltales was the feel of the other's presence.

As the key was turned in the lock and the door cracked open, Loa Wei Fen allowed the knife to turn in his right hand. His left was pressed flat against the surface of the top of the armoire, upon which he was hiding. "Always attack from above." The leap would be awkward unless the policeman, who was now dressed like a peasant, moved one step farther into the room.

Loa Wei Fen had been waiting on top of the armoire for over two hours. The police search finished over three hours ago. He had watched the search while crouching on the tile roof across the way. There were so many police and then none. This troubled him. So he waited for a full hour before slipping into the apartment.

He too had felt the former solidity of the place. Anger surged through him and he reached for his knife.

Fong stood in the door, a slash of light from the hallway across the apartment's carpet. What was wrong here? The police had been here, yes. But that was not all that he was sensing. What else was here? He couldn't tell. All he knew was that his body was preparing him to run. And that's what he did. Leaving his apartment without entering, without closing the door, he raced to the basement and out a rear door into an alley. He threw himself over the now locked gate of the academy. Pushed through the crowded Marco Polo club across the way. Barged into a washroom and pried open a window. Then he leapt out. He could only hope that he finally lost whoever or whatever was following him as he merged with the traffic on Yan'an.

Loa Wei Fen followed as fast as he could. The basement, the gate, the club all were no problem. When he saw the policeman racing toward the washroom he knew that the man would be looking to crash out a window so he headed back out of the club and ran toward the side of the building. But Loa Wei Fen was unlucky this time. An electrified fence awaited him. Its fourteen-foot height prevented him from following the escaping figure of the policeman who, emerging from the high window, looked so much like a serving man escaping from a princess's boudoir.

Fong had no idea whether he'd fully thrown off his ghost. His fear was still very real. He grabbed the phone from one of the public kiosks and threw a five-jiao note at the owner. Amanda picked up at the top of the second ring.

"Are you all right?"

"Never better, but I'm not coming back there this evening."

"What about your promise, Mr. Policeman?"

There was mockery in her voice and a seductive taunt. For a moment he considered going there. Then he saw Loa Wei Fen half a block down the street walking slowly, sectoring the area with his gaze. Searching. Searching for him.

"I'm being followed. I don't want to lead him to you."

"The man in the picture?"

"Yes. Go to the Portman tomorrow and find out what room he's in." He didn't wait for an answer. Loa Wei Fen was too close. His gaze moving with terrifying precision.

The half-demolished, three-story Victorian house stood empty — more accurately forceably emptied — at the junction of Yan'an and Nanjing. Across the way the compact car stood on its metal pedestal, some sixteen feet in the air. The wrecking ball had taken a bite out of the circular balcony at the top of the house. No glass remained in the windows, no wood panelling on the walls, or fixtures on the doors. Red tiles, seemingly defying gravity, balanced precariously on the now sodden roof. Outside the building was a vast hole, the beginnings of a mega-story building. Inside, in the one remaining corner of a third-story room, Fong sat and tried to stop shivering. He was safe until morning. His mind knew that, but his body was still filled with adrenaline.

Then a wind picked up from out of the east. A breath from the Mongolian steppe travelling pure and cold, blowing aside for a moment the haze of Shanghai summer. It surrounded him in the bleak of night and roused him from his stupor — the way she used to. With a subtle change of the air pressure Fu Tsong was there. All around him.

It didn't help that Fong knew that this was only a dream. It didn't help because he'd had this dream many times before. And it would not stop at his command. Each time the dream supplied him with more bits of the memory that he had so desperately tried to erase.

This night it began with him racing out of the theatre, with Geoffrey Hyland's voice ringing in his ears. "If anything happens to her, I'll chase you wherever you go. Wherever you go I'll find you and get my revenge."

He had to think clearly. Fu Tsong was gone. She had gone to the theatre to get a cab. She was carrying a small bag.

Where would she go?

Back at their apartment, Fong called Wang Jun and got him to start tracking down the cab. Fong had to consciously steady his thoughts as he hung up the phone.

She took a small suitcase. Which one? He opened the armoire in the bedroom where he kept their few suitcases. The small brown wicker bag was gone.

It was so small, what could she take that she couldn't have just carried? The phone rang. It was Wang Jun. The cab company had given him the probable cab number and a general vicinity in which to look. Dispatcher shifts had changed since the cab was sent out and since the dispatcher had no radio link with cabs and no records are kept after a call, they had to find the off-duty dispatcher. Wang Jun said they already had a lead on his whereabouts. Then he hung up.

What would Fu Tsong have put in that small wicker suitcase? Fong opened her drawers but, like most men couldn't tell what was missing or not missing. Then he opened her closet. Everything seemed to be there, but as he went to close it his eyes were drawn to an empty hook on the door. His heart almost stopped.

Fu Tsong owned two bathrobes: a beautiful silk one that she wore all the time, which was still there, and a tattered plaid terrycloth robe that was too big for her, but which she would wear whenever she was ill. "It makes me feel safe and warm while the sickness rages inside. It's my way of helping everything get fixed," she'd often said.

That robe was gone. The empty hook seemed cruel.

His mind was afloat, lost in a wash of terror. He forced himself to answer more questions. Where would she go to get fixed? *The Pudong* rose in his throat like a round hard thing. He swallowed it down and forced himself to concentrate. Fu Tsong's life depended on it. His baby daughter's life depended on it. His whole world depended on it.

Where exactly would she go? The Pudong is a big place. She'd never been able to remember an address in her life. She'd write it down. But she'd hide something like that from him. Where, though? He started with her desk in the living room corner. No, couldn't be! It was too open to him. Where would she hide something from me? She's smart! Where did she know I'd never accidentally look? Nothing on her bedside table. Nothing in her closet or clothing. Nothing in the medicine cabinet over the sink. . . but even as he went to close the cabinet he knew where Fu Tsong would hide something she really didn't want him to find.

On the shelf over the toilet Fu Tsong kept a set of brushes, some face cream, and an unusually shapeless bag with a zipper. In the bag she kept her spermicide and her now unused diaphragm.

He pulled out the beige diaphragm case. It opened with a plop. He picked out the plastic dome revealing a cheap business card on the bottom of the case. On the card was printed a name and an address in the Pudong. Below the address was a guarantee of satisfaction in its services "for women desirous of giving birth to male children." For a moment Fong's knees went weak.

The phone rang in the other room.

He listened to Wang Jun's voice say that they had located the dispatcher and had sent a car to get him. Fong hung up before Wang Jun was finished.

Pelting rain against the windshield of his police car. Hand held down hard on horn, flashers going, siren piercing the downpour. Screams of anger as he whipped past hundreds of bicyclists in their cheap plastic ponchos that made them look like coloured pyramids on wheels, and sped down Yan'an.

The address in the Pudong was in the north sector. He roared toward Beijing Road. A traffic jam at Nanjing Road and Xian brought him to a screeching halt. It was solid for almost six blocks in all directions. Something had spilled or stopped or someone was hit. He was still over two miles from the Pudong address where his wife and daughter were. Abandoning his car, he ran like a wild man, screaming and shouting, toward the overhead walkway. Racing up the rain-slicked steps he leapt over a prone beggar and got to the centre of the strangely elegant structure.

Only a supreme act of will kept him from stopping in the middle of the overpass spanning the busiest intersection in Asia and screaming *Help me, help me, help me!*

Charging toward the Xian side he slipped on the wet overpass pavement and careened down the forty-five steps to the street below. Then he was running again. A sharp pain in his hand drew his attention. Two of the fingers of his left hand must have landed awkwardly in his fall. One dangled backward at a peculiar angle. The other had been pushed back over the knuckle. The former he ignored. The latter, with a yell of pain, he yanked back to its original length.

At Beijing Road he flagged a cab, pulled the driver

out and dumped the surprised man in the gutter. Before the cabby could open his mouth to complain Fong was speeding away from him toward the Bund.

Inside the cab, Fong floored the late-model Santana and controlled the fishtailing as he careened toward the river. In a flash of lightning he saw the huge television tower across the Huangpo River. And momentarily thereafter he smelled the river. Even in the rain once you crossed Delicious Food Street the river announced its imminent presence.

He turned south. A second traffic jam, this one a half mile of cars trying to get onto the new suspension bridge heading toward the Pudong. Once again he abandoned a car and took to foot, this time racing toward the suspension bridge across the Huangpo.

Anyone paying attention would have marvelled at the lone running figure clearly etched against the darkened, lightning-streaked sky. So tiny, insignificant when com- pared to the suspension bridge's massiveness. The bridge swayed in the wind as the tiny figure dodged and weaved and at times climbed over cars stalled by the intense downpour.

At the end of the bridge, Fong was in the Pudong. Instantly the familiarity of home flooded him. It was like the Old City where he had grown up. In the downpour few people were on the streets to ask for directions. He finally found a steamed bun shop open and raced in, shouting the address at the old lady behind the counter.

If the sight of the soaked, broken-fingered man surprised her she didn't let on. She simply pointed farther down the street. Running in the direction the woman pointed, Fong turned a sharp bend in the road and was instantly greeted by the new Pudong: towering cranes, massive construction sites, mud and mud-coated haulers of progress. No one seemed to know where the address was that the short madman was shouting at them. Finally a foreman, drawn by the ruckus, came up and, hearing the address, pointed toward the one remaining shanty in the midst of the moonscape of construction sites.

Fong ran directly toward the ancient structure, not bothering with roads. He raced into a construction site, across it and up the other side, and then through, across, and up a second until he stood panting at the closed door of the old house.

The building was bathed in the eerie glow of the construction site's arc lights.

Fong was about to yell Fu Tsong's name when he heard her moaning.

The door burst open under his running thrust, and he was greeted with a vision from hell.

The baby must have been in the breech position. A botched attempt to "untimely rip." Something had ruptured. The butcher fled — and left this.

White walls, grime encrusted. Aluminum table. A single lightbulb swinging wildly from the ceiling. Rain pouring through the roof. And there in the midst, on the table, wrapped in her tartan bathrobe, a small line of her blood dripping off the table onto the already blood-rich earthen floor, Fu Tsong clutched a blood-and mucus-covered thing to her—and screamed for the mercy of death.

Fong felt his heart click in his chest.

Then everything stopped. Fu Tsong's eyes opened wide for an instant, her arm swung off the side of the table and something infinitely cold filled the room.

Fong felt himself falling, plumeting through darkness, utterly, totally alone.

Even as Fong was fighting his night demons, Wang Jun was remembering how he had found his young friend that night four years ago in the Pudong. It was a vision Wang Jun could not easily forget.

A lightning flash had silhouetted Fong against the open back door of the shanty. The outline of the small man, his feet seemingly stuck to the mud floor of the horrible little room. Then a scream filled the confined space. And the small man moved with terrible speed. Before Wang Jun could intercede, Fong lifted the inert bodies of his wife and unborn child and raced out the back door into the rain.

When Wang Jun finally caught up to Fong, the younger man was standing alone on the lip overlooking the construction pit. Sixty feet beneath him was the newly poured cement foundation of a huge building. Even as Wang Jun looked over the edge, the bodies of Fu Tsong and her baby were swallowed by the grayish muck. The sash of Fu Tsong's bathrobe floated incongruously on the surface—gently in motion as if catching life from the rain itself.

He stared at Fong.

Fong stood very still for a long time. The rain increased. The thunder roared its approval. Fong seemed to take it all in. For a moment his eyes brightened, then the light behind them dimmed. As they did he shouted to the sky. "You win! You win! I have delivered her to you. Take her. Take her for my sins!" Then he tilted back his head and spat well out into the pit.

Wang Jun rubbed his eyes, chasing away the image. As far as Wang Jun knew that was the last time that Fong had ventured into the Pudong. But it was all one now. It was late. They'd find Fong tomorrow. They most certainly would.

Fong awoke from his nightmare covered in sweat. The dream had ended the way it always did. Him alone. Them gone. A truth. But not the complete truth. Not yet.

Breathing heavily he looked out at the city. In the Shanghai dawn the smog clings quilt-thick to the buildings. Roads, still passable, await the coming assault of day. For a breath the bamboo-coated construction sites let out a sigh of relief between shifts—restful, but only for a moment. For the tumult would begin again, as it must, if Shanghai was to continue its assault upon the sky. And, just for a moment, Fong thought, To have been an ant in its midst, a moment of its time, the slightest ripple in its stream has been an honour. Then he spat and faced the reality of a dangerous dawn after a terrifying night.

DAY NINE

The Portman, like every other major hotel in Shanghai, had extensive security in its lobby. Discreet but extensive. Also like most Shanghai hotels, at the Portman you could sit in the lobby if you ordered a drink or a cup of coffee. It was too early for a drink so Amanda ordered coffee. She was not surprised that the cup of bitter coffee cost more than the entire lunch she and the two policemen had eaten at the Old Shanghai Restaurant on the day of their dead man's walk.

She sipped the rancid stuff as she watched the human traffic in the lobby. After fifteen minutes she knew that this would get her nowhere. There were too many elevators to watch and besides even if she saw the man in the picture how would she find his room number?

She finished her coffee and went over to the concierge's desk. A young man with pimples, reasonable English, and a well-cut suit stepped forward to help her. She asked for a city map and was given a small piece of paper that was almost decipherable. She looked at it closely and put on a puzzled expression. "Is there a problem?" the young man asked her. Amanda bit her lower lip. Why do men like that?

"Well, there is, actually."

"May I help?"

"I hope so." She pulled out the picture of Loa Wei Fen from her purse and put it on the table. "Do you know this man?"

The young concierge nodded.

"He's staying here?" Once again he nodded. Then, with seemingly uncontrollable excitement, Amanda bit her knuckles. "Bobby Tol is staying here? Really?"

"Who?"

"Bobby Tol, the Okinawan singer, here in this hotel?" The young concierge looked at the picture again and said, "I guess he is." It was clear that he didn't know who Bobby Tol was but it was also clear that he was more than a little taken with Amanda.

"Would you do something for me?" Amanda said and marked the effect of her words on the young man.

He replied weakly, "What?"

"Take some flowers up to his room for me. I don't want to invade his privacy but I'm such a fan. Would you take care of delivering them?" He nodded eagerly. If he were a dog his tongue would have been on the pavement.

"You're great, thanks. I'll be right back with the flowers." With that she touched his hand gently. He spluttered and reddened and looked ready to drop to the ground and kiss her feet.

• • •

There was a florist in the arcade on the west side of the hotel. She bought an enormous basket of flowers and winced when she saw the price. Oh well, the better to follow you by, she thought. She carried the flower basket back into the Portman lobby, smiling back at all the questioning looks.

By the time she brought the flowers to the concierge, he had regained his composure. He took the basket and asked if she wanted to send a card as well. She declined and after thanking him profusely retreated to the far end of the lobby. The concierge called over a uniformed bellhop and gave him the flowers and a room number.

It was not difficult for Amanda to follow the enormous basket of flowers to room 2714.

Li Xiao was in a fury. The object of that fury was Wang Jun. The two men sat alone in the big conference room.

"It was a mistake," yelled Wang Jun.

"All our men just happened to take a break at the same time? Is that what you are trying to tell me? That the three men detailed to stake out Zhong Fong's apartment just happened all to be called away. I'm supposed to believe this?"

"Talk to Commissioner Hu if you have a problem," snapped back Wang Jun.

"You're telling me you didn't do this, Wang Jun?"

"I'm telling you this isn't any normal investigation in case you haven't figured that out yet."

"We have new testimony from the Canadian director,

whatever his name is, and so we reopened the investigation. Right?"

"Sure, if you have to believe that, believe that. But just for the record, I wouldn't get carried away by the idea that you are in charge of this investigation. Everything here is going through his Hu-ness. He may look stupid, but he's cleverer than you and me put together."

"If that's so, why did our cops miss Fong yesterday?"

"Because his Hu-ness had another surprise waiting for Fong."

"What?!"

"Even you can't be that young, Li Xiao. Fong's a dead man. One way or the other, he's a dead man."

"I thought he was your friend, Wang Jun."

"Funny how that works, isn't it?"

Fong *was* Wang Jun's friend. His only real friend. But things being what they were, Wang Jun would go to the wall to catch his friend and put him behind bars in a prison from which he would never emerge. The New China was growing and Wang Jun wanted to live his last days riding the shoulders of the giant rather than ground beneath its heels.

Amanda almost screamed when Fong slid up beside her on the busy street corner.

"You have the room number?"

"Don't do that! You'll scare the panties off a poor girl."

"Do you?"

"2714."

"Good, let's go."

"Where? To the Portman?"

"Where else?"

"Is he there?"

"Would we be going there if he was there?"

"Well, then where the hell is he?"

"Looking for me."

"Oh," she said and began to pick up her pace to keep up with him. It occurred to her that if Loa Wei Fen was looking for Fong, then he might in fact be following them now. It made her laugh.

"What's funny?"

"All of this is. Yet it isn't, is it? I used to know but now I'm not so sure."

Fong smiled. "Welcome to China."

"What exactly do you mean by that?"

"If you have to ask the question you wouldn't understand the answer," he replied.

But Fong was wrong. Amanda asked her question out of a sense of etiquette rather than out of any real need to know. The paradoxical nature of it all was not lost on her. Far from it. What she didn't know, though, was that as Shanghai worked its awakening magic on her, it also brought her to the attention of the true centres of power in this ancient land.

They approached the Portman from the back and Fong led her through a maze of tunnels beneath the building to a freight elevator. He was about to step in when he said, "Go up to the lobby and take the elevator there. I'll meet you at the twenty-seventh floor." To her inquiring look he simply said, "I would look out of place in the lobby elevator. You would look out of place in here."

They met in front of room 2714 without incident. He had her watch the bank of elevators as he deftly picked the lock. Within a minute they were inside Loa Wei Fen's room.

"What are we looking for?" she asked.

"A trail. Something that helps us get from the assassin to the one who bought his services. The one who owns him." As he talked he was methodically opening and searching each of the drawers of the desk.

As Fong went about his by-the-book search Amanda checked the bathroom, entirely devoid of cosmetics; the closet, two very expensive suits, finally the bed side table with the square carrying case. She opened the case and took out a computer notebook.

"What have we here?" She put the computer on the end table and fired it up.

"You know how to work things like that?"

"This is more complicated than I'm used to but they're all basically the same." The computer went through its virus check and came to an opening menu. Six down the menu was e-mail. Before he could point to it, she had already selected it.

It required a password.

She went back to the menu and transferred to the operating system. From there to the drivers. Each layer of the computer opened under her command. Finally e-mail access appeared. There was a single character beside the code.

"What does it mean?"

"*Tao*. The way."

She backtracked and went to e-mail again. This time she supplied the English letters for the character. The screen lit up as if it were happy to see her.

"How do you know how to do that?"

"I used to write but I didn't want Richard to see what I wrote so I got very knowledgeable about computer things like passwords and other protective devices. I used all of them."

"You really didn't want him to see your work."

"I told you that already." She returned her attention to the monitor. "What am I looking for?"

"His messages."

"The ones he sent?"

"No, the ones sent to him."

With the stroke of a few keys, up came the message that instructed Loa Wei Fen to kill Zhong Fong and then disappear for a very, very long time. Fong paled as he scanned the screen. Amanda looked closely at Fong, but before she could say anything he asked, "Who sent it?"

"You don't care what it says?"

"I care. Who sent it?"

"Give me a second." She backtracked to the operating system and worked through several screens. Finally she looked at him and said, "And the winner in Peoria is . . . E-M-29-7976."

"That's a code?" he asked, but his mind was far away. E-M-29-7976. Where had he seen that before? "Get his e-mail address and then let's get out of here."

They were outside the room a minute later. But as Fong was about to close the door, he stopped himself and headed back into the room. There, to Amanda's amazement, he upended the bed and threw Loa Wei Fen's few possessions into the toilet. As he emerged there was a strange smile on his face. All he said was "Our friend likes leaving messages, so I thought he might find it interesting to receive one. You've got his e-mail address?"

She had never seen this side of him before. She liked it.

Outside the Portman, he turned to her and said, "Can you get me the street address that goes with that e-mail number?"

"In North America I'd say no, but here the servers are so antiquated that I've got a chance. Back at the Equatorial there's a business centre. They've got computers, I'll give it a shot."

"Can you send an e-mail message to him?"

"That I know I can do. What do you want to say?"

"'Loa Wei Fen, they're trying to kill us both. We both have a lot to lose in this stupid game.' Sign it Zhong Fong."

She repeated the message and he nodded. "Where'll you meet me?"

"How long should it take?"

"Sending a message, almost nothing. Finding the address of E-M-29-7976 could take a long time. Sorry."

"When a screen has that number flashing on it, is the screen the sender or the receiver?" asked Fong.

"Why do you ask? Have you seen the number?"

"Yes, I think I have," he said. Then slowly he added, "I believe the address is 29 Zhongshan Road, seventh floor, suite 976."

"Are you sure?"

As if weary from it all, "Yes, but check it for me, will you."

"Whose address is that?"

"The commissioner of police, Shanghai District." Fong felt dizzy.

The upended bed and the general disarray of his few possessions didn't penetrate Loa Wei Fen's calm. The reversal of roles, however, did. He had been in their rooms, both of their rooms, but he was not prepared for them to be in his. The flashing light on his computer notebook caught his eye. When he punched through to e-mail and read the message from Zhong Fong, he had to control his twisting anger. Then he called up the program that would tell him the address of the sender of the e-mail. When it came up on the screen he smiled.

He would go to the Long Hua Temple. He would meditate into the eyes of the lion cub on the roof. Then as the darkness fell he would revisit the Shanghai International Equatorial Hotel, the address from which the e-mail had come.

Breaking into police headquarters would have been simple for Fong to do alone, but with a tall blond woman it proved a challenge. But he had no choice, he needed her computer expertise. So they went together. And since there was no real way to hide they just barged in.

It was the end of the workday and his Hu-ness never stayed past 3:00. They had been lucky and avoided Li Xiao, Wang Jun, and Shrug and Knock so that although they received some pretty strange looks they were not challenged. That is until they got up to his Hu-ness's secretary's office. Then the challenge was momentarily loud. Loud because the secretary screamed. Momentary because Fong grabbed her and stuffed almost an entire box of tissues into her face, before tying her to her swivel chair.

Even as he was doing it Amanda was getting the e-mail messages off the machine.

"Is this always so easy? Aren't there security codes and stuff?"

"There are, but the machines here aren't new. China's been sold a stack of old machinery. Unused. But old. Old enough that the security features are rudimentary enough for me to dismantle." As she finished she punched up a series of e-mail messages. There had been seventeen in the last twenty-four hours. Sixteen had been from the same address. She wrote it down.

Leaving the office they almost bumped straight into Shrug and Knock. Fong wouldn't admit, even to himself, how much joy he got in cold-cocking his former assistant.

It was dark by the time they got back to the Equatorial. Amanda had to do some pretty fancy talking to get herself and Fong into the business centre a second time that day. "There is much demand for these services," she was informed by the silk-bloused receptionist.

"May I see your supervisor?" Amanda said, smiling pleasantly. Within minutes of meeting the male supervisor, Fong and Amanda were being led into the interior of glass-walled office spaces. As the supervisor left them alone in the glassed-in office she turned to Fong and with a smile said, "It's hard to say no to a tall blond."

To which Fong responded straight-faced, "I wouldn't know anything about that."

When Li Xiao got back to the office it didn't take him long to identify the blond lady who had arrived with Fong. Wang Jun identified her in three words and a two-handed gesture. "Tall? Blond? Tits?" His hand gesture accompanied the last. Then he said, "She's at the Equatorial."

Loa Wei Fen used his most cultured voice on the phone. "Does the hotel have a computer centre?" He nodded at the reply and said "Thank you." He hung up, took one last look at the dishevelled bed and slipped out of Amanda's room, heading toward the computer centre in the lobby.

The eight-by-ten-foot glass enclosure in which Amanda and Fong were working was spartan but functional. Two chairs, a computer and printer setup, modem, and fax hookups. The computer once again was brand new but badly out of date. Someone had clearly pulled a fast one on the Chinese. Like the guy who sold English-language welcome signs to hundreds of Shanghai restaurants which read COME ON IN BIG BOY. That guy at least had a sense of humour.

Fong marvelled at the length of Amanda's fingers as they raced across the keyboard. Suddenly her fingers stopped and hovered, poised over the keys.

"Problem?"

"I don't think so . . ."

"What's the but in your voice?"

"How's my time?"

"Why?"

"There's a fast but risky way and a slower but safer way. Your pick, copper."

On the monitor the phrase SELECT FUNCTION was flashing.

"Fast. I'm not sure it's possible to be in a riskier situation than we're already in."

The beautiful fingers moved from their poised position. Keys were struck and information about the source of the sixteen e-mail messages on Commissioner Hu's computer began to emerge. Suddenly the screen began to blink.

"I've hit a trap."

"A what?"

"There's a request for a second password. If I don't get it right the computer will report us back to the e-mail number that we're searching."

"Like a booby trap?"

"More like a snitch."

"Could it be a fake?"

"Could be."

"The first password you found was New Life, right?"

"Right."

Fong thought for a moment and then said, "There is no second password. New Life in Shanghai is everything."

Amanda hit the Enter key. The blinking stopped and addresses began to scroll. When they finally stopped, one was highlighted. As the address appeared, the fingers of Fong's hand clenched so tightly on her shoulder that she winced in pain.

"What?" she almost yelled.

"That is the address?" he said, pointing at the highlighted line on the monitor.

"Yes. What is it, Fong?"

Fong's voice cracked as he said, "It's in the Pudong." Completely at a loss as to what this reaction meant, Amanda replied, "That's what it says. That industrial place across the river, right?"

In a faroff voice, his eyes clouding, he responded, "Right." Then after a long pause he added, "I haven't been to the Pudong in over four years."

Before Amanda could respond the far wall of the glass room exploded. A pellet from the shotgun blast sliced through her cheek and then shattered the computer screen in front of her. A second and third blast rang out. The smell of cordite filled her nostrils. All she remembered was Fong grabbing her hand and yanking her out of the chair, glass flying everywhere. And shouting. And Fong pulling, pulling her through one shattered computer room after another. Then darkness.

Fong had actually seen the policeman's image reflected in the computer screen, the Pudong address seemingly plastered across his forehead. He heard the first blast and saw the blood flower from Amanda's cheek before the computer screen exploded into shards of glass and useless metal bits. Fong heard Li Xiao shouting at his men to stop firing. He also heard volley after volley of shots. One of the blasts must have shorted out the electric main line. In the darkness he and Amanda managed to slip into the shopping arcade and then run free out onto Hua Shan Road.

Loa Wei Fen had arrived at the business centre in the lobby just as the first shot was fired. He sized up the scene in a glance and realized that if Fong and the blond woman were to escape it would have to be through the shopping arcade. So he went into the food store at the far side of the complex and, munching on macadamia nuts, waited for them to appear.

When they did, he followed them. Tracking the bloodied twosome was not difficult.

Back in his hiding place Fong looked closely at Amanda's wound. He had removed the glass shards from her hands and knees. The cuts bled but were not deep. However, the gash on her cheek had ripped the flesh clean down to the bone. She was pale but not in shock.

"Does it hurt?" he asked as his fingers gently touched the skin above the wound.

"No. Will it get infected?"

"Too early to tell."

"I carry antibiotics, I've been taking them like vitamins since I arrived."

"Don't trust the food, huh?"

"If you get offended I'll clock you one. I've heard the water in this town is pestilential." She fished out a small vial of pills and held them out to Fong. For a moment he couldn't open the childproof bottle but then he saw the arrows and aligned them. He ground a tablet to powder in his palm, and shook it carefully into the open wound on her face. When he finished she reached for the vial and popped a tablet in her mouth. "Damn."

"What?"

"I can't swallow it. I've got no spit."

Without comment he gently tilted back her head. She parted her lips. His spittle tasted of old Kent cigarettes.

Fong knew that it was past midnight. In the city's night glow he could make out Amanda's face, her head nestled in his lap. Her body had retreated to the sanctity of sleep. He ran his fingers through her hair and marvelled at the lunacy of all this.

All this now.

How easy it had been with her. How even that first time, her head had tilted and her lips parted accepting his tongue as a part of her. How her body fit with his, every inch top to bottom. How the musk rose from her, a flower releasing its pollen, in a puff of wet scent. So unlike Fu Tsong, who was tiny. So unlike Fu Tsong whom he could lift with a simple movement of his hands. And yet Amanda Pitman fit too. More accurately he fit to her. No, he could not lift her and there was not the tightness that was Fu Tsong. But there was a clutching, holding reverence between this woman and him. An exactness of feeling and an aliveness taking place between them in the desolation of the formerly beautiful room on the third story of the now half-demolished Victorian house across from the elevated car on the sixteen-foot pedestal.

While Fong was lost in his contemplations, Loa Wei Fen crouched on the other side of the wall, and waited. Waited and wondered what he was waiting for. Why he simply didn't kill them now. Why? Confusion reigned. Then he began to fall inside himself.

That night with Amanda's head on his lap and Loa Wei Fen on the other side of the wall, Fong's dream started with him standing over the great construction pit in the Pudong holding Fu Tsong in his arms — the baby still on her chest, her robe open, a smear of blood on her abdomen. He felt the lightness of death in his arms. Coals without heat. Noise which only love could resurrect as music. Orsino hammering on the piano never aware that his salvation slept beneath his feet. Then, for the first time, his dream allowed him to see himself fling the two of them far out into the pit. He saw Fu Tsong, the baby still on her body, seemingly come to life as she passed through the beam of the first of the mercury vapour lights. He lost sight of her when she left the light and entered the darkness. But then she entered a second beam. Fong shuddered. The memory so long buried was now garishly alive. In the harsh beam of the second light Fu Tsong raised her arm toward him. Her mouth opened but no sound came. Still falling, she repeated the arm gesture, her mouth continuing to move soundlessly. Then she disappeared into darkness — until the dream opened one last hidden door. This door allowed him to see the concussion of bodies on the freshly poured cement slabs. The swallowing in cold obstruction of Fu Tsong and their baby — only the sash of the bathrobe left afloat on the surface.

He heard himself crying in his sleep but he couldn't awaken. His eyes were drawn to that sash. For a moment it was still, but then it rose up and flared its back. A king cobra as thick as a man's arm. And he was not above it now, but beneath it. In a bamboo construction-elevator shaft. The great serpent, its hood flooded with blood, its eyes remorseless, bore down upon him from above. Its armless body finding purchases unseen by man as it descended toward Fong.

Loa Wei Fen could hear the tears on the other side of the wall. For him they were the tears of Wu Yeh, the opium whore, as she cried for her African lover. They were the tears of the woman from whom he was taken when he was six. They were the tears deep inside him that were begging to come out. The tears that would bring him to the edge of the roof from which this time he must indeed jump or fall forever.

DAY TEN

The buses began their morning shriek. It was 4:00 A.M. Loa Wei Fen took a peek at the sleeping lovers as he soundlessly rose from his squatting position and made his way out of the destroyed building. The thud of the city was picking up as he moved eastward along the dusty streets toward the Old City. Shanghai was little more than a mirage to him now. But in that mirage there was an oasis of truth. A place of momentary peace in his hopeless dream. An opium whore whom he loved.

Moments after Loa Wei Fen entered the Old City, Wang Jun awoke from a fitful sleep. He got out of bed, careful not to wake the couple who slept on the other side of the drawn curtain. The water spat from the street spout as he turned it on. Its colour didn't please him so he let it run until the colour thinned. Then, ducking his head, he allowed the water's chill to waken his sleepy brain. Turning, he drank from the stream. "Might as well drink this shit, it's already in our veins," he thought. Spitting out the last of the water, he sat down on the pavement and looked at the Shanghai alley along which he had lived for the past twenty-two years. He had been twenty-nine when he first came to Shanghai. He was sixty-two now. And what did he have to show for those thirty-three years of work? A place to throw his weary body after a wearying day's work. Little else. Oh yes, he also had a friend, Zhong Fong. A friend whom he was betraying even as he sat here. His cellular phone rang. He took it from his coat pocket and for a moment stared at its flickering lights. Then he punched it on. "Wang Jun." The furious voice of his Hu-ness cracked the morning stillness. Wang Jun did not so much listen as endure the tirade. All he could do was hold on and allow the anger to wash over him. He noted that this kind of behaviour no longer hurt him. There was a time when his skin was less thick. A time when betraying a friend would have given him more pause.

Li Xiao was in the office by 6:30 and the pressure was already on. It was hard to answer the questions about yesterday's failure to apprehend Zhong Fong. It was more difficult getting answers as to why the officers fired without his command. It was most difficult for him to accept that he was nothing but a pawn in this game — that he was head of this investigation in name only.

Late last night he had challenged Commissioner Hu on that point. All that the commissioner had said was "No one is beyond expendability here. China is bigger than anyone person. You will do what you are told to do or you will go away. The choice is yours." He chose to say nothing. In China that choice means that you accept.

Now, the next morning, he was dealing with the consequences of his choice.

The old man with the hoarse voice was not used to yelling. He was almost incapable of it. But he yelled at Commissioner Hu that today was to be the end of it all. That both men were to be dead by the end of the day or Commissioner Hu would be the commissioner of a rat-infested jungle outpost in the south. Commissioner Hu's silence pleased him. It was assent and understanding. It felt very good to hang up on the commissioner. Such men were important to the system but left a foul taste in one's mouth when one had to deal with them.

The man with the cobra on his back had hurt her. How badly she didn't know. The opium was still alive in her bloodstream. Its neural lubricant had allowed her into another place as he ranted at her. Hurt her. But now the pain was welling up. So, as the man continued to sleep on the palate in her cubicle, she slipped out into the hallway and hobbled toward the front. She was aware of the blood slipping down her legs. She didn't care. She got to the front and pulled the policeman's card out of the drawer beneath the phone. She dialled the number on the card. When the phone was answered she asked for Lily. She was met by a lengthy silence and then a woman's voice came on the time.

Lily only got in a few words before she was pushed aside by Shrug and Knock. "This is a call that the commissioner should hear about, isn't it?" Lily sat stony still as Shrug and Knock forced answers from the opium whore. Lily wondered if this job was still worth having. She'd miss Fong.

Fong awoke from his cruel night's sleep. His back ached from the crunch of the brick behind him. Amanda was still asleep with her head in his lap. He looked at her facial wound and breathed a sigh of relief. The wound was clean. It had crusted smoothly. He reached into her pocket and pulled out the bottle of antibiotic. He crushed a tablet in his fingers and powdered the wound again. Her colour wasn't bad and there still seemed to be no fever. For a moment the phrase "Luck is on our side" popped into his head. But he pushed it away as soon as it arose. Luck had kept her alive through the night. No luck would keep them alive today. Only thought and action. She was five feet eleven inches tall, white, and blond. Hard to hide in a city where the average height was five foot six, where there were few whites and no blonds. Where do you hide an albino giant in a city of short dark folks?

Loa Wei Fen had heard Wu Yeh leave the cubicle. He didn't move but he listened closely. His mind supplied him with a map of the opium den and the environs. He heard the click of the phone as she hung up. The snake rose on his back. Her padding feet were making their way back to him. The swolta seemed to move toward his hands. She who loved the black man would not see this day's night. He who loved the opium whore would not see tomorrow's dawn. At least not on this earth. Of both these things he was sure.

The padding feet stopped outside the cubicle.

• • •

Fong pushed Amanda's head down as she hunched in the back seat of the taxi. As they were stepping into the cab, Fong had seen a woman with a red armband race out of a nearby building. Her ferret eyes locked on him and Amanda. She would file her report in less than a minute. "To the North Train Station and hurry," he yelled at the cabbie. The small red car took off with a lurch and blared its way into traffic.

The call reporting Fong and Amanda was taken and transferred to Li Xiao's cellular line. The young detective picked up the call just as he hopped out of his car and headed toward the door of the opium den. He barked into his cellular, "Get the cab number out to all the wardens and keep this line open. Send out everything that comes in to the police units on their radios and patch it through to this number as well." He left the phone in the car and headed toward the opium den.

He paid no attention to the small man crouched against the storefront across the way.

But Loa Wei Fen, now dressed in the rags of an opium addict, paid more than a little attention to the policeman. As the patrol cars arrived from every side and surrounded the opium den, Loa Wei Fen watched. Watched and felt himself moving closer to the edge of the roof. Ready at long last for the jump.

The gore of the opium whore was enough to turn Wang Jun's stomach. Li Xiao cursed and stomped around. There were too many policemen for the tight corridors. The whole thing was out of hand. The commissioner was yelling for him somewhere off to one side. There was shouting and screaming everywhere. No one noticed the beggar man across the street rise and cross towards Li Xiao's police car.

And no one noticed him reach inside and take the cellular phone.

The North Train Station was filled with people — but not filled enough to hide Amanda. Fong was faced with a hard choice. He was sure that the warden who saw them get in the cab had reported what she saw. If she had good eyesight she'd be able to supply the cab number. If so, Fong knew that they should change cabs. But if they got out of the cab Amanda would attract attention again. Then he saw them, bands of police officers moving quickly through the crowd. The recently arrived peasants moved out of the way as the police pushed their way through. "The bus station on the west side," Fong snapped at the driver. When the driver paused, Fong reached into his pocket and threw a wad of kwai onto the front seat. The cab lurched forward. It was just past noon. Daylight was not their friend.

Fong leaned out the window. There was a slight mist

hovering over the Huangpo. The promise of the first summer storm hung in the air. He wondered for a moment if they'd be alive to see the rain. To drink in its liquid hope.

The call from the North Train Station came in to all units. Wang Jun got it in his car. His Hu-ness was told of the call while yelling at Li Xiao in the corridor of the opium den. Loa Wei Fen got the call as he moved along Fang Bang Road and admired the building clouds to the east. Rain was going to come. A deluge to wash him over the edge.

The bus station was as stupid an idea as the train station. Fong didn't even allow the cabbie to slow down before he shouted a new destination. The cabbie looked around at him like he was a nut. "The theatre?" he demanded. Fong turned to Amanda who held out a handful of money. Fong took it and tossed it to the driver.

The cab swung out into traffic and phones rang all over the city.

Fong spotted the roadblock before the cabbie did and yelled at him to pull over. Before the cab stopped moving Fong had the door open. He threw money at the driver and shouted an address far in the other direction. He didn't really believe that the cabbie would bother to go where he was instructed. Fong didn't need that. Just a five-minute head start. Just get the police to follow the cab for five minutes and he'd have a place for Amanda and himself to hide for the rest of the afternoon. The cab pulled a dangerous V-turn and sped away. As it did a police car roared after it but Fong didn't stay to watch the show. Racing through the crowd and onto the overpass, he and Amanda crossed over Xian and then headed down a back alley. At the end of the alley, in front of a low door, he stopped. He looked back. There was no one following. A gnarled old man answered his knock. He looked at Fong inquiringly. "I'm Fu Tsong's husband." The ancient's face lit up and he opened the door. They stepped inside.

Just as they did, a woman with a red armband leaned out her window to place her laundry out to dry. She thought she saw a small Chinese man with a tall white woman enter the back door of the theatre. That's what she thought she saw. And she knew her duty: to report what she saw, thought she saw, or wanted others to believe she saw. She completed hanging her bamboo pole strung with laundry and then headed down the five flights of stairs aiming her bent figure toward the alley's mouth and its phone kiosk.

Amanda was amazed. They were in the wings of an old theatre. Onstage were some of the sets of the Shanghai branch of the classic Peking opera. Before them dozens of actors in classical makeup and costume were readying themselves for rehearsal. Fong was standing to one side talking to one of the actresses. After a moment, she ushered Fong and Amanda into a small room, telling Amanda (with Fong interpreting) that she was "Su

Shing, a dear friend of Fu Tsong's. Fong's wife." She opened a large closet and removed an elaborate costume and pots of makeup. Fong had already removed his outer clothing and was sitting in front of the makeup mirror. Su Shing gave a slight bow and left the two.

"What are we doing?"

"Hiding. It's the only place I could think of where you wouldn't stand out. You might have noticed that you look somewhat different from almost everyone of the fourteen million people in this city."

"Yeah, I noticed that."

"Good. Put on the costume. I'll do your makeup for you."

"You'll put on my makeup?"

"That's what I said, unless you know how to do the Peking opera makeup for your character."

"How do you know how to do this?"

"My wife was an actress." She noticed him falter for an instant. Then he added, "For a long time." After another clearly troubled moment he spoke again. "She was a great actress. She liked me to do her makeup for her. She taught me. I learned."

Amanda was sitting now. Fong stood facing her with one of his legs between hers. His delicate hands pushed aside her hair. "Hold this back." She did. He reached for the pot of white makeup. "I've got to go over your wound. It'll hurt. Okay?"

She nodded and took tight hold of his leg. He took a large swath of the white ointment and spread it over her cheek with a smallish trowel. When it touched the wound her nerves sent shards of pain straight down the bones of her face to her chest. She bit her lip to hold back a scream.

He saw it but kept on. With her face covered in the white paint, he reached for the costume's headdress. Its long feathers swayed as he placed it over her blond hair and tucked in the tendrils. Tears were running down her cheeks as the pain continued. He ignored them and helped her out of her blouse, skirt, and shoes and into the elaborate costume, adjusting the many hidden straps. Finally he slipped her feet into the black and white platform shoes.

"Stand up."

As she did, he took a step back and looked at her in the mirror. Even without her makeup completed, she was exquisite. He quickly applied the covering base makeup to his own face and then put on the costume of the serving man. When he was finished he stood beside her and looked into the mirror.

The two of them stared at the couple in front of them.

Slowly she reached up and touched one of the feathers on the headdress.

"Draw it down slowly and bend it into your mouth," he said.

She did as he said, drawing the feather down and placing part of it between her lips. A buzz of pleasure shot through him.

"Who am I?"

"You're you."

"No, I mean who am I dressed as?"

Fong was about to say "You are dressed as you" but stopped himself.

"A beautiful princess from the coast who was promised in marriage to a prince of the west."

"And you?"

"The serving man entrusted with taking you across three thousand miles of China. Across snow-covered mountains, swift wide rivers, and vast deserts to bring you to your new husband."

"And do you?"

"I do."

"And do we fall in love on the journey?"

After a silence in which both of them heard each other's shallow intake of air, "Yes."

"Do we consummate our love?"

"In our own way, yes. In the three-year journey we only touch once. When I break my leg crossing a river. You insist that I ride the horse. You help me onto the horse's back. Our hands touch for an instant."

"Our consummation."

"Yes."

"And what happens when we finally get to the court of the west?"

"Your new husband is there. He is indifferent to you. You are only a pawn in a game of politics. But he takes you in. He completes his part of the game."

"And what happens to you?"

"I turn around and walk three thousand miles back to the sea."

She touched his hand. It felt dry like rice paper.

"Did your wife play this role?"

"In a way, yes."

He began to complete her makeup. "She's dead?" He nodded yes and continued with her makeup, being as careful as he could to avoid the wound on her cheek. She put a hand into his free hand. For a moment he didn't respond to it. Then he returned the touch. Jolts of feeling leapt between them, their touch a full consummation.

Li Xiao was in the middle of grilling the cabbies who had driven Fong when the call came through. Li Xiao called for a map. Wang Jun said, "Fuck that, follow me." The parade of cops spun about and headed back toward the theatre.

Withdrawing her hand from his, Amanda looked up at this strange man from this distant country. She could feel a third person in the room with them. "What was her name, your wife?"

"Fu Tsong." He pronounced the name simply but to her ear with immense delicacy and sadness.

"How long ago did she die?"

"Years, days, minutes. Sometimes she's not dead at all," he said in a flat, faraway voice. Tears were in his eyes.

"Tell me."

And he did. How they met. How he loved her. How his careless words led to her death. How he found her on an abortionist's table. How he was never sure whether she loved him. Each phrase hit the centre of the still pond between them, sending perfect circles out in all directions.

After he stopped speaking she allowed a lengthy silence. Finally she asked, "Why did you take me here?"

"To hide you."

"I already told you that you're a bad liar. Why am I here? "

"To produce a memory."

"Of what?"

"Of you."

"Why?"

"This is China. There is no way to escape here. I will be caught shortly and I will be sent to prison for a very long time. I need a memory for the nights when the darkness gets too great for me to bear. I'm sorry. Sorry for everything."

"Don't be. What'll they do to me?"

"They'll try to frighten you. Probably deport you. They don't care about you. They do care about upsetting your government so nothing serious will happen to you. Just be brave and you will be home in a week."

"You're sure?"

"Of that? Absolutely."

"And of other things?"

She saw his mind return to Fu Tsong. She knew that he was fading from her.

She reached for him. The clouds parted and he was with her again.

"Don't go away like that."

"I loved her very much and hurt her very badly."

What was Amanda to say to that? The truth of what he said was etched clearly on his face. So clearly that makeup couldn't hide it. In fact, as was the beauty of Peking opera makeup, his emotions were conveyed with startling clarity.

She reached for his hand again. This time when they touched, they just touched hands.

Bones and skin and sinew failed to transcend this world's realities.

Onstage Su Shing was working with several actors and actresses. All the women were dressed and made up as the princess in *Journey to the West* and all the men as the serving man. The musicians played a section of the opera as Su Shing illustrated a moment in the journey in which the princess, in fear, pulls down her left feather with her left hand while shooting her right leg straight forward. Su Shing then hit a high note and contracted into an exquisite pose. As she did, the cymbals sounded and, as if on cue, the police entered from the back of the theatre. Wang Jun was in the lead with Li Xiao and Commissioner Hu right behind. At the same time several burly northern cops came from backstage. One stepped forward and called to the back of the theatre, "There's no one left backstage on this side, we're checking the other side." He made no reference to the stage-door man. Fong stood at the back of the group of actors dressed as the serving man. As half the cops moved across the stage he scanned the wings. He knew what had happened to the stage-door man. He didn't know exactly how he knew but he knew in his bones that Loa Wei Fen was in the theatre too. That he had followed them somehow and killed the doorman to get in undetected.

Su Shing stepped forward, berating the policemen. "This is a rehearsal, not a police station. There is a performance of these apprentice actors in less than half an hour and they are going through their final preparations."

His Hu-ness yelled back, "There will be no performance today. We are the representatives of the people. The people own this theatre, not you. You work for them. So work. Act and we the people's representatives will watch."

Amanda slipped out of her platform shoes. She was now the same height as the rest of the actresses in theirs. Su Shing screeched a command to the musicians. The music began and two of the actors moved forward. They enacted a section of the play where the serving man guides his charge across a raging river. Li Xiao and his Hu-ness were moving toward the stage.

As they got close to the group of women, Fong spotted Loa Wei Fen high in the flies over the stage. A reptile on the hunt.

Li Xiao was looking closely at the women. Amanda didn't know it, but the wound on her face was bleeding through her makeup.

Fong caught Amanda's eye. He canted his head slightly to the left. She looked and saw that the left side of the stage was not covered by the police, all of whom seemed intent upon examining the women. Amanda smiled slightly; as she did, she raised her arm slightly toward Fong.

Fong almost swooned. Something rose up inside him. A terror. A memory. The simple arm gesture from Amanda moved something deep inside him, as if his body organs had shifted as he stood.

Amanda repeated the gesture and said silently, without moving her lips, "Goodbye, Fong, and thank you." Then she looked at the young detective who was near her. She slipped her platform shoes back on, making herself a full foot taller than he. She took a deep breath and then shouted in English, "Back off, pipsqueak."

Li Xiao was so startled at the advance of this enormous woman speaking in a foreign tongue that he almost fell backward. Before he could get his balance she was advancing on him, blood pouring crimson on her white makeup.

"Yeah, you, I'm talking to you, you yellow devil, you monkey in a suit, I'm talking to you, you fucking son of a bitch, you cocksucking dog fucker." Then she saw the man she assumed was his Hu-ness and charged at him. "I'm talking to *you*, you puny-dicked moron, you. . ."

It was enough. She'd caused the one thing the Chinese cannot handle. Chaos. There was screaming everywhere as her words were translated with as much delicacy as possible. When she grabbed his Hu-ness by the lapels, all hell broke loose. Cops were moving everywhere.

It was not hard for Fong to slip out. He didn't delude

himself into believing that Loa Wei Fen in the theatre's flies would be fooled. So he ran. But as he ran he savoured the memory of Amanda Pitman calling his Hu-ness a puny-dicked moron.

Fong didn't remember much of what happened next. It had begun to rain. Traffic was horribly snarled. He ran. Darkness fell. The storm broke in all its fury as he entered the tunnel under the Bund at Beijing Road. He had no idea how it had gotten so late so quickly. All he knew was that he could run no more.

The tunnel was empty except for the old musician and his filthy child.

"Just let me sleep here, grandfather. Betray me if you must." The beggar child moved from his blanket rag and approached Fong with his hand out. Fong reached into his pocket and gave the boy every yuan note he had left. The boy neither smiled nor frowned but delivered the money to his father, who began to play. As the haunting music echoed in the tunnel, Fong leaned back against the coolness of the tunnel wall. He breathed through his open mouth, his eyes misting. Without a sound the beggar boy came over to him and curled up in his lap. The warmth of the boy on Fong's body sent a sob through his being. With his hand in the beggar boy's hair, he drifted off to sleep with one final thought: if there is a god, he is laughing now.

Fong's dream that night began with the cobra. Its steel coils were snaking their way down the hallowed-out shaft of the construction site elevator. Fong was at the bottom, completely walled in, and despite his frantic efforts to pry open the elevator doors they refused to budge. Outside the elevator shaft Fong could see the rattan wrapping and the massive bamboo scaffolds. His screams for help were drowned out by the screech of the storm and the thunder of the cranes. Above, the mighty snake flared its hood and descended the cables of the elevator — never fast but constant. Suddenly the mercury vapor arc lights switched on, converting darkest night into frozen day. The reptile's unblinking eyes glinted red. Without warning the mighty snake dropped itself from the cables directly onto Fong's now almost paralyzed body.

His scream must have awakened the beggar boy, who was patting Fong's hair and whispering that things were going to be all right.

It was very late at night. There was little traffic in the tunnel. The old string player was shovelling a small bowl of rice into his toothless maw and staring at Fong. He finished his rice, stood up and, taking the boy by the hand, headed out of the tunnel. Fong could have sworn that the old man said two words over his shoulder: the Pudong.

Then things happened in a blur. Wang Jun was at his side. The two of them were running. Sirens crowded the night, competing with the roiling thunder. They jumped into Wang Jun's car and headed across the suspension bridge. "What are you doing, Wang Jun?"

"I'm being dangerously sentimental. I'm saving your sorry life."

As Wang Jun's car careened off the exit ramp from the suspension bridge, he headed away from the sirens — into the heart of the Pudong.

• • •

Li Xiao and Loa We Fen got the report of the escape from the tunnel at the same time. The difference was that Li Xiao was on the Shanghai side of the Huangpo River, Loa Wei Fen on the Pudong side. . . waiting.

Wang Jun slammed on the brakes, skidding his car to a stop not two feet from the police roadblock. With a precision that identified them as federal troops, the men at the roadblock advanced on Wang Jun's car.

Fong looked at his old friend. Wang Jun didn't seem to be unhappy. "Where will they put you, Wang Jun?"

"In hell with you, no doubt."

"That's only true if they catch us."

Wang Jun reached inside his jacket and took out his gun. He held it out to Fong and said, "You're younger."

With that, both men slammed open their doors, rolled out onto the pavement and bounded to their feet before their would-be captors could react.

As he ran Fong heard the gunshots and the thud of Wang Jun's body slamming to the pavement. He didn't hesitate or look back. He ran deep into the mystery of the old area. Deep into the heart of this terrifying place. He didn't stop until his legs would take him no farther.

He found himself in the midst of a large muck-filled construction site.

He leaned against a stack of bamboo, his breath ragged in his chest. Raising his head he saw two great arc lights far across the vast construction site. Their beams were focused on a solitary bamboo elevator shaft. He took a step toward it before it struck him like a sledgehammer blow to the chest. His heart leapt in fear. It was the elevator shaft from his dream.

Before he could move he heard the slosh of a foot sliding in the muck behind him. He instinctively ducked to his left. The swolta tore through his quilted jacket and sliced across his left breast just to one side of his nipple, continuing down to rip through sections of Fong's left leg.

For a moment he looked at his attacker, who had slipped to the muck-covered ground, then he ran and slid and yelled and fought the pain until a darkness seemed to envelop him.

He had to rest. His body was soaked with blood and sweat, the pelting rain mixing the two in an unholy froth.

He leaned back against a solid surface that gave slightly against his weight. It was bamboo. He turned slowly, a tingling fear electrifying his blood.

He was at the base of the solitary elevator shaft, the construction lights full in his eyes.

Loa Wei Fen looked down. Beneath him was the end of his quest. Directly below, blinded by the bright construction-site lights, it crouched warily, its head moving

left and right but never up. Never up the bamboo elevator shaft. Never to where Loa Wei Fen lurked and
patiently waited, like a lion cub on a roof, ready to jump.

"Above, Loa Wei Fen, always attack from above," the
voice of his old teacher whispered in his ears. So remov-
ing his muddied shirt, he began. His hand reached for
the swolta. The knife hilt rolled slightly and fitted itself
to its master's palm. Then down, down the bamboo
bracing he slithered, his prey never suspecting danger
from above.

• • •

After the first attack Fong's mobility was reduced to a
hobbling gait but there was still spring in his step and
although the knife had severed muscle it had missed
tendon, so the leg still responded to his will. When he
fell his gun had filled with thick mud. Now, as he braced
himself against the bamboo elevator shaft, he tried desperately to clean the gun barrel. His enemy was clearly
stronger and quicker than he. Only the bad footing had
saved his life on that first attack. Now he would have to
survive by his wits.

"Loa Wei Fen," he shouted into the harsh lights. "Loa
Wei Fen, we know who you are. We know your school
in Taipei. We have pictures of you." He waited. There
was no response. The rain picked up again.

On one side of the tall bamboo shaft low-voltage electric lines hissed slightly as the rain caused shorts where
the cables were jury-rigged together. The lines led to a
major power source high up on the shaft. On the ground

muck and puddles covered most of the area except for a slightly raised cement pad upon which the elevator car would eventually come to rest.

Fong took aim at one of the two large arc lights and fired. The gun kicked hard to the right and the bullet pinged harmlessly off the side of the light's casing.

"They gave you to us, Loa Wei Fen. They've used you, and now they want you gone. They gave you to us, you stupid shit."

Loa Wei Fen was slightly surprised by the gunshot but encouraged by the miss. The lights were to his advantage as they were aimed down at the quarry, not up at the hunter.

He felt the cobra markings on his back begin to fill with blood. Without conscious thought, he spread the muscles of his upper back, opening the cobra's hood. He slid down to the sixth floor of the bamboo shaft. His quarry was directly beneath him, hollering at the wind.

"They used me too. We're both just pawns for them," Fong screamed into the now sheeting rain. He aimed and fired a second time. This bullet found its mark and one of the two arc lights snapped off.

Like the taking out of an eye, the blinking off of one of the lights robbed Loa Wei Fen of his depth perception in the middle of his swing to a central strut of the fifth floor. His fingers reached and found only air. For a moment he plunged, but instinct saved him as his other arm, in full extension, struck and held a cross strut. And there he hung by one arm as the wounded man below him began to yell again.

"We don't mean anything to them! They don't give a shit! They want us both dead, you idiot!"

Fong fired three times at the remaining light and missed each time.

Loa Wei Fen, after hanging for almost thirty seconds, pulled himself up by one hand and then continued his progress down. The shouting man was directly beneath him, looking tiny through the curtains of rain now blowing almost parallel to the ground. Loa Wei Fen put the hilt of the knife in his mouth and tasted the acid of the snake's skin. Blood engorged the markings on his back so they stood out like brilliant red welts.

His next move downward knocked free a low-voltage auxiliary electric cable.

The slender power line popped and hissed in the puddle at Fong's left. He leapt aside and traced the dangling wire upward. And there, two and a half floors above him, was the great cobra of his nightmares, its hood spread, its sinuous body ready to drop on him from above. Fear coursed through him so strongly that he soiled his pants and dropped his gun into the puddle beside him. It glowed blue in the electrified water.

With an expert push, Loa Wei Fen, swolta in hand, began his spinning fall toward his prey, arms outstretched, legs spread, knife ready.

Fong saw the approaching, twisting shadow, framed perfectly by the elevator platform. As the snake's head rose, its single fang glinting in the arc light, Fong reached high up on the diagonal piece of bamboo that supported the major electrical cable, and pulled with all his might.

Below him Loa Wei Fen saw the man reaching up toward him, beckoning—like the little monk on the peacock at the end of the strut of the Jade Buddha Temple. The little monk below. He, the fearful lion cub, above. This finally was the leap to the path.

The bamboo snapped free and severed the heavy cable. The exposed end of the cable touched the scaffold. The electricity, offered a new avenue of escape, leapt up the soaking bamboo toward Loa Wei Fen. With the same speed it raced down to the arm of the small man now almost knee deep in the mud.

The electricity hit both men at the same time. For a moment both were lit by a ghostly fire. Muscles involuntarily knotted in response to the jolt. The voltage surge threw Fong to his back on the cement slab, his limbs twitching. It forced Loa Wei Fen to bite through his tongue as he plummeted earthward.

Then the electricity crossed the thick main cable high up the scaffolding. Bamboo burst into flame. Sharp lengths of the solid vine plunged like spears toward Fong.

Fong's eyes snapped open. Lightning bolts of flaming bamboo were streaking down at him and in their midst the huge snake twisted its body, trying to turn, even as it fell directly at him. Fong never felt the bamboo spike pierce his left biceps and splinter against the concrete slab. He didn't feel it because the cobra's tooth, the swolta, was free falling, point downward, directly toward his heart.

The cobra completed its turn. For a moment the two men locked eyes. One on his back on the slab, the other plunging face down toward the earth, the swolta between the two.

Fong instinctively reached up to protect himself from the falling knife.

Loa Wei Fen saw the little monk signalling for him to follow. And he understood. At last he understood how to make the leap to the path. He lunged downward toward the plunging swolta and with a flick turned the blade upward toward himself.

Loa Wei Fen's body crashed limb for limb on top of Fong. There was no cry, only a solid thud and the ripping sound the swolta makes as it slashes through bone and muscle.

Loa Wei Fen's left hand fell off the slab into an electrified puddle. The electric current jolted through his body a second time, scorching the snake from his back. As he smelled the odour of his own seared flesh, Loa Wei Fen had a momentary clear vision of the little opium whore in the back alley with the large black man. Of the thrill on her face as the black man caressed her breast. And with this vision clearly in focus, his mind came alive with joy—his body a chimera of electrical impulses.

Fong felt the world spin. As the bamboo shaft burned away it revealed a horizon of tall buildings where once the old town had been. Where once people's lives were their own to live. Where once he had held his wife and their unborn baby above a yawning maw in the ground. And then committed them to space and eternity — her arm gesturing to him, her mouth alive with silent words.

Loa Wei Fen moved on top of him. Their bodies were fitted together piece for piece. He could feel the man's laboured breath on his cheek. Something was pooling, thick between them. He reached around the man and felt the point of the swolta protruding a full two inches out of the man's back. He pushed with all his remaining strength and Loa Wei Fen rolled off him and lay on his back. As Fong struggled to his feet he saw the snake handle of the knife standing above Loa Wei Fen's sternum, as ungodly a gift as ever offered man.

Loa Wei Fen smiled up at Fong. He moved his right shoulder and his hand lifted from the ground. It moved toward Fong and then back to himself.

Fong blanched.

It was the exact same movement that Fu Tsong had made as she fell toward the construction pit. It was the terror awaiting him at the end of each nightly horror excursion back to the Pudong.

The hand came up and made the same motion again.

Fong couldn't move.

Loa Wei Fen's mouth was moving, blood and bits of tongue bubbling on the lips but no words.

For a moment Fong was on the edge of the construction pit again. Fu Tsong was in the air falling, with the baby, her arm moving exactly as Loa Wei Fen's was moving now. Fu Tsong's mouth had moved too but there were no words. Nothing to explain what the hand movement meant.

Loa Wei Fen tried one more time. Tried to communicate to the little monk to complete the job—to set him free. The little monk didn't seem to understand.

With the howling of the storm in his ears, Loa Wei Fen forced words into his throat.

"Thank you," came out cleanly. Then with great effort, "You've set me free."

Fong saw the blood trace the words on the lips of the dying man. He saw the arm gesture again mated perfectly with the words.

And then he wasn't there anymore. But with Fu Tsong. In midair her arm tracing the same path. But this time her lips moved and there was both sound and meaning. As clear as a lover's sigh she said to him, "Thank you. You've set me free."

The rain slashed down on him. His tears mixed with it. His sobs came up from the earth and roared out of his mouth. His sides cracked and suddenly he was on the ground, digging in the mud. Throwing it over himself. Burying himself in the cold obstruction. Trying with all his might to avoid the laughter of the heavens that drowned his sobs.

And there he lay until a thought grew in his mind. A thought that warmed his being. Set his mind strangely at rest. Knowing what Fu Tsong had being trying to say to him as she fell allowed him, for the first time in his life, to fully accept that Fu Tsong had loved him. Loved him enough to thank him for a death that was surely his fault. With her arm movement she was not being set free. She was setting *him* free.

He arose from his would-be grave and stood in the pelting rain for a moment longer. Then he stepped toward the charred body of Loa Wei Fen. There was a smile on the dying man's face. Scraping the mud from his hands, Fong reached forward and pulled the knife from Loa Wei Fen's chest. A bubble of blood came up with the blade, "Thank you," bubbled from his shattered mouth as Loa Wei Fen, still smiling, repeated his hand gesture.

Then the man's eyes opened wide and he exhaled one long breath. The smile on his face became luminous.

DAY 889

In Ti Lan Chou Prison, Fong never knew if it was day or night, winter or summer, time for another brutal work shift or time to confess his political sins once again. On occasion a cellmate left and did not return. He accepted that. Like all modern prisons, Ti Lan Chou echoed with the clanging of metal on metal. But it also possessed a strange stillness. A stillness wherein meaning loses its potency and memories fade.

Fong used the stillness to find some peace. Finally, his dreams calmed.

On the one hundred and forty-ninth day of his third year in Ti Lan Chou Prison he was awakened by two guards and led down corridors that he had never seen before. Then, out a door into a courtyard. Into the night.

Above him were the first stars that he had seen in more than two years. Real stars. And a night breeze. He forced himself to face the cold wind. Then he forced himself not to cringe as he fought down the urge to beg to go back to the stillness of the prison.

A gate opened and an ancient man in a heavy over-coat ambled toward him.

The man stopped five feet from Fong and stared

at him for a very long time.

"You have strong friends, Inspector Zhong." The voice was hoarse, blood filled, near its end.

"I have no friends."

"No friends here, perhaps. But you have a friend in the West. A writer whose book *Letters from Shanghai* has made her a powerful woman. She has, as the West is fond of saying, championed your cause."

Remembering Amanda hurt him.

"I've looked forward to meeting you," the man croaked.

"Have you really?" It came out feebly.

"Yes. As have my many associates in this great venture. All send their regards."

Fong lifted his chin and felt the wind on his cheek. He savoured the smell of the living earth. Then the old man put his hand on Fong's shoulder and walked him to the courtyard door. "Now I expect you want an explanation as to what all this was about."

"It was about ivory," Fong spat out.

"Nonsense," spat back the hoarse-voiced man. "Who could possibly care about the tusks of elephants enough to murder men? It's about that." He opened the door, revealing a breathtaking view of the night lunarscape of the Pudong, the planet's largest construction site. The place of Fu Tsong and Loa Wei Fen's deaths.

"But. . ." Words refused to come to him.

"Once a child is born it must be fed. Once a city is reborn it must be fed. Once a nation arises from the ashes it must be fed. Those buildings grow on a very special diet, a diet of money and trade. Both from the West. The West that is so sentimental about the health and well-being of large tusk-bearing mammals."

He handed an official-looking envelope to Fong.

"You're a talented individual, Zhong Fong. China may need your skills again at some future time." Fong opened the envelope. "It's a promotion, Zhong Fong. You seem to like playing sheriff. Well, there is a town on the Mongolian border which needs a sheriff and we have decided that you are just the man for the job. Your train leaves from the North Train Station at dawn. It's an eight-day train journey. Unfortunately in these tight economic times we could only afford a hard seat for you. Safe journey to the west, Zhong Fong."

Shock saves the body from experiencing pain too great to bear. Numbness saves the mind from a similar fate. So it was in a numb stupor that Fong approached the apartment that had been theirs, then his, and now not theirs or his. To his surprise the place was empty.

No. They had emptied it. They had known he would come here.

The furniture was gone, the paintings, all of Fu Tsong's things. How small a place seems without furniture. On the bathroom floor he found Fu Tsong's complete Shakespeare.

They knew him. They owned him.

He picked up the book. The smell of fresh urine rose from the pages. The acidity momentarily brought a welcome pain back to him.

His scream shook the windows of the bathroom, scared the snotty theatre students pretending to be angry in the statued courtyard and only faded when it reached the din of the traffic on Yan'an.

As Fong made his way through the throngs to the North Train Station he walked by a restaurant window with live snakes on display. As Fong passed, a large cobra raised itself up to its full height and flared its hood. For a moment Fong paused. Then he laughed. Here was an animal that thought it was important. Thought it was power itself. Fong stepped up to the windowpane and stared into the cobra's unblinking eyes. Then he rapped the glass sharply enough to make it ting. As the snake darted away in fear, Fong hissed, "You're only important and powerful until some man comes along with enough money to skin and eat you live."

On the eighth day of the train ride, hard seat, Fong opened Fu Tsong's Shakespeare for the first time. He read through *Twelfth Night*, hearing Fu Tsong's voice in every one of Olivia's lines.

He searched in vain for his voice in the play. If we are all in the play, who am I?

At last, as the train pulled into his new town, he came to the very end of the play. To his surprise it was Malvolio who had his voice. His pain. And as the train whistled to a dusty stop he shouted Malvolio's final line, "I'll be revenged on the whole pack of you."

It felt good on his lips in both English and Chinese.

ABOUT THE AUTHOR

David Rotenberg has directed in theatres throughout the United States and Canada as well as theatres in Cape Town and Shanghai. Since returning to Canada in 1987, he also works as a master acting teacher at the National Theatre School of Canada, Equity Showcase Theatre in Toronto, and at York University. The lessons that Geoffrey Hyland teaches in the novel are part of Mr. Rotenberg's unique approach to acting, which is used by a great many successful actors in Canada.

He has two new novels awaiting publication and has published another Zhong Fong mystery, *The Lake Ching Murders*.

As a side note to this novel, his production of *Rita Joe* in Shanghai was received with reserved politeness; however, his *Twelfth Night* was hailed by critics and audiences as a masterpiece.

He lives in Toronto with his wife, Susan Santiago, and their two children, Joey and Beth.